COLLEEN GLEASON

THREE TOMES BOOKSHOP

PURSES CURSES AND HEARSES

0 9 8 7 6 5 4 3 2 1

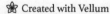 Created with Vellum

1

Jacqueline Finch had been in love with books since she was five and first started to pick out the words in *The Cat in the Hat*.

By the time she was ten, she'd go to the library and check out an entire stack of books—sadly, fourteen was the maximum—take them home, and read them within three or four days. Then she'd go back for another stack of Nancy Drews or Trixie Beldens or Cherry Ameses or Boxcar Childrens or whatever she could get her hands on. Her librarian had been so wonderful, always helping her to find new authors and series to read, that Jacqueline decided she wanted to be a librarian someday.

And so she did.

She worked for twenty-five years, mostly as a reference librarian, at the Chicago Public Library before her life took a severe one-eighty turn...on her forty-eighth birthday.

On that day, she not only got pink-slipped from her library job, but her reputation was shattered by a completely untrue and offensive rumor that she'd tried to seduce a married man...and then she got home to discover that the owner of her cute little rental had sold the house with no warning and very little lead time for her to vacate it. Not only that, but her so-called best friend, Wendy, had had the gall to *believe* the rumors about Jacqueline and Desmond Triplett.

Fortunately, the universe wasn't completely hard-hearted, for on the very same day—almost as if it were planned that way—Jacqueline discovered she'd inherited a bookstore in the touristy town of Button Cove, located on Lake Michigan near the pinkie tip of northern Lower Michigan.

Three Tomes Bookshop was the perfect establishment for someone who loved books as much as Jacqueline did. Located in the downtown of touristy Button Cove, the shop was a large Victorian-style house with seemingly unending nooks, crannies, and alcoves, all lined with shelves of books—new, used, vintage, and even antiquarian—organized by genre and subject. There were working fireplaces in most of the rooms on the main floor, and another very large one in the cozy tea room on the second floor—a contained, blazing fire and nearby reading chairs being, in Jacqueline's mind, basic requirements for the perfect bookshop.

Yes, Jacqueline loved books, and she'd landed in the perfect realm for someone like her...except for one thing.

Mrs. Hudson and Mrs. Danvers.

"That's really two things," said Nadine Bachmoto as she rested her elbows on the counter in the front of Three Tomes. She owned the yoga studio on the second floor across the street from Three Tomes, and she had befriended Jacqueline almost as soon as she arrived in Button Cove nearly three weeks ago.

With a grimace, Jacqueline shook her head. "Not

really, because they go together. There's no one-with-
out-the-other with those two. They're constantly bick-
ering and competing and trying to tell the other what
to do."

"But Mrs. Hudson's always so helpful and cheery,"
Nadine said. She was dressed in her usual attire: yoga
pants, sports bra, and t-shirt, all of which showed off a
lot of round, bulgy curves. Also in her late forties, Nadine had light, creamy skin and rich brown hair in a
stylish, layered cut—currently caught up in a ponytail
—along with big, dark eyes.

"She is pretty darned convenient to have around,"
Jacqueline admitted.

Mrs. Hudson basically ran the tea room upstairs,
which was a godsend. Customers thought she was
very entertaining, with all of her talk about Mr.
Holmes and Dr. Watson and what it had been like
living with them at 221B Baker Street in London as she
served them scones and other pastries and insisted
that tea was a far better option than coffee. (An
opinion with which Jacqueline firmly disagreed.)

What the customers didn't know was that Mrs.
Hudson *was actually* Mrs. Hudson, not an employee
playing a role. Somehow, she'd come out of a book of
Holmes tales—quite literally—and, by all indication,
never intended to slip back onto the pages. Jacqueline
had no idea how it had happened, and she certainly
didn't have any inkling of how to undo it.

"Danvers, on the other hand..." said Jacqueline,
grimacing as she glanced over to make certain the
sharp and condescending housekeeper from Daphne
du Maurier's *Rebecca* wasn't lurking about, as she
tended to do.

"She is creepy as hell," said Nadine. Her eyes
widened and she suddenly looked over her shoulder.

Jacqueline had also caught the movement from the corner of her eye, and she turned. But there was no sign of the housekeeper, who still talked about Rebecca de Winter as if she were some sort of goddess. Instead of the arrogant, pinch-faced woman with hair scraped back so tightly it looked like it would cause one hell of a migraine, it was the two shop cats making their appearance. They normally meandered up to the front when it was time to open the store, and as it was only five minutes to nine, they were right on schedule.

"Good morning, Sebastian," said Nadine, stooping to pet the soft, fluffy, golden-haired feline. He obliged by twining himself in figure eights around her ankles, then he jumped lightly onto the counter for even more attention. His purring was loud and smooth as he butted her hand flirtatiously with his head. "Don't worry, I'll keep you away from that mean old Mrs. Danvers."

Max, the second cat Jacqueline had inherited along with the shop, Danvers, and Hudson, was a sleek black creature with an arrogant expression. He rarely deigned to allow attention to be bestowed upon him, instead preferring to watch the goings-on from a favorite perch on the highest shelf in the front room. With the grace and power of a small panther, he bounded his way up to his spot and settled there, eyeing everyone with cool gray eyes.

"How is everything going, getting ready for the grand reopening tomorrow?" said Nadine as Sebastian sat neatly on the counter.

Jacqueline smiled even as she pushed away a little tingle of nerves. She'd been trying not to worry about tomorrow's big event, but she couldn't help be a little anxious. "I think I have everything under control. I just hope people come."

"Oh, they'll come," Nadine said with a smile. "Suzette and I have been telling everyone about it, and passing out save-the-date cards. There's a lot of interest. Everyone loves Three Tomes."

Jacqueline felt another flutter of anxiety. What if she didn't have enough food? And drink? What if she had too much? What if no one showed up? What if everyone came and ate and drank but didn't buy anything?

What if something *weird* happened—like all the weird stuff that had been going on since she arrived?

At least she didn't have to worry about the books being ruined with food and drink. That was one of the special things about Three Tomes: crumbs, flakes, frosting, and liquid of any kind simply evaporated or fell off the books, leaving absolutely no residue whatsoever.

"Thank you so much," Jacqueline said to Nadine. Her heart swelled with emotion. She'd only known Nadine Bachmoto and Suzette Whalley—who owned the bakery beneath the yoga studio—for a few weeks, but they'd already forged a loyal and enjoyable friendship. Of course, the three of them witnessing a witch having a hissy fit might have helped clinch the deal. "I really appreciate all of your support. I just hope Danvers doesn't scare everyone away. She's just so...you know." She shook her head, in case the housekeeper was lurking or listening. The woman always showed up from out of nowhere—usually when she wasn't wanted.

Which was pretty much all the time.

"What *is* her deal, anyway?" asked Nadine, lowering her voice as she too looked around. "I mean, I've never read *Rebecca*."

"You should. It's a fantastic gothic novel," Jacqueline told her.

"I barely have time to read my email and the latest Nora Roberts—that woman alone puts out enough books to keep me busy all year—and TJ Mack books. I probably won't get to *Rebecca* anytime in the near future, so just give me the gist," Nadine said with a flap of her hand. "That's why I have a librarian for one of my BFFs."

Absurdly pleased to be described as a BFF after only three weeks, Jacqueline said, "The book takes place in the 1930s in England. Danvers was the housekeeper for the first Mrs. de Winter—the eponymous Rebecca—and after Rebecca died tragically, she didn't want anyone else to take her place. So when Max de Winter—who was wildly rich, of course, and lived in this huge, creepy house called Manderley—brings home an ingenuous new bride, Danvers makes the woman's life living hell because she's still loyal to her previous mistress. Kinda of like what she does here," Jacqueline said, glancing over her shoulder again to make sure the creepy bitch hadn't sneaked up when she wasn't paying attention. "Funny thing is—we never learn the name of the second Mrs. de Winter in the book; it's told from her point of view, and no one ever calls her anything but Mrs. de Winter."

"Sounds really creepy."

"It is...in a good way. There's nothing like a suspenseful gothic novel," Jacqueline said, thinking fondly of all the Barbara Michaels, Mary Stewart, and Victoria Holt novels she'd enjoyed over the decades. "Even if you don't have time to read it, you could watch the movie. Hitchcock made an Academy Award-winning film adaptation of it. There was a recent remake too, just within the last couple of years."

"Okay, I'll put it on the streaming list. Anyway, Suzette and I can't wait for the party," said Nadine. "We'll be here to help you—I'm getting a sub for tomorrow night's classes, and Suze has someone to run the counter. Hey," she said suddenly, looking out the front window of the shop. "There's that hearse going by again."

Jacqueline followed her gaze and saw a battered old hearse driving slowly down Camellia Avenue toward the court end. "That makes, what, the third time in the last week? Are there that many people dying in Button Cove?"

"I don't know, but if that's the case, surely the undertaker could afford a nicer-looking hearse than that," said Nadine.

Jacqueline bit her tongue and didn't correct her to "mortician." She was just getting to be good friends with Nadine and Suzette and she didn't want to come across as too pedantic, even though, as a reference librarian, she was a font of information about pretty much everything. Instead, she said, "The car does look awfully shabby. Are we certain it's actually used as a hearse? Sometimes people just like to drive those cars around for effect. There's no business name on the side."

Nadine looked at her. "That's a good point. But either way, why does he—it looks like a guy driver—keep going up and down our street? Camellia ends in the court, so he always has to turn around."

"Looking for parking?" Jacqueline replied. "Maybe they work around here."

"And drive a hearse. That's special," Nadine replied with a giggle. "Whoever he is, he fits right in with the three crones at the end of the street, and you with your witchy cousin."

Jacqueline sighed. She'd been trying to forget about Egala Stone, a distant cousin who was, yes, an actual witch, and who thought *she* should have inherited Three Tomes and had recently tried to scare Jacqueline into giving up the shop. "Thanks for that reminder. At least she hasn't come back and stalked me."

"I'm certain it's only a matter of time," said Nadine with another giggle. She seemed to find Jacqueline's witchy problems amusing—even though she'd witnessed a furious Egala creating an indoor tornado, which, at the time, was pretty damned scary. Jacqueline's dark red hair had curled. Literally. And it had yet to go straight again. On bad days, she looked like Little Orphan Annie had stuck her finger in a light socket. On good days she almost resembled the heroine on a romance novel cover.

Too bad she had more bad days than good days.

"Please don't say that," Jacqueline retorted with a groan. Unlike her distant cousin, she didn't have one bit of witch ability in her genes. At least as far as she knew. She shivered at the thought; she had enough to contend with and didn't want to have to learn magic or anything like that. "I've got enough to deal with with Danvers."

Holy crap. The thought just struck her. What if Egala showed up tomorrow?

Jacqueline's stomach pitched and swung like a heavy pendulum, and she swallowed hard. It was one thing for customers to believe her employees were playing the role of literary characters; it was another thing to have an actual witch show up and whip a bunch of books into a cyclone in the middle of the room. Which Egala had, in fact, done in this very room the first time they met.

Jacqueline felt sick. Maybe she should cancel the event.

"Anyway, I can't help but be curious about the hearse driver," Nadine said, blithely unaware of her friend's anxiety. She was peering out the window again.

The long black car was on its way back from where it had turned around at the end of the street. It looked like something someone from the Addams Family might have driven—and as soon as the thought struck her, Jacqueline immediately quelled it.

She did not need any more characters showing up out of books. Although she had to admit that Little Miss Muffet had been very helpful when there was a little spring spider infestation last week. Fortunately, the little blond curds-and-whey eater hadn't stayed for more than a few hours, and when she was finished running off the spiders, she disappeared—presumably back into the Mother Goose book that had tumbled off the shelf earlier that day. After that, the old, raggedy book had simply shown up on the front counter, closed, which seemed to indicate that Miss Muffet had returned to her tuffet.

Jacqueline had been here less than a month, but she'd learned the portent that a random bookish character was going to show up: an old tome spontaneously (as far as she could tell) would fall off the shelf and land with its pages open. It had only happened a few times since she'd taken over the shop, and she fervently wished it would stop. So far, the few characters who'd shown up had been manageable— although Miss Gulch, who'd kept Jacqueline prisoner in the cellar during a terrible thunderstorm, had been very unsettling. And Paul Bunyan, of all things, had shown up last week.

Though not as gigantic as Jacqueline would have imagined, he was still a big-ass guy, with shoulders so broad he barely fit through a doorway. He clunked his head every time he walked into one of the genre rooms and had to duck beneath most of the hanging light fixtures, but at least he kept his ax hanging from a loop in his belt.

Jacqueline wasn't thrilled to have the big guy lumbering about her shop—a bull in a bookshop was an apt description—but at least he hadn't brought Babe the Blue Ox, putting a literal bull in her bookshop. Fortunately, he disappeared after a couple of days, having only knocked over three stacks of books during his tenure while spending the rest of his time barely fitting on a bench that was meant for two people, staring morosely out the window. She still had no idea what he'd been doing in Three Tomes, but she was glad he'd gone back into the book of tall tales from whence he'd come.

"I think I'll mosey on back to the studio," said Nadine. She was still watching the hearse, which was rolling slowly down the street. "Is he *looking* for something?"

"Parking, probably," said Jacqueline, wondering why her friend was so fascinated by the hearse. It was just a car. "Or maybe he's searching for a particular address."

"I should go on out and see if I can help him," Nadine said, starting for the door. "Or at least find out who he is. All right, I'll be here about three tomorrow to help you with the setup. Ta!" she called as she slipped out, the bell overhead jingling pleasantly behind her.

Jacqueline shook her head, smiling. Nadine was a ball of energy all the time, and she was a lot of fun to be around. She also didn't make Jacqueline feel guilty about not having come over for a yoga class yet, even though Nadine bought tea and books from Three Tomes, and Suzette's baked goods were featured in the tea room upstairs.

Jacqueline sighed. She really did need to start doing some sort of exercise other than a few basic stretches in the morning. Everyone said that once you hit forty, strength training was really important. And so was cardio. And so was doing puzzles, to exercise your brain. And so on, and so on, and so on.

Couldn't she just enjoy being over the hill without worrying about everything she should be doing to keep herself there?

She sighed again. For now, she had some boxes of books to unpack and stock before tomorrow's party—that was exercise, wasn't it? And she could run (well, walk; no need to get crazy here—although her inner thighs rubbing together might disagree) up and down the stairs to the tea room and the apartment on the third floor, which was about to become her new home.

Nothing like biting off a big hunk of life at one time.

Since it was early and the shop had just opened, she didn't have anything pressing to do besides shelve the new titles. Things would get busy in an hour or so and stay that way for most of the day—something that Jacqueline considered nothing short of miraculous, having always heard that small bookstores usually had to struggle to stay afloat—so now was a good time.

But the cart filled with boxes of books she'd left in the hallway was gone. That usually meant Mrs. Danvers had taken it upon herself to see to the task, and Jacqueline had mixed feelings about the housekeeper's efficiency. On the one hand, it was work she didn't have to do herself—or pay someone to do. On the other hand, the woman was such a buzzkill to have around.

Since she didn't have books to stock, Jacqueline decided to walk through the shop and just...bask. She would bask in the pleasure of knowing she owned this lovely, charming, magical place, and that she could take any book off the shelf and read it or keep it or borrow it...she could talk books all day long with people...she could pore over publishers' catalogs and request advance copies of whatever she wanted...and do it all while surrounded by books, books, and more books. It was a dream come true—a dream she hadn't realized she'd had until she came here.

With a smile, she started down the hall that connected the sunny, open front area with the back entrance and parking lot. There were several rooms on either side of the hall, each one on the left containing novels organized by genre: romance, science fiction and fantasy, general fiction, and teen reads. On the right side, the rooms were nonfiction topics like history, natural history, biography, science, and so on.

She loved going into the science room, because that one had several doors and little alcoves that led to other rooms and alcoves, and more nooks and seating areas and shelves tucked in everywhere... They were all somehow nestled into each other like the chambers of a spiral seashell. The rooms and alcoves went on and on and on, yet still somehow contained by the boundaries of the house.

Instead of browsing among the zoology section, she went into the mystery and suspense area. It was one of the rooms with a fireplace, and she'd positioned two blue damask chairs, one on either side of it, for browsers to sit while they flipped through their potential purchases. It was the first week of May, so there was still a chill in the air here in Northern Michigan—which meant there was already a lovely blazing fire... which had been set and lit by Danvers.

Jacqueline sighed. She supposed it might be worth the lurking buzzkill to have an unpaid staff member who just did things that needed to get done. Heck, Mrs. Danvers knew more about the inventory and how to manage the computer system than she did!

Jacqueline skimmed an affectionate hand over the spines and fronts of the rows of Agatha Christies and Louise Pennys and Alyssa Maxwells, absorbing the energy she knew lurked inside those covers and behind the spines. She removed an old favorite from the shelf —*Into the Darkness* by Barbara Michaels—and sank into one of the chairs, opening it to the middle. She'd read it so many times that she could pick up anywhere, read a little bit, and then put it back.

Maybe a comforting read right now would help ease some of her anxiety about tomorrow.

The fire blazed happily next to her, and she felt the gentle warmth play over her arm and leg closest to the hearth. The only thing missing was a cup of coffee.

Jacqueline was so very happy at that moment: she owned this wonderful place, she had begun to make friends, and she really felt as if she belonged here.

And then she saw the foot on the floor behind one of the shelves.

2

J acqueline lurched to her feet, setting *Into the Darkness* rather roughly on the table next to the chair, and stared.

The foot was shod in what looked like a ratty old boot, and it appeared to be attached to a trouser-covered, supine leg that extended from behind a freestanding bookshelf that jutted into the room.

The question was whether the leg and foot belonged to a living, breathing person or a dead body.

She was, after all, in the mystery and thriller room.

Jacqueline's heart thudded hard in her chest as she tiptoed hesitantly toward the unmoving body part. "Hello?" she said tentatively.

The boot and trousered leg didn't move.

Great. Just what she needed.

"Hello there," she said, moving closer.

Still no response.

With a sigh and an overwhelming feeling of dread, Jacqueline stepped all the way to the bookshelf and peered around it.

The foot and leg belonged to a man in his teens who was slumped against the wall and the bookshelf.

The softest snore emitted from his nose, easing Jacqueline's initial fear that he was dead.

"*Hello,*" she said again, louder this time as she prodded his boot with her foot. "Ahem."

When he didn't move, she finally gave the sole of his boot a solid kick, and that did the trick.

He jolted awake. "Oi! Whadyer do that for?" Glaring at her, he sat up and reached for the battered top hat that had fallen off and was squashed between him and the wall.

Her estimate of his age went up to about sixteen, based on the bristling but patchy stubble on his chin. Obviously he hadn't used a razor recently. A small frisson of nerves sizzled down her spine when she got a good look at his clothing. It was old—old in style, fabric, and wear. The fact that he'd spoken with a Cockney accent only made her more nervous. The carnation wilting from his coat lapel made her even more anxious.

"You're sleeping in my shop," said Jacqueline firmly. She was reminded of the times she'd had to waken students or researchers who'd fallen asleep in their carrels when the library was closing.

"Wot's it to ye?" he said, then suddenly gave her a charming grin that displayed a crooked tooth in the front. "Ye wouldn't deny a warm crib to the likes of a foin gennulman, now, would ye?"

Oh crap. She definitely knew who he was.

Jacqueline sighed. She really didn't need this right now. There was just too much going on with the party tomorrow and her moving into her apartment. But what choice did she have?

"Jack Dawkins, I presume," she said as he leaped lithely to his feet, hands-free, reminding her of a dancer or gymnast.

"At yer service, milady," he said, sweeping into an exaggerated bow.

Jack Dawkins, a.k.a. the Artful Dodger from Dickens's *Oliver Twist*, who was known for his pickpocketing skills—that was, his "artful dodging" of the bobbies and his lightening of the gentry's pockets with his talented fingers. He was dressed in fine gentlemen's clothing that were obviously castoffs from his Victorian world. Coat, trousers, boots, a waistcoat or vest, and a grimy white shirt beneath it all. His neckcloth was loose and the strings that tied the shirt at the neck hung free as well (buttons hadn't been used on men's shirts until the mid-1800s). Everything he wore was just slightly too big for him: the cuffs of his coat, which was long and had tails, hung nearly to the tips of his fingers, and the hems of his sagging trousers puddled a little on the floor around him. He snatched the wilting flower from his lapel and offered it to her with a flourish.

"Ye can call me Dodger," he said, giving her a wink and another of those charming grins—which Jacqueline somehow found difficult to resist. He had sandy-brown hair with a lot of red glints that would probably get brighter if he ever washed it, and he was far too slender for his frame, likely due to the poor diet of the children who lived on the streets of London during that time period.

"*There* you are!" cried a strident voice behind them.

Dodger's grin faded, and he sighed as he and Jacqueline turned to face Mrs. Hudson. She was attired in her normal ankle-length dark dress covered by a white apron. Her graying hair was pulled back into a neat bun with one tiny wisp that had come loose and curled in front of her ear. Her face was flushed with irritation, and she narrowed a lethal gaze on him.

"I was just catching a bit o' a snooze," Dodger told her. But his winsome smile didn't seem to have a positive effect on the landlady of 221B Baker Street.

"You get your lazy bones upstairs and finish mopping up that floor," said Mrs. Hudson in a voice that brooked no disobedience. "And when you're done with that, you'll be washing cups and drying them."

"Oi! Ne'er thought it'd be that 'ard for a bloke to be goin' straight." Dodger gave Jacqueline a pained grin, but to her surprise, he gave one more theatrical bow and then loped off—presumably to do Mrs. Hudson's bidding.

"What's he doing here?" Jacqueline demanded. She hadn't seen a copy of *Oliver Twist* fall off the shelf. "How did he get here?"

Mrs. Hudson shrugged. "Why, the same way they always do, dearie. We've discussed this before." She gave Jacqueline a patient smile laced with just the faintest bit of exasperation.

"Yes, yes, I know, but usually I see or at least hear the books when they fall off the shelf, and then I have a warning that—um—someone is going to show up. But I didn't see his book anywhere," Jacqueline told her.

How was she going to figure out this shop if the freaking rules kept changing?

"That Danvers creature probably picked it up and put it away," said Mrs. Hudson. "She's sneaky like that."

"Well, she's going to have to stop doing that," Jacqueline said, already imagining the murderous Bill Sikes showing up. Just in time for her grand reopening tomorrow. *No, please...* "Or I'll—"

"Yes, ma'am?" The cold voice from behind had Jacqueline's heart leaping into her throat, dammit.

She turned to see Danvers standing there, looking, as always, like a bad-tempered crow. Her neat blue-black dress was belted at the waist and her inky hair was scraped back into its usual no-nonsense knot. Jacqueline hadn't ever gotten close enough to look, but she suspected that neither a gray nor a white hair would even consider marring that dark, shiny expanse. Mrs. Danvers's features were sharp and angular, and her mouth was set in a pale pink line. She wore heavy, dark hose—which was testament that she was definitely from a different time—and sensible black shoes, along with tiny jet bead earrings at her ears. She carried a ring of keys at her belt that *should* have jingled when she walked, and thus announced her presence, but for some reason never did.

"What is it you wished to speak to me about." Danvers framed her words not as a question, but as a challenge—which was par for the course. She didn't like to take direction from anyone except her beloved Rebecca.

"Jack Dawkins has arrived from *Oliver Twist*," Jacqueline said, forcing herself to keep eye contact with the housekeeper. "And I didn't hear the book drop or see it. Did you?"

Mrs. Danvers sniffed. "If there is a book on the floor, of course I am not going to *leave* it there." She was no taller than Jacqueline, but she somehow managed to look down at her with those glittering dark eyes.

Jacqueline gritted her teeth. "Yes, of course. But if it's a special book—"

"A *special* book?" Danvers gave her a look of condescension and delicate confusion.

Jacqueline *hated* that she felt flustered. Why should she? After all, *she* was a real person, and the creepy scarecrow in front of her was only a figment of Daphne du Maurier's imagination. "Well, the, uh, sort of book where the—"

"Aw, come off it, ye old hag," Mrs. Hudson exploded. "Ye know what she means, now, don't you? And you just picked up that book on purpose so she wouldn't see it, now didn't ye?"

"If you're not satisfied with my work," Danvers said, fixing Jacqueline with a haughty look, "then you should certainly dismiss me."

Oh, if *only*!

"Ma'am," Danvers added with a touch of maliciousness.

Jacqueline wanted nothing more than to dismiss Mrs. Danvers and send her back into her book. (Not that she knew where the book was, which was part of the problem.) She felt Mrs. Hudson fairly quivering next to her, ready to crow what would surely be a victorious cry if Jacqueline did so, sending away her nemesis and leaving her to reign supreme over Three Tomes and its tea room just as she had done at 221B Baker Street.

But Jacqueline couldn't do it. The warring thoughts rattled through her mind in a matter of seconds—she really did need the extra help, and Danvers really did do a good job, and Jacqueline didn't have to do payroll for her, which was a *big* bonus. But the real reason she didn't send the woman away was simply because she didn't think Danvers would actually go.

Or, if she *did* go, that she'd set the bloody bookshop on fire on her way out the door. Jacqueline shuddered at the thought of all her beloved tomes going up in a Fahrenheit-451 blaze.

"Not at all," Jacqueline said, adopting a lady-of-the-manor tone. Perhaps Danvers would respond better to that sort of persona. After all, she'd worshipped Rebecca. "But if one of the old books falls off the shelf and lands with its pages open—you *know* what I'm talking about—I want to know about it." She gave the housekeeper a firm look.

For a moment, it appeared Danvers was about to dismiss herself. Clearly, even the lady-of-the-manor tone wasn't to her liking. But then the housekeeper bowed her head—more insolently than deferentially—and said, "Of course, ma'am."

Mrs. Hudson, who'd been watching eagerly, deflated like a forlorn balloon and muttered something it was probably best that Jacqueline didn't hear.

"Very well. Now, have there been any other books that have fallen and might be heralding any new, er, newcomers?" Jacqueline asked. She was also wondering whether more than one character could come out of a single book that fell.

Perhaps she'd ask the ZAP Ladies—the three old women who were probably witches who lived at the end of Camellia Court—about that, instead of further engaging with Danvers and Hudson.

"No, ma'am," said Danvers sullenly.

"Very well. You may proceed with whatever you were doing," Jacqueline said, still trying for the airiness of a wealthy woman ordering her servant about.

"That is why I came looking for you," said Danvers, clearly expecting that Jacqueline should have read her mind and already known the reason for her appearance. "There is an individual who wishes to speak to you."

"I see," Jacqueline said. "At the counter?"

"Of course," replied Danvers.

Jacqueline didn't exactly flee, but she wasted no time making her way to the front room. As always when she walked in, she was suffused with delight by the way the sunshine poured in through the large bay windows, whose platforms were filled with books on display. A round table in the center of the room held another display of titles—mostly new fiction—on a circular, tiered shelf where Sebastian often found a spot of sun in which to park himself, heedless of the hair he left clinging to page and spine.

She saw the back of the woman who was browsing through a book by the window. She had a head of short, curly mouse-brown hair, and there was something familiar about her.

"Hello," Jacqueline said pleasantly. "How may I— *Wendy?*"

"Jacqueline." There was a bit of hesitancy in the other woman's voice—which was not surprising, since the last time Jacqueline had seen her so-called best friend back in Chicago, Wendy hadn't been very nice. In fact, she'd been downright awful. "Hi."

"What are you doing here?" said Jacqueline, confused and trying not to sound unwelcoming. She wasn't, of course, being unwelcoming, but she was just so surprised by the non sequitur of her old friend showing up. Jacqueline hadn't thought much about Wendy Tract and the life she'd left back in Chicago over the last three weeks.

But all of a sudden the memory of that day—that terrible, horrible, no-good day when her life made a one-eighty flip—rushed back to her mind. That was the last time she'd seen Wendy, and she supposed she *was* still hurt and angry over it. But not enough to be rude or even cool to her. Jacqueline was very good at being a people pleaser, and she avoided conflict like the plague.

"I wanted to see your shop," said Wendy, still hesitant as she clutched her purse close to her side. "And... well, we left off on a—a sour note, and I felt bad about it."

She was right. On that terrible day, Jacqueline had been given her pink slip—literally—from the Chicago Public Library, and was on her way out of the building carrying a banker's box filled with her personal effects when she'd run into her friend. Jacqueline tried to say goodbye, but Wendy had simply given her a disappointed, condescending look and said, "I would never have expected it of you, Jacqueline."

Wendy was referring to the rumor that Jacqueline had tried to seduce—or had actually completed a seduction; Jacqueline never quite got the details—one of the male coworkers at the library. Who was married.

The fact that Wendy had not only believed such a thing, but hadn't warned Jacqueline about the rumor, really stung. Her dismissive and judgmental comment had really stabbed Jacqueline in the gut.

But not long after Jacqueline settled in at Three Tomes, Wendy had texted an apology. Jacqueline replied with a "no worries" message, but no other exchange had happened...until now.

"It's all good, Wendy. We're good. And, well, welcome to Three Tomes," said Jacqueline. She did a self-check and was pleased that her smile was, in fact, mostly genuine and that she didn't harbor any significantly bad feelings toward Wendy. There was some awkwardness, true, and maybe a bit of the emotional bruising lingered, but she could certainly be pleasant for the short time Wendy was here at the shop.

The truth was that Jacqueline thought she'd

been happy in Chicago—that she'd had the perfect life—but even after less than a month here, her life here in Button Cove was far better than anything she'd ever imagined...even considering Mrs. Danvers.

"You look good," Jacqueline went on, feeling the need to fill the space with words. "And I love your purse!"

"Oh, thank you," Wendy said with a smile, glancing down at the bag hanging from her shoulder. It was sleek and curvy, made from rosy-pink leather that looked soft as butter. It had a flap that folded up, over, and down, clasping on the front at a large metal medallion with an intricate design of vines and flowers twining around an ornate E. There were matching metal bumpers with tiny feet on the bottom corners of the bag so it wouldn't get scuffed or dirty if it was set on the floor—not that Jacqueline would set a bag like that on the floor. It looked soft enough to ooze into a puddle of suede, but yet it kept its shape perfectly.

"It's from an up-and-coming designer," Wendy went on, pushing her red-framed glasses back up onto the bridge of her nose. "I actually won it in a raffle—I could never have afforded to buy it, you know."

"It's gorgeous," Jacqueline said, still looking at it and feeling a little twinge of envy. She wasn't a big lover of handbags, but this one really caught her eye. And it looked large enough to hold her smartphone, e-reader, wallet, and reading glasses, along with the myriad other necessities she carried in her purse. She might have to splurge...though probably not, considering all the extra costs associated with moving into a new apartment.

Maybe she could buy herself one for Christmas if

the store did well enough. She wondered who the designer was. Probably someone with the initial E.

"This is the most charming bookshop I've ever seen," said Wendy, breaking into Jacqueline's thoughts and looking around avidly. The tenseness had evaporated from her expression and she seemed more at ease. "Oh, and you even have a shop cat!"

Sebastian had made his appearance, and he accepted Wendy's affections as his due. Wendy had always lamented that they couldn't have a cat at the library. "Cats and books simply belong together," she'd say. "Along with cups of tea."

Jacqueline introduced Wendy to Sebastian and Max, the latter of whom was currently sitting in the window display next to the new Charles Finch and Stephen King. "Would you like to see the tea room? It's upstairs. We could sit and have a cup and catch up."

Wendy visibly flinched. "You have a tea room? Is it in the actual bookshop?" The brown eyes behind her scarlet-framed glasses were wide with dismay, and she made a quiet sound of distress.

Jacqueline hid a smile. She'd had the exact same reaction upon first learning about the café upstairs. But she couldn't tell Wendy that the books were protected magically. Nor could she tell her that Mrs. Hudson was, in fact, Mrs. Hudson.

"Our customers are very careful," said Jacqueline as she led the way upstairs. "And we encourage them to purchase the books before they sit in the tea room." That wasn't precisely true, but she felt she had to say something so that Wendy wouldn't think Jacqueline had abandoned all her bookish scruples now that she was out of the library world.

"I see," replied Wendy.

When they reached the top of the stairs—which

rose from the side of the front room on the first floor into a wide-open space on the second level—Wendy gasped.

"Oh my!"

Jacqueline had had a similar reaction the first time she saw the café. It had the high ceiling popular in Victorian homes, and there were tall, narrow windows through which the April sunshine poured. A large fireplace was situated on the front wall, and a sofa and two loveseats created the perfect U-shape for customers to sit and enjoy the blaze. There were some café tables furnished with mismatched chairs, and more sofas and armchairs arranged throughout. A long counter that ran about a third of the length of the front room had three stools for customers, along with rows of stainless-steel tins filled with loose tea. Several three-tier stands covered by glass domes displayed the pastries from Sweet Devotion, Suzette's bakery. Between the windows and fireplace, framed blow-ups of well-known books were mounted on the wall.

"Why, it's just perfect! Simply perfect!" exclaimed Wendy. "Jacqueline, I'm so very happy for you!"

And with that, she burst into tears.

3

"So...she just showed up, ordered tea, and started bawling?" said Suzette.

It was after nine o'clock that evening. The book-shop had just closed, but Jacqueline had been working on preparations for the celebration tomorrow, and Suzette had wandered over from across the street to see if she needed any help.

Jacqueline shook her head. "We didn't even get to the tea. She was bawling before we stepped off the stairs."

"Why was she crying?" replied Suzette, shaking her curly head. Her skin was dusky olive and her hair was a mop of curly black liberally streaked with gray. She had sleek, cut shoulders and biceps from her work kneading and shaping dough, and a long, lithe figure of average height. Her dubious expression fit the pragmatic personality Jacqueline had come to know and appreciate. Less emotional and more cut-to-the-chase than Nadine, Suzette was a get-'er-done kind of person—and, clearly, exploding into sobs in the middle of an old friend's business wasn't her idea of kosher behavior.

"I'm not really sure," Jacqueline replied, still

feeling as if she'd been clocked in the head. "She never really said what was wrong, just kind of mumbled and sobbed. I think she said something about being cursed—but I didn't take it literally," she said quickly when Suzette's eyebrows shot up. "I don't *think* she meant it literally. Of course she didn't mean it literally. Still, it was very strange."

"What did Mrs. Hudson do?"

"Oh, you know—the normal thing," Jacqueline replied with a laugh. "She made her a strong cuppa with lots of milk and sugar and insisted Wendy sit in front of the fire and drink it. Wendy finally collected herself, apologized to me, and then she left." She shrugged. "It was pretty odd, really. She just showed up, broke down, then fled."

"She must really feel bad about how she treated you back in Chicago," said Suzette.

"Maybe. I don't know. I just don't know what to think about it, so I'm going to put it out of my mind." Jacqueline hesitated, then went on. "I got the impression Wendy is staying here in Button Cove for a few days. Maybe she'll come back in and we'll have a coherent conversation."

"Did she buy anything while she was here?" asked Suzette, looking around grimly as if she would be personally affronted if Wendy hadn't.

"No," replied Jacqueline, wondering how she should feel about that. After all, she did own a business and had to think about things like the bottom line nowadays. Nadine and Suzette always insisted on paying for their tea when the three of them sat in the café—even when Jacqueline waved them off. And Wendy hadn't even thanked her for the tea Mrs. Hudson had given her, let alone offered to pay for it— not that she would have allowed her to do so, since

Jacqueline had invited her up there, but still...it seemed odd that she hadn't even offered.

The whole event was really quite strange.

Just then, the shop's door rattled in its frame, and Jacqueline looked up to see Nadine's nose and splayed hands pressed to the window and her eyes comically wide above them.

"Now I'm going to have to wipe off your nose print from the glass," Jacqueline teased as she opened the door.

Nadine fairly bounced in. "I just came over to make sure everything was under control for tomorrow. It's gonna be *big*, Jacqueline. I just know it's going to be a great success. What are you bringing?" This was directed toward Suzette. "I'm watching my carbs, but tomorrow is Free Day Sunday."

"That's right—Sunday's always a free day because it's pizza night," Suzette replied, laughing.

"It is. And tomorrow is a super, extra-special Free Day Sunday because it's Jacqueline's open house even though we're not officially doing pizza night. So, what have I been saving up my carbs for? Blondies, I hope?"

Suzette nodded. "Yes, of course. Just for you. Cut into small, bite-sized pieces. I'm also doing little pizza turnovers, each about as big as your pinkie. And I'm making tiny raspberry tarts—each one the size of one perfect raspberry. Andromeda supplied me with the berries, and each one is huge—as big as my thumb."

"And out of season," Jacqueline said wryly.

Andromeda was one of the so-called ZAP Ladies who lived in the robin's-egg-blue Victorian with the tangled gardens at the end of the court. Jacqueline didn't quite know how the three women managed it (actually, she could guess), but their tiny plot of land produced an unbelievable amount of fresh fruits, vegetables, herbs, and even some nuts and spices year-round. She suspected they helped the gardens with a spell or a charm or maybe some other sort of earth energy.

"It all sounds super yummy," replied Nadine. "I'm going to starve myself all day tomorrow!"

"And there will be wine, tea, and some soft drinks as well," said Jacqueline. "I couldn't get Mrs. Hudson to agree to coffee, but I'm going to sneak some in. I've also got tea sandwiches coming from Orbra's Tea House down in Wicks Hollow. I haven't been there, but I hear it's got the best high tea around."

"It does," replied Suzette. "We have to go some-time. Orbra is a hoot, and her friends Maxine and Juanita are real pieces of work. You'll love them. Any-way, I've got to be heading out. It looks like you have everything under control, Jacqueline, and as usual, I've got an early morning tomorrow!" As a baker, she rose at four thirty to start work for the day, even when she wasn't catering a grand reopening party.

"Thanks for coming by. I'll have a check for you tomorrow when the food is delivered," said Jacqueline.

"No rush, but thanks," replied Suzette, heading for the exit.

"But I just got here," said Nadine mournfully.

"Sorry, chica—I've got to get my beauty sleep." Suzette blew a kiss and slipped out the door.

"You can help me move this table," Jacqueline said to Nadine, gesturing to the large, round table. "I just decided to move it out of the way, against the wall over there, because it might get too crowded tomorrow and people will bump into the display. At least, I *hope* it'll get too crowded. Am I being too optimistic?"

"No!" said Nadine. "Think positive, Jacqueline!"

Mrs. Hudson and Mrs. Danvers had disappeared, as they usually did every evening, and Jacqueline hadn't seen the Artful Dodger since Mrs. Hudson shamed him into getting back to work. She wasn't certain whether to be nervous or relieved.

She and Nadine had just finished sliding the table aside, cramming it into the corner near the front counter, when she heard a familiar thud.

Crap.

"Did something just fall back there?" asked Nadine.

"Yes," replied Jacqueline grimly. "A book."

"Did the cats— Oh." Nadine winced. "Do you think it's *that* kind of book?"

Jacqueline sighed. "We'd better check."

"How do you know if it's that kind of book?" asked Nadine. "The kind where someone comes out."

"Because," Jacqueline said, already at the doorway to the room from where the thud had come, "there's no way that book just fell off the shelf, and, see—it's open. No one was in here, including the cats. Even if a book were to get knocked off the shelf, it rarely would land wide open like that." She sighed.

Nadine started toward the splayed book, then stopped. "Can I touch it? Pick it up?"

"Hasn't killed me yet," replied Jacqueline, eyeing the open tome with a very annoyed look. She didn't need any more characters showing up here! Although she hadn't seen Dodger for a while, so maybe he'd gone back in....

"*Grimms' Fairy Tales,*" said Nadine, crouching next to the book. "Can I close it?"

"Yes," said Jacqueline, looking at the ancient volume. It was so old that the binding was frayed and the pages were yellowed and crackling. When Nadine closed it, there was a soft puff of dust and mildew smell. Jacqueline could hardly read the title on the dirt-brown cover; the embossed imprint was faded and had been smoothed nearly flat. "Oh, wait...what fairy tale was it open to?"

"Oh crap, I didn't notice," replied Nadine with a grimace. "I'm sorry. Does that matter?"

"It might give me an idea of who's going to show up," replied Jacqueline.

"Do you mean anyone from Grimms' fairy tales could show up? Like, the giant from 'Jack and the Beanstalk'?" Nadine's eyes bulged. "Or the wolf from 'Little Red Riding Hood'?"

"I don't think 'Jack and the Beanstalk' is a Grimm tale," Jacqueline said faintly. But Red Riding Hood was...

"What about 'Snow White'? Could the dwarfs show up? I mean, that might not be too bad..." Nadine gave her a pained smile. "They're hard workers."

"I don't really know how this actually works," Jacqueline replied helplessly. "All I know is that someone from that book is going to show up...sometime. I don't know who or when or how. And I've already got the Artful Dodger sneaking around here somewhere."

"Wait. The pickpocket from *Oliver Twist*?"

"The one and only Jack Dawkins," said Jacqueline. "Mrs. Hudson had him working upstairs for her, and I haven't seen him for a while."

"Do you think she brought him here?" asked Nadine. "Can they do that? I mean, if they can, you know, I have a real big crush on Roarke from the In Death series. Any chance they could, you know, get him to visit...?" Then she shook her head and waved her hands frantically. "Never mind, never mind. Eve

Dallas would jump from the pages and slice me to bits. Maybe I'd be better off going for Sargent Blue from the TJ Mack books instead. He's my second book boyfriend crush."

Jacqueline's smile, prompted by her friend's antics, faded. She shrugged. "I don't know if anyone can call them or bring them or how it works. I really don't know all the rules yet. I do know that Danvers picked up *Oliver Twist* and closed it, so I didn't even know the book had fallen until I found the Dodger sleeping in the mystery/thriller room."

"Wow. That kind of sucks, doesn't it?" Nadine said, looking around. "Not knowing the rules."

"Well, it's not great," Jacqueline replied. But despite the sense of foreboding she'd been feeling ever since this morning, and the upheaval of falling books and materializing characters, she couldn't help but *love*—just *love*—Three Tomes and her new life. She'd ended up here because of her family's roots, and she knew there was a reason for it. She just wasn't quite sure what it was she was supposed to do with this very special magical bookshop.

She slid *Grimms' Fairy Tales* back onto the shelf among some of the other vintage tomes and hoped that Rumpelstiltskin wouldn't show up tomorrow and ruin her party.

4

The next morning, Jacqueline was a little hesitant as she opened the back door and stepped into Three Tomes.

The shop spilled before her—the corridor that led to the front, studded with all of its doorways along the way, was dim and quiet. There was no sign of life, including the cats, and Jacqueline felt a little tremor of unease. Usually at least Sebastian greeted her when she came in, and more often than not, she could hear Danvers mucking about in the back room or making noise somewhere in the depths of the place.

But today, it was like a tomb: still, empty, shadowy. She closed the door silently behind her and locked it, for it wasn't yet time for the shop to open.

"Is this the first time I've been in here alone?" she wondered aloud in a whisper that was hardly more than the movement of her mouth.

The first time since the day she'd arrived, anyway, when she stepped into the eerie, dusty, and shadowy shop. Since then, Hudson and Danvers seemed to always be lurking about somewhere.

Jacqueline set down the insulated coffee mug she'd taken to sneaking into the shop because Mrs.

Hudson steadfastly refused to have coffee upstairs in the café. Then she hung up her light jacket—even a sunny April morning next to Lake Michigan was still quite chilly—and was just about to head up to the front room when she glanced at the door to the cellar. A little prickle of something—not nerves so much as awareness, or even anticipation—skittered over her shoulders and down her spine.

She hadn't been down in the cellar for weeks. Not since that first time. But something pulled her to go down there now.

She hesitated, looking down into the darkness, then flipped the wall switch. A spill of light illuminated her way down the steps and into the concrete-floored, mason-bricked cellar. She began to descend.

The basement itself wasn't scary. It *had* been scary when Jacqueline was trapped down there with Oz's Wicked Witch of the West three weeks ago.

No...the basement wasn't scary at all. It was special. And unique.

So why had she avoided coming down here ever since she'd discovered how special it was?

Jacqueline's heart thudded wildly in her chest. It wasn't because she was afraid she'd encounter a rodent or walk into a spider web, or, worse, have a spider *land* on her. It was because she knew the space *needed* her, and she didn't really know what that meant.

A small channel, no more than six inches wide, wound through the floor near one corner of the room. Water tumbled gently inside the channel, winding with a pleasant gurgle around a circle of exposed earth in the floor. Just beyond the water and earth was part of a tree trunk, protruding from one of the basement walls. She knew the tree had been there first, long before the walls were built, and that the mason bricks had been carefully set around the trunk. A bit of root angled up from the floor next to it, and as Jacqueline drew closer, she could make out the marks on the tree trunk...some of them ancient.

The tree was a cedar, and its gnarled, rough bark had been peeled away to expose smooth, fragrant red wood. Jacqueline's handprint, made in red when she was only five and hardly remembered it, was a symbol of her inclusion in the female ancestral line of the Stone family, which was descended from women of the Anishinaabek. The other, older handprints hadn't faded over time—over the centuries, perhaps even millennia—but hers was the most recent, and its image stuck out to her even amidst the other marks.

The strangest thing of all was that when Jacqueline had first seen her handprint on the tree trunk three weeks ago, it was the size of a child's palm. But once she saw it and recognized it—and remembered placing it there—the print had metamorphosed into the current size of her hand, as if to confirm: *Yes, it's you, and you belong here.*

Three Tomes Bookshop was a special place, located on a piece of earth filled with unique and powerful energy. And this area, this cellar, was a center of that energy...a sacred place.

To the Anishinaabek, cedar, raw earth, and running water were powerful elements of nature, sacred and filled with energy and wisdom. These indigenous people had lived in the area for millennia...and it was from those wise women that Jacqueline had descended through the maternal line of the Stone family.

"I'm here," Jacqueline said aloud, then wondered why she was compelled to do so. But even as the thought sifted through her mind, a little pleasant prickling rushed through her body, as if to say, *Welcome.*

Still uncertain what precisely she was supposed to do about this place, Jacqueline sank onto the uneven concrete floor next to the circle of exposed earth. It was delineated by a frame of bricks set into the ground, as if to ensure it wasn't mistaken for anything other than an altar. *Altar.*

Jacqueline tilted her head and thought about it. She decided she liked the idea.

But she still didn't know what it was she was supposed to *do* about it. It was just a flat, circular area of ground.

"I get that I'm related to all these—I don't know, wise women? Shaman? Crones?"—she refused to say witches—"who came before me. From whom I'm descended," she went on, speaking to whatever energy was listening. "But what am I supposed to *do* with it? With this space? With this entire place?"

When no response was forthcoming, she trailed a fingertip in the burbling water, thinking how strange and beautiful it was to have a little creek running through the basement of her home. She didn't worry that it would cause a flood someday, or that the protruding cedar would weaken the foundation, or that anything would come up from the exposed earth...she simply *knew* that she didn't have to be concerned about that.

It was a sacred, special place, and it was protected because Mother Nature herself was being honored within.

But that didn't mean Jacqueline fully understood what she was doing there.

Perhaps she was just a guardian of the space.

And that, she thought, was reasonable. That she could do.

The sounds from above told her that someone—Danvers, most likely—was about, and that she had a party to prepare for.

Jacqueline took one more moment to touch her hand, palm flat, to the circle of dirt she'd called an altar. She closed her eyes and swore she felt the heartbeat of the earth.

I'm here, she thought again.

And then she rose and, with one final look around, started up the stairs.

Back on the main floor of the shop, Jacqueline swept into the whirlwind of party planner. It was just ten o'clock (the shop opened late on Sundays), and although the grand reopening didn't start until three and she had everything planned and organized, she felt anxious and nervous and excited. She unlocked the back door and flipped the sign to *Open*, then walked up to do the same at the front.

Sebastian and Max were in their usual spots, overseeing the shop with their sharp feline eyes. The soft clinks and clatters from above indicated that Mrs. Hudson was at work as well.

To Jacqueline's delight, Mrs. Danvers was nowhere to be found, which helped her to relax a little as she booted up the computer cash register for the day. Still, she was waiting for someone from Grimms' to show up at any time, and fervently hoped it wouldn't be the likes of the "Hansel and Gretel" witch.

She had enough witches about.

At that moment, as if her thoughts had done some conjuring, the front door rattled sharply in its frame, then clunked back into place before opening with a little jingle from the bell above it.

Jacqueline looked up to see three old women crowded in the entrance, right below the picture of the Witches Three from *Macbeth* (sadly, not the least bit coincidental, she'd come to realize) that hung over the doorway. It was almost comical, for the trio seemed to all be trying to step across the threshold at the same time and got themselves wedged in the opening. It reminded Jacqueline of a Three Stooges scene, but in this case, it was the three crones—better known as the ZAP Ladies.

"You'd think you'd know by now that you have to push the door, not pull it, Petey," one of them was grumbling. She was slender and lean with golden skin and elfin features. Her pale blue hair was styled appropriately in a pixie cut. She wore cropped pants and a *Flashdance*-style top that hung over one crepe-wrinkled shoulder, revealing the wide strap of a sports bra.

"I always forget," replied Pietra, who was the shortest, roundest, and most fair-skinned of the three. Somehow, she managed to squeeze her way in first. She looked like a luscious grape in the shimmery lime-green maxi dress she wore. She had a pretty face with sparkling eyes and soft, round cheeks, chin, and nose topped by a head of soft brown hair. "Hello, Jacqueline! Did you see that hearse going down the street again?"

"Well, hello there, handsome," said Andromeda, the woman with the spiky blue hair, before Jacqueline could reply by wondering aloud why everyone was so concerned about the hearse. Andromeda was speaking to Sebastian, who'd risen from his seated position on the counter in order to receive her affectionate greeting.

"Good morning, Jacqueline," said the third arrival.

She'd been the first to extricate herself from the madcap comedy that was the trio's entrance, stepping back onto the sidewalk so that her friends might make their entrance. Zwyla was a smooth-skinned Black woman who stood over six feet tall, often taller when she wore platform heels. She wore a gold turban embroidered with jet beads and an A-line dress hemmed in beaded fringe that rattled pleasantly as she glided into the shop. "We brought you a housewarming present."

Oh joy. Jacqueline's smile froze on her face. *Oh dear.*

To the three old ladies—all of them in their eighties—a housewarming present could be anything from a bundle of dried sage for smudging and banishing bad energy (which Jacqueline would actually welcome), to a month's supply of eyebright tea (which was definitely not one of Jacqueline's favorite things), to a jar of dried newt or pickled snake eyeballs or whatever other weird thing was in the little herbary workshop they used for...whatever it was they did. Which she didn't like to think about.

"How sweet of you." Jacqueline kept her other thoughts to herself, however, and smiled more genuinely as she closed the door behind the women.

Despite their collective determination to offer unsolicited advice like a group of nosy grandmothers, she enjoyed the ZAP Ladies (so named because of their initials) and their antics. Even Zwyla—who, at six foot two and counting, could come across as intimidating at times—was kind and interesting.

Pietra, on the other hand, was like a motherly apple of a woman, and she was one hell of a baker. Maybe she'd made some of her glazed blueberry scones, in which case Jacqueline decided she would definitely not share them with customers via the tea room or at her party. After all, they were her favorite.

"I won't be settled into the apartment for days. Maybe even weeks," Jacqueline said. She was speaking of the third floor at Three Tomes, which was a large and spacious flat with its own working fireplace. It was the fireplace that had sold her on living above her shop when she initially resisted the idea of being so close to her work. "Because of the grand reopening today. Ask me why on earth I decided to do both things in the same week."

"Why did you—" Pietra started before her friend interrupted.

"We're really glad you decided to move in up there," said Andromeda, giving Pietra a roll of the eyes. "Haven't you ever heard of rhetorical questions?" she muttered to her friend.

"It wasn't a question, it was a command, Miss Grammar Queen," Pietra retorted. "She said, 'Ask me why—'"

"Fine, it was a rhetorical *command*," Andromeda said with a huff. "Same thing."

Pietra gave her friend a little shove, then turned her attention to Jacqueline. "It'll be so much easier having you nearby all the time," she said eagerly, sending a shiver of dread down Jacqueline's spine.

Oh, man. Did this mean the ZAP Ladies would regularly be inviting themselves to dinner upstairs at her place? At least now she could escape and go back to her hotel room at night...

"Well, I'm here all the time at the shop anyway..." Jacqueline said uncertainly.

"Yes, of course, but this way you'll be here *all* the time." Pietra beamed and, to Jacqueline's relief, thrust a small wicker basket at her. "Oh, and I brought blueberry scones—glazed, of course. I know they're your favorite, so don't you *dare* share them at the gathering today. And underneath the napkin are some catnip biscuits for your shop-mates." She smiled at Max and Sebastian. "Don't eat them all at once, you silly things," she told them. "You'll start hallucinating." Even Max seemed interested, for he jumped down from the top of the bookshelf and landed lightly on the counter. He didn't preen like Sebastian did, but he did deign to lower his head for a quick pat before sniffing genteelly at the basket.

"Thank you so much," Jacqueline said, taking the basket. "And I won't!"

"Shall we bring it upstairs for you?" asked Zwyla. She was extricating something from the large, tote-like purse she carried over her shoulder.

"Bring what upstairs?"

That was when she saw the too-large parcel Zwyla had pulled slightly out of her far-too-small bag to show her. Jacqueline shook her head; she'd learned not to ask questions about such strange things.

"It's a little bulky," said Zwyla, tucking it back inside. Jacqueline noticed the purse didn't seem to move or sag from the item's significant weight.

"Besides, I want to see what you've done to the place," said Andromeda. "You've got all those tall windows—I'm going to get you some nice plants to put on the sills. Probably some rosemary, and maybe a pothos. If you let the pothos go, it'll grow all along the window's edge, so be sure to cut it back to keep it in line."

"Sure," replied Jacqueline. Plants would be a housewarming present she'd love, although coming from Andromeda, she might be concerned about the pothos getting a little crazy. "I'll see if Mrs. Hudson will come down and watch the counter."

"There's no need for that," said a stony voice.

Jacqueline's heart jolted, and she turned to see Mrs. Danvers standing there.

"*I* will handle it," said the housekeeper with a sniff. "Ma'am."

"And scare everyone off at the same time," muttered Pietra, probably too quietly for Danvers to hear.

But when the housekeeper trained a pointed look at Pietra, Jacqueline knew she'd been wrong. Pietra glared back at Danvers, lifting her pudgy chin...but she also stepped a little closer to Zwyla.

"At least someone will update the inventory properly," continued Danvers, giving Jacqueline a dark look.

Only too happy to remove herself from the housekeeper's dark, sardonic presence, Jacqueline led the way to the service elevator in the rear of the house that would take them to the third floor. She only hoped Pietra was wrong and that customers wouldn't be scared off by the crow-like woman.

"Oh, my! You've cleared everything out and painted already," said Andromeda as she walked down the apartment's hallway, which ran along one side of the building, to the front room. "I love the dusky sage for the wall around the fireplace! It's so cozy."

"I didn't need Cuddy's furniture," Jacqueline said. "It—uh—wasn't my style." She'd been glad to get rid of all of the old, musty furnishings from the previous owner, who was her benefactor and distant relation. And whom she'd never met, let alone even heard of before this inheritance. Jacqueline was especially relieved that the large, round mirror that had hung over the fireplace in the living room was gone. '

The mirror had been possessed by another witchy ancestor of Jacqueline's—Crusilla—and it was only after the glass had been broken that the creepy old witch was banished.

As if reading her mind, Zwyla said, "This will go perfectly above the fireplace." She set down her tote and began to pull out the parcel. As it emerged from the bag, the item became impossibly wider and taller. It was wrapped in brown kraft paper and tied with string.

"Go on, open it!" cried Pietra, fairly dancing with excitement once the flat, rectangular item was fully extracted.

Jacqueline loved presents. Who didn't? But she was, admittedly, a little nervous about what the large, rectangular package contained. She hoped it wasn't another mirror...there was no way she wanted to take the chance of some spirit living in the mirror and watching her all the time.

But she didn't hesitate. It was, after all, a *present*.

"Oh!" she cried with real enthusiasm when she tore the paper away and saw the painting. "It's gorgeous!"

She was immediately and truly enamored. The picture was at least three feet wide and two feet tall, and the painting was done in oil of a beautiful cedar tree with intricately gnarled branches and a knobbly trunk. It was a simple yet stunning depiction of a sprawling tree created in blues and greens and grays... and immediately Jacqueline felt a shimmer of *something*—some sort of energy—as she brushed her hand over the picture.

The cedar that protruded into the basement grew mostly unfettered in a courtyard out in the back, where she could see it every time she walked into the shop. It felt simply perfect, simply *right*, that Jacqueline would have an image of the tree honored by her ancestors in her living space as well.

"Thank you," she said, blinking rapidly and hoping no one would notice. "It's absolutely perfect."

"And you won't have to worry about anyone possessing it, like the mirror," said Andromeda, patting her arm.

"Thank heaven for that," said Jacqueline, still staring at the image. The longer she looked at it, the more details became clear to her. The background of the tree was dim and shadowy as if it were deep in a forest, but there was a spill of light just beyond, as if sunshine filtered down and limned the delicate edges of its branches and made a small pool of yellow-gold on the ground. She discerned birds among the cedar's branches, the subtle shapes of butterflies and bees, clusters of icy-green-blue berries. She could almost smell the scent of fresh cedar, too.

"Shall we help you hang it?" asked Zwyla. A smile of pleasure quirked her mouth.

Jacqueline agreed readily; she suspected it would be much simpler to let them do it than to try to struggle with it herself. It was quite heavy, with its thick, ornate frame of some carved wood. Besides, she'd end up hanging it crookedly anyway—she always did.

"Our friend Wayren did most of the painting," said Pietra in a low voice as her statuesque friend lifted the painting with one hand, as if it were no heavier than a piece of paper. "But we all helped a little—Andi and Z and me. Each of us added our own little bits to it to make it personal." She was beaming with pleasure, and Jacqueline's eyes began to burn again, dammit. "It's a very special piece."

"It's gorgeous," Jacqueline told Pietra, her voice a little rusty with emotion. "I couldn't have asked for anything better."

"We're just so glad you're here, and that you've begun to settle in," said Andromeda. She'd folded her arms over her middle, but the tip of her nose was suspiciously pink, and she seemed to be blinking more than necessary as well.

"There we go," said Zwyla, stepping back to survey her handiwork.

"Thank you. I love it. It's the best housewarming present ever," Jacqueline said, eyeing the painting in its new location over the dark maw of the fireplace. It looked perfect above the creamy brick of the facing, surrounded by the dusky sage of the walls. She couldn't wait to get her cornflower-blue velvet sofa in front of it.

"You're very welcome. You're part of us now, you know," said Zwyla. Even she seemed to be blinking more than necessary. "Here on Camellia Court. See there, in the bottom right corner? Those are camellias."

"We had to add them because...well, because camellias represent so much of everything about this court," Andromeda said in a voice that was a little rusty. "What you're a part of."

Jacqueline nodded, not trusting herself to speak... and not exactly sure she fully understood what it meant to be part of them. But she felt too foolish to ask. She knew that the mystical energy from camellia flowers was supposed to enhance divine femininity and friendships, confidence and prosperity. All things she'd found since coming to Button Cove.

At last she collected herself. She swallowed and said, "Yes, thank you for making me feel so welcome.

Now, I'd best get downstairs and make certain Danvers isn't scaring away customers," she added briskly, to cover her emotions.

"Good luck with that," Pietra muttered.

Jacqueline led the way back down the hall to the little elevator. "I have no idea how the movers are going to fit my sofa and queen-sized bed in this elevator," she said as they squeezed into the tiny box. She could smell different floral scents emanating from each of her companions, and wished she could identify them. "They might have to come up the stairs."

"Oh, we can help with that. Especially Zwyla," said Pietra eagerly.

"Of course, if you like," replied Zwyla. "We could take care of it today before the party."

Jacqueline's eyes bugged a little. "Really? That would be amazing!"

"Certainly," replied Andromeda. "What are friends —and crones—for?"

They were laughing companionably when the elevator door opened to the second floor tea room.

"Oi, beg your pardon, my lady," said the Artful Dodger, stepping back in surprise. He looked only slightly less disreputable than he had yesterday. Perhaps Mrs. Hudson had made him comb his hair, though it was hard to tell under the hat, and at least the streaks of grime were gone from his face and hands. But he still wore clothing that was too long and baggy for him, and his top hat slouched grumpily on his head. Yet his white shirt didn't look quite as dingy, and he'd somehow acquired a fresh carnation. White, this time, and probably from the vases Mrs. Hudson put out on the tables every morning.

"Good morning," said Jacqueline, noticing that

Dodger was holding a large box of teacups and saucers. "Are you taking that downstairs?"

"Aye, my lady," he said, looking into the elevator with bright eyes. "Ain't never seen anything like'at before. Jus' push a button and go! 'Ard to berlieve!"

Jacqueline and the ZAP Ladies filed out of the elevator to allow Dodger his fun.

"You come right back up here, you hear me, young man?" Mrs. Hudson appeared, holding a dishcloth and wearing a forbidding expression. "None of this riding up and down all day like ye did yesterday."

"Yes, mu'um," he said, but Jacqueline saw the gleam of excitement in his dark eyes just before the elevator doors closed.

Mrs. Hudson must have seen it as well, for she gave a gusty sigh. "More trouble'an he's worth, ain't he now."

This was Jacqueline's opportunity. "Why is he here?"

"Why, you needed help for the party," replied Mrs. Hudson, sounding annoyed. "I can't do it all meself, you know, and that Danvers creature just makes things all the worse."

"Yes, of course," Jacqueline said, hoping to forestall a snit. But she wanted to know more and had to ask. "So were you the one who, um, summoned him?"

Mrs. Hudson planted her fists on her aproned hips and gave Jacqueline such a dark glare that she thought the woman might actually quit her job (such as it was). "I certainly did *not*." Mrs. Hudson sniffed, as if it were a travesty that Jacqueline had even suggested it. "But far be it from me to turn away any good help—though calling the likes o' him 'good help' would be a stretch. Now, if you don't mind, *I've* got work to do."

Clearly, the snit had not been avoided.

Jacqueline glanced at the ZAP Ladies, who'd watched silently and with great interest. Why weren't *they* more forthcoming about how all this worked?

"I suppose we'd best get on with our own work," said Andromeda, already starting for the stairs that led to the main floor. "That queen-sized bed isn't going to move itself."

"Oh, I, um..." Jacqueline fumbled a little. What were the logistics when a trio of eighty-somethings offered to move your stuff? Should she be worried? She probably should... "I suppose I should give you the key for the storage unit."

"That would be helpful," Zwyla said dryly. "It's not as if we're wizards or sorcerers or anything like that."

Jacqueline eyed her, unsure whether the woman was joking. But Pietra's light giggle clued her in, yet still left her no closer to knowing whether they actually needed the key or directions to the storage place or not. Nonetheless, Jacqueline hurried down the stairs in the wake of Andromeda's jaunty blue hair and extracted the key from her purse.

"I really do appreciate it," she said, handing it off to Zwyla. "Do you...uh...need anything else from me?"

Zwyla gave her a pitying look, then shook her head.

With that, the three crones hurried out of the shop with a jangle of the bell, leaving Jacqueline to wonder whether she'd made a mistake by basically turning over to them the entirety of her possessions.

Before she could worry over that, a customer came in and distracted her by asking for a good chapter book series for her ten-year-old son.

Jacqueline was *delighted* to help.

She spent the next hour or so helping the steady stream of book buyers that came into the shop, enjoying every minute of it. The first customer bought three Percy Jackson books, a couple who came in together bought the new Stephen King and Chrissy Teigen's cookbook, along with a tin of apple ginger tea from upstairs, and a handsome businessman was looking for the latest Malcolm Gladwell book, but also walked out with the first Harry Bosch novel because he was a fan of the TV series.

By the time twelve thirty came around—she was going to close at one until the party—Jacqueline had sold a dozen hardcovers, fifteen paperbacks, and a true first edition of *The Clue of the Velvet Mask*—the Nancy Drew mystery that had blue silhouette endpapers, which were rare for this title—for a hundred and seventy-five dollars.

Not bad for a book that probably would have cost less than a dollar in 1953. It was also the last book that had been written by Mildred Wirt Benson, the original ghostwriter for the Nancy series, and that was part of the reason it remained one of Jacqueline's favorites.

She sighed happily and slid onto her stool as the latest customer walked out accompanied by the pleasant crinkle of a book-filled shopping bag.

She was just reaching for the insulated coffee mug she'd sneaked past Mrs. Hudson's watchful eye when a woman rushed into the shop.

The woman slammed the door so hard it felt like the entire house shook. Her eyes were wide, and she backed herself up against the door as if to protect it from opening again. She was breathing heavily.

Jacqueline found her voice. "Is everything all right?"

"No. It's my husband...he's trying to kill me!"

5

"**G**ood heavens!" Jacqueline flew into action. "Do you want to hide? Is he after you? Does he have a weapon? I'll call 911!" She had the phone in her hand before she heard what the newcomer was saying.

"No, no, don't call 911." The woman, who looked as if she was in her early thirties, seemed to be slightly calmer. "He's—he's not following me. I don't think, anyway." She peered out the glass, trying to look down the street without opening the door. "Sorry—I just wanted to get in here without anyone seeing me, so I kind of made a mad dash once I got out of my rideshare car. Which is another whole thing...did you know it's a hearse? They don't even have Uber or Lyft up here, so you have to ride in a hearse! It's really weird riding in one. I hope it's not an omen." She gave a little shiver. "Anyway, I-I didn't mean to..." Her voice trailed off, and Jacqueline saw the glistening of tears in her eyes. "I didn't mean to startle you."

"All right," Jacqueline replied cautiously. "Why don't you tell me what this is all about? Do you want to sit down somewhere?"

The woman nodded. "Yes, thank you. I'm really

sorry to just barge in on you like this, but, you know, it's sort of what you do here, isn't it?"

"Mmm...yes, I suppose that's true," replied Jacqueline, thinking of all the self-help books on the shelf—although she didn't know that any of them were necessarily about relationships where husbands tried to kill their wives. (*Was* that what the woman was trying to say? Her words had been so disjointed.)

She supposed *The Gift of Fear* by Gavin de Becker was a little along those lines, though if someone read that book, they probably would see the warning signs early and not marry the asshole in the first place. The book was all about listening to a person's innate sense of danger, and it was brilliant. She recommended it to every woman she could, and currently had five copies on the shelf, with more on order.

The bookshop carried books that taught self-defense techniques as well, so maybe that would help the poor woman. Already Jacqueline's librarian mind was darting to the shelves to pull certain titles. And then, of course, a nice, cozy mystery might be in order too, for an escape—but she'd make sure it wasn't one where the husband killed his wife.

"Yes," Jacqueline said more firmly. "I'm certain we've got something here that will help."

She gestured the young woman into the mystery and thriller room because the tall-backed blue chairs in there were particularly cozy and right next to the fireplace. Plus she could see into the front room from where she would be sitting, in case the husband or another customer came in. Jacqueline could always take the woman to the self-help section later. Fortunately, there weren't any other customers around, and nor was Mrs. Danvers lurking.

"All right, now first...why don't you tell me your

name?" Jacqueline said as she settled into the tall wingback chair next to the young woman.

"Oh, yes, right. My name is Amanda Gauthier." She seemed calmer now, and she looked around. "This is such a cozy little room. I just *love* a real fireplace." Her eyes trailed over the mysteries Jacqueline had put on display—*Still Life*, *The Widows of Malabar Hill*, *Forgotten in Death*—then seemed to linger on *Gone Girl*, leaving Jacqueline to wonder whether that was an accident, interest, or an indicator of Amanda's situation. "I've got a gas one in my office, but there's nothing like a real, wood-burning fireplace. Though it's a lot less messy, and all I have to do is twist a knob to turn it on." She gave a weak smile. "I'm always cold, and my office is on the shady side of the building, so..."

Jacqueline refrained from advising her that in about fifteen years, she wouldn't always be cold, and to enjoy being able to cuddle by the fireplace whenever she wanted because before she knew it, she'd be dealing with sudden trails of sweat running down her spine.

Amanda, whose nervousness seemed evident by her babbling, was a slender woman with shoulder-length brown hair and attractive features. Her clothing was expensive and stylish—the kinds of things Jacqueline couldn't afford and knew wouldn't look good on her forty-eight year-old body that just couldn't seem to lose that extra fifteen pounds—well-cut merino wool slacks in rich sable, with the subtlest of plaid pinstripe, a cashmere twinset of dusky pink tastefully trimmed with beads and seed pearls, and a cream-colored shearling and suede coat to take the edge off the April chill. Amanda also carried a large Dooney & Bourke bag that probably cost half of Jacqueline's library salary, but wasn't even as nice as the pink leather one Wendy had been carrying yesterday. The wedding ring Amanda wore was a large, square-cut diamond surrounded by a frame of smaller ones that made it look massive.

She probably can't wear gloves with that rock, Jacqueline thought without an ounce of envy. Diamonds weren't her thing, and neither was marriage...though she'd nearly married her own asshole twenty years ago. Thank goodness she'd dodged that bullet.

"Thank you," Jacqueline said, responding to Amanda's compliment about the room. "Now, are you certain you don't want to call the police?"

"Oh, no, no," Amanda said, shaking her head. "It wouldn't do any good. They'd just... They wouldn't believe me."

Jacqueline was beginning to feel a little out of sorts. If the woman wasn't in any imminent danger, and she didn't want to call the police...why was she here? Just for a book? Not that Jacqueline didn't believe books could solve just about anything, but if she thought her husband was trying to kill her, a bookshop was not the first place she'd go.

So she remained silent, hoping that it would prompt Amanda to tell her a little more.

"You see, I *know* he's trying to kill me—Kenneth, I mean, my husband—but I don't have any *proof.*" Amanda's eyes were wide and earnest.

"All right..." Jacqueline said, letting her voice trail off in encouragement.

"I mean, he stole my asthma inhalers. I *know* he did. I have severe asthma, so there's always an inhaler in my car and one in my purse, one by my bed, and one in the kitchen. I started having an attack the other day—I was taking my car to the mechanic for some work—and I couldn't find either of my inhalers in my purse or in the console of my car. They were just gone. They're *never* gone." Her voice rose with tension. "I could have *died.*"

"What did you do?" Jacqueline asked.

"I managed to get to urgent care—thank God I was close by—and they gave me an inhaler there, but I should have had one with me. I *always* do. It's like tampons—you don't leave home without it."

"That does sound strange," Jacqueline said. She hardly ever needed tampons anymore, but she still carried one with her just in case. "I'm glad you were able to get help at the urgent care. Did you find the inhalers later?"

"No," replied Amanda, her gaze sharp. "No, I didn't. I dropped the car off at the mechanic and took a really good look and they weren't anywhere in the car. I asked Kenneth about it, and he acted very concerned and offered to go to the pharmacy and pick up some new ones for me. He even helped me look around the house for them. We didn't find any, of course. Because he took them and hid them."

"I see." Jacqueline actually didn't quite see. Not that she didn't feel compassion and concern for Amanda Gauthier, but she was still very confused why the young woman was telling her all of this.

"It was attempted murder," Amanda said firmly. "There's no other way to look at it. For all I know, he put something in the—you know, the heating and cooling vents—in my car. Something that would *make* me have an asthma attack while I was driving and couldn't get help. Because it came on pretty suddenly."

Jacqueline nodded, horrified. "You should file a report with the police."

"They won't believe me. They'll just pat me on the

head and tell me I forgot where I put my inhalers—*as if*. Besides, there's more." She drew in a shaky breath, leaving Jacqueline to wonder whether there would be a need for Amanda to pull one out right now. "I was walking down the road. We—well, his family—own one of the wineries just outside of town—Big Bay Vintage. It's a curvy, hilly road that leads up to the office at the vineyard, and I like to walk along there. It's a two-mile round trip and it's got hills and it's pretty and shaded—anyway, I usually go right before dinner. It was getting dark, and I was walking along like I usually do, and suddenly a car came out of nowhere and roared up behind me. I barely jumped aside fast enough; I *felt* the heat from the engine as it went past. He tried to run me down," she said in a shaky voice. "There's no doubt about it."

"What makes you think it was Kenneth?" asked Jacqueline.

"I saw the taillights. They're pretty distinct—he's got a Tesla."

"Maybe he didn't see you," said Jacqueline.

"*See?*" replied Amanda, her eyes glistening with tears. "That's exactly what the police would say. But I *know* it was him, and I know it was on purpose."

"All right, then...if that's the case, then why would your husband want to kill you?"

"Does a ten-million-dollar life insurance policy give him a motive?" she replied icily.

"Whoa. I'd say so." Jacqueline didn't know anyone who'd be worth a ten-million-dollar life insurance policy.

"Exactly." Amanda's fingers shook as she clasped them in her lap. Jacqueline couldn't help but notice her nail polish: an eye-catching red-violet color. "I don't have any way of proving he's doing this, but it sure seems obvious to me. The winery is doing really well, but he and his dad are talking about putting in a boutique inn at the vineyard, and they need a big cash infusion to do so." She spread her hands and grimaced. "And that would be me, DOA. He'd probably even name it after me—the Amanda Inn or something —to make it seem as if he was doing it out of grief."

"Well," said Jacqueline. Her head was spinning and she wasn't quite certain what to do about all of this information. "It does sound very sketchy. But I'm not quite sure why you're telling me about it." She didn't want to sound as if she wasn't willing to assist, but what could *she* do anyway?

"Because, you know..." Amanda twirled her fingers around to encompass the room. "You help people."

Jacqueline frowned. "I've got lots of self-help books, if that's what you mean. I'm always happy to assist someone to find a good read, but I don't think that's going to be enough for you."

Amanda laughed, her eyes crinkling charmingly— not agedly—at the corners. "I understand. I get it. You *have* to say that. But I *know* about this place." She smiled conspiratorially. "So, that's fine...you just find me a good *book*"—she gave an exaggerated wink— "and do whatever else you have to do."

Jacqueline had a sinking feeling she was beginning to understand. Her hands had gone clammy and her insides were roiling. "So...um...where did you get this idea that, well, this is the place to come for... uh...help?"

"Why, lots of us know about it. I mean, lots of us *women*. Obviously, it's all about women helping women, right? Wise women helping their sisters, and so on. *Camellia* Court, right? It's named that for a reason. But we keep it on the down-low for obvious reasons—men don't really need to know how powerful we are. Or, at least, some of us are. You're even on a website—"

"A *website*?" Jacqueline felt faint. "What website? And what exactly do you mean?" She felt dizzy and a little sick.

"Well, it's a website about wise women," said Amanda. "With resources listed. Three Tomes is listed as one of them."

Holy shit. Holy crap.

"I...see," Jacqueline said faintly.

"Everyone knew about Cuddy, so we were all really worried when she passed on, you know, that things might change. But when we heard that *you'd* taken over—that you're her blood kin, and that you were going to continue on with everything—we were so relieved." Amanda smiled. "So, you'll help me?"

"I..." Jacqueline simply didn't know what to say. Obviously, Amanda was in some sort of danger. *Someone* had to help her. But what could *Jacqueline* do?

This is why you're here, said a voice in her head. *This is why Cuddy Stone left this place to you.*

No, no, no... Jacqueline screamed internally. *I just want to be a bookseller!*

"Oh, thank you!" cried Amanda, and Jacqueline realized she must have given some sort of affirmative response without meaning to.

Definitely without meaning to.

"Thank you *so* much!" Amanda rose from her chair and surged toward Jacqueline, hugging her even while she was still sitting down.

"Now," she said, with eyes that sparkled, "what are we going to do about that bastard Kenneth?"

～

JACQUELINE DIDN'T REMEMBER how she managed to put off Amanda. She guessed she said something vague about having to think on it, or make a plan or something.

She did remember a little pang of apprehension as she sent the young woman on her way, hoping she wasn't thrusting Amanda back into danger. But she simply couldn't focus her thoughts on how to proceed —not only did she have *no clue* what to do, but she also had a big party about to happen in less than two hours.

Two hours! Good heavens. Her stomach pitched again.

She turned around. She'd intended to lock up the shop at one o'clock for final preparations, and it was past time to do so. She'd been so distracted by Amanda and her story. Fortunately, no customers had come in during that time...at least that she'd noticed. If they had, Mrs. Danvers had likely attended to them.

Jacqueline locked the front door and put up the sign she'd made explaining that the shop would re-open at three o'clock for the party. Just as she was preparing to do the same at the back entrance, she saw someone walk out of one of the nonfiction rooms.

The woman was definitely not a customer, for she carried a metal pail. Inside it was a floor brush and a small dustpan that might be used for sweeping up minor messes.

Or fireplaces.

Jacqueline's chest tightened a little. *No. No. No!*

"Hello," she said, and the young woman turned toward her.

"Oh, hello," replied the stranger. She had a faint accent that Jacqueline couldn't place; something with a formal lilt to it that didn't sound British. "I hope I didn't disturb you. I was just cleaning out the fireplace."

Jacqueline's heart sank.

The young woman was around sixteen or seventeen, and she had large blue eyes set in a pretty, delicately featured face. Her hair was mostly covered by a sort of kerchief, but a few light brown wisps had escaped from the covering. Her clothing—a long-sleeved shift that fell past her knees with a supple leather corset laced over the bodice to give it shape—was neat and clean; however, it was clearly old and well worn and definitely not the type of clothing people wore in the twenty-first century. There were patches and worn spots, and one small burn mark in the front. Her hands were slender and pale, with long fingers, but they were the hands of work and covered with scars and calluses. No nail polish.

"Cinderella, I presume," said Jacqueline, trying to tamp down the panic that threatened to rise. If this crap kept up, she was going to have a heart attack.

"Yes, my lady," the teen replied, and curtsied gracefully.

"Um...what are you doing here?" asked Jacqueline. *And where can I hide you for the rest of the day?*

Maybe she could lock Cinderella, Dodger, and Danvers in the cellar. She'd keep Mrs. Hudson roaming free for obvious reasons.

"I was cleaning out the fireplace in that room— Oh, there were so many books!" Her eyes sparkled. "I've never seen so many books, even at the castle." The sparkle dimmed a little, but her smile remained. "I'll finish the other fireplaces right away, my lady, and—"

"I'm not a lady," said Jacqueline. "I mean, I'm a

lady, I identify as female, but I'm not a *lady*-lady, so you can just call me...um...Jacqueline."

Cinderella looked at her skeptically. "Just Jacqueline?"

"Yes. Um, *Miss* Jacqueline if it will make you feel better," Jacqueline said, thinking of what some of the younger patrons at the library used to call her. Then she wondered why the hell she was wasting time discussing her form of address. "And what I meant was, what are you doing here, in my shop—here, in Button Cove?"

"Oh, I see. Well, I'm not...I'm not quite certain," Cinderella replied with her lilting accent. The sparkle in her eyes faded completely. "I was trying to get away from Anton, and the next thing I knew, I was sort of tumbling in midair...and then I was here—and there was quite a bit of work to be done." She smiled, and her face was suffused with such loveliness that Jacqueline understood exactly why the prince had supposedly fallen in love with her on sight at his ball. "But I don't mind it, really. I'm used to hard work, and I'm good at it. It keeps me busy. You seem far less—er... What I ought to say is, I'm used to being ordered about and shouted at, and you seem far less...loud."

Jacqueline picked out one bit from her speech. "Anton? Who is this Anton you were trying to get away from?" She didn't remember a male villain in the Cinderella tale, but there were always stewards or friends of the prince hanging about in every version of the tale she'd ever seen or read. Which version was this one? She supposed Anton might even be the king, which would be very unfortunate.

"Anton is the man I am—was—supposed to marry," replied Cinderella.

"Oh," replied Jacqueline. "Well, that's unfortunate. He was someone your stepmother chose for you?"

Cinderella looked at her in shock. "No, of course not. Anton is *Prince* Anton. And I have no intention of marrying him."

6

Jacqueline stared at her. "You don't want to marry the prince."

"No," replied Cinderella.

"You'd rather...um...clean fireplaces and dress in patched clothing than marry Prince Anton and live in luxury?" Jacqueline just wanted to be clear. She must be missing something. Maybe there was more than one prince?

And what was it with troubled marriages—or marriages to be—today?

"This is the guy who searched you out with the glass slipper and all, right?" she went on. "After you ran away at the stroke of midnight? Anton is the one who fell for you at his ball—the ball you went to with help from the Fairy Godmother."

"Yes, of course, Miss Jacqueline," replied Cinderella. She was polite, but Jacqueline could see the faint impatience in her expression. "There's only one prince in Leidelland. I was supposed to marry Anton after all of that—the ball, the glass slipper—but I realized I didn't really want to. It's so *boring* at the castle. And stuffy. The clothes they want me to wear make it very difficult to move around and do anything—not that there's anything to *do* but sit and talk to people and eat fancy meals and be polite."

"But Anton...he's handsome and rich, and—and he's kind to you, isn't he? Or isn't he?" Jacqueline's hackles went up. There were plenty of men—and women—who were kind and loving and gentle until *after* the wedding. And then, like Kenneth Gauthier, they turned into ogres.

She stopped that thought immediately. *I do not need Shrek or any of his fictional relatives showing up here too.*

"Oh, yes, he's very kind. He's so sweet and attentive...but he wants to do everything for me. Why, I went down to the kitchens once to see about helping the cook, and you would have thought I'd taken a dagger to Anton's favorite steed." Her eyes were wide with distress. "Of course, I didn't realize I'd done anything wrong. I just really like to make soup! And I make the best brown bread my stepmother ever had. She told me that once."

"That was nice of her," said Jacqueline dryly, but Cinderella, apparently, was unleashed—for she went on, hardly pausing to take a breath. Jacqueline sincerely hoped this speech wouldn't end in another hug...

"And then I wanted to spend some time sewing—I really enjoy making up ideas for gowns and frocks, and sewing them with whatever bits of fabric I can find," Cinderella rattled on. "Usually old gowns from my stepsisters. Even the doves and mice help me— they'll bring back little scraps of trim or cloth they find and lay them on my windowsill. I had this wonderful idea for a cloak. The outside would be dark blue velvet that would fall like silky water, and the inside lining would be decorated with pale blue roses, each flower made from twisted pieces of velvet and satin... They would completely cover the inside of the cape, as if you were wrapped in a blue rose garden!"

The sparkle was back in her eyes.

"I see," replied Jacqueline. "So you were bored at the—"

"What on *earth* are you doing?"

The snappish tone had both Cinderella and Jacqueline jolting.

Mrs. Danvers stood there, a harder than usual glint in her eyes as she skewered Cinderella with them. "Have you finished the fireplaces yet?"

"No, ma'am," replied Cinderella, straightening her shoulders as if she were a soldier about to report for duty. "I was just about to—"

"Then I see no reason for you to be standing about gawping and gossiping," continued Danvers, leaving off the words that Jacqueline could almost hear: *with the likes of* her.

"Yes, ma'am," said Cinderella. She rushed off down the hall, brush and dustpan clinking inside the pail.

"That was quite unnecessary, Danvers," said Jacqueline in a chilly voice.

The housekeeper stiffened, then, to Jacqueline's surprise, bowed her shiny, dark head. "Yes, ma'am. I do apologize. I simply wished to make certain all is in readiness for your gathering this afternoon."

"You needn't be so curt," Jacqueline went on, gathering her courage. "We all know Cinderella is an excellent worker. It's not as if she's going to—well, blow off her job."

"Blow off, ma'am?" Danvers replied, still in a deferential voice.

"It means to not do it," said Jacqueline.

"Yes, ma'am."

A strained silence hung between the two of them, and Jacqueline sensed the housekeeper was waiting for something. "Um...is there anything else, Danvers?" she said. "Surely you have things to do."

"No, ma'am. Yes, ma'am." And Danvers gave a little bow.

A *bow*.

Jacqueline knew her eyes widened in shock, but the woman had already turned to go off and probably hadn't seen it. She stared after Danvers, wondering and suddenly a little worried. It was very unlike the housekeeper to be so subservient and deferent.

In *Rebecca*, the only time Danvers seemed apologetic and helpful to the second Mrs. de Winter was when she schemed to manipulate her new mistress into making a fool of herself...at a large, very important ball being held at Manderley.

A shiver skittered down Jacqueline's spine, and her stomach pitched unpleasantly. Today was a most important "ball" here at Three Tomes.

She certainly hoped Mrs. Danvers didn't have anything up her tight black sleeve.

~

BUT JACQUELINE COULDN'T DEVOTE much time to worry about Danvers and her machinations. Even though the shop was closed for the moment, Jacqueline felt as if she couldn't even breathe a sigh of relief. She couldn't think of anything that needed to be done, but surely there *had* to be something. And she felt guilty about posting the signs on the doors announcing the temporary closure of two hours and reminding customers of the party.

Mrs. Danvers and Mrs. Hudson joined forces to arrange the food up in the tea shop, although Jacqueline was hearing a good bit of stomping of feet, thumps, clinks, and clatters—and furious exchanges wafting down from above. Danvers wanted the tables there; Hudson wanted them *there*, and so on...

However, when Jacqueline came up to the café to check on them, the women subsided into disgruntled silence and continued their work of folding napkins and setting out plates and flatware, for both of them had vehemently overruled Jacqueline's intention to use paper or plastic serving ware, including napkins.

The Dodger, who'd been arranging tables (and re-arranging them as the housekeeper and landlady argued about layout) had removed his top hat but was still wearing a coat whose cuffs hung down over his hands—leaving Jacqueline to wonder how he was such a successful pickpocket if his fingers were always encumbered—and trouser hems that dragged on the floor. Once the party started, he was supposed to be assisting Mrs. Hudson here the tea room—busing tables and refilling trays with tiny tea sandwiches, bite-sized blondie brownies, and pop-in-the-mouth pizza bites, and Jacqueline didn't want him to look sloppy.

When he went to the back room on the second floor to get more chairs, Jacqueline decided to say something to Mrs. Hudson. Maybe Sherlock's landlady had an idea of something else he could wear. And aside from that, Jacqueline was wondering if it was even a good idea to have a light-fingered pickpocket hanging about the party.

But before Jacqueline had the chance to say anything about Dodger, Cinderella's kerchief-covered head appeared at the top of the stairs.

"Miss Jacqueline," she said as she finished her ascent, "I was just finishing the book display you wanted in the blue room when I heard someone at the back door. It was a woman, and she seemed quite insistent on coming inside."

"I'm certain she can wait for another...forty minutes," Jacqueline said, looking at the clock. "Don't you think?" She looked around at her companions.

"Of course, miss," replied Cinderella as Hudson nodded in agreement. Danvers muttered something— probably unpleasant—but then nodded as well. "Should I tell her to come back then?"

"If you would, thank you...but maybe see if you can find out what's so urgent. Just in case," Jacqueline added. She felt horribly guilty about turning away a customer.

Just then, there was a loud thud. They all turned to see Dodger standing near the back of the tea room. It appeared he'd dropped or tripped over the stack of chairs he'd been carrying.

"*Gor*," he breathed, and that was when Jacqueline saw that his eyes were fastened on Cinderella. There were stars in them.

He started toward them, then stumbled again, as if forgetting he was carrying a load of chairs.

"Jack," said Mrs. Hudson sharply. "What on earth is wrong with you?"

"Oi" was all he said. Still staring.

By now, Cinderella was looking back at him. "Why are you wearing a coat that's too big for you, sir?" she said.

"I..." Dodger shook his head like a wet dog, but no other words came out.

Jacqueline decided it was past time to intervene. "Dodger," she said, stepping between the pickpocket and Cinderella so as to obstruct his vision, "those chairs need to be put in their places."

"Yes, mu'um," he said, craning his neck as if to look around her. "'oo's 'at there?" he asked in a low voice.

But the young woman heard him. "I'm Cinderella."

"I'm *very* pleased to meetcha, my lady," said Dodger, having recovered. He released the chairs none too gently onto what had been a polished floor and swept a dramatic bow to Cinderella. When he rose, he was holding the perky white carnation from his lapel, which he offered to her with a gallant flourish. "Ain't never seen such a vision o' loveliness in me 'ole life."

"Well, that's very kind of you, sir, but I am still wondering why you're wearing a coat that's too big for you," replied Cinderella, taking the flower. "And your trouser hems are dragging on the floor."

"Oi, my lady," replied Dodger soulfully. "'Tis true. I keep tripping on them, I do. But these are me finest togs! Makes me look like a toff, they do." He straightened proudly. "Better'n wot that ol' codger Fagin would 'ave me wearin'."

Jacqueline had an idea. "Cinderella, do you think you could alter his coat sleeves and trouser hems rather quickly? Before the party?"

"Of course," she replied. "It wouldn't take long at all."

"*Gor...*"

"All right, then, Jack," said Mrs. Hudson brusquely. "Stop a-gawking and give the girl your clothes!"

Still gawking, Dodger slid quickly out of his coat and handed it off to Cinderella. He seemed ready to reach for the strings that tied the waist of his trousers when Jacqueline intervened. "Not here," she said sharply. "Go into the storage room there and take them off. You can stay in there—with the door closed—until she's finished."

He gave her such a woebegone look Jacqueline nearly laughed, but nonetheless, he complied.

Jacqueline sighed as Dodger disappeared into the storage room. This was shaping up to be worse than when she'd been scheduled at the library on Teen Study Night during exam time and found a used condom in one of the study room trash cans.

"Shall I go down and tell the woman at the door to come back in a little while?" asked Cinderella, seemingly unmoved by the Dodger debacle. She was still holding his coat.

"Yes, thank you. I'll bring down his trousers," said Jacqueline, resisting the urge to run a hand over her head. It used to be comforting to touch the neat French twist into which she'd normally fashioned her dark red hair daily, but since her encounters with Egala and Crusilla—her distant and witchy relatives—and her hair had gone curly, touching it only reminded her of how untidy it appeared and what had caused it to be that way. She didn't like the Orphan Annie look. Today, in honor of the party, she'd stuck a sparkly hairpin in it to hold back the part that liked to fall in her eyes.

As soon as Dodger's hand emerged from the storage room, offering up his trousers, Jacqueline took them and hurried downstairs. It was less than thirty minutes until the party was supposed to start, and her palms were sweaty and her insides churning.

She had nothing left to do but worry and obsess.

The front door rattled in its jamb, and she glanced

over to see Nadine and Suzette waving excitedly at her through the glass.

The sight of her friends eased some of Jacqueline's nerves. With a smile, she opened the door, and they surged inside.

"We're here!" cried Nadine. "Everything looks great, Jacqueline! You've moved a lot of things—but there are still books everywhere. It's perfect. Where are the blondies? I've been saving myself for them all day, and I want to get some before they're gone. Because they *will* be gone, cuz Suzette made them."

Jacqueline laughed. "Upstairs, of course. Good luck sneaking one with Mrs. Hudson on the job."

"Here," said Suzette, removing a small plastic bag from her purse. "I saved these for you." When she handed Nadine the package, which contained a few of the butterscotch brownies, her friend's eyes went wide and then teary.

"Oh, Suze! Thank you. I swear, if we were lesbians, I'd run off with you." Nadine was already opening the package.

"And I'd go," replied Suzette with a fond smile. Her wild, gray-streaked curly hair was pulled back from the middle of her forehead with her own jeweled barrette. "You know how I feel about men right now. However, much as I hate to admit it, women don't do much for me in the bedroom department, so I'm stuck with dating apps or my vibrator. And lately, Tinder and Bumble aren't cutting it. But...there is a guy who might show up today that I've sort of been talking to," she said, blushing faintly.

"Ooh!" said Nadine around one of the brownies. "Do tell!"

Before Jacqueline could urge the same, her friends' attention turned to the back hall. She glanced over and saw the trim figure walking toward them. "Guess who showed up from the Grimms' book," she said dryly. "Just in time for the party."

"That's got to be Cinderella," said Suzette. "The, uh, brush and pail...and the dress."

"Yep. And guess what—she doesn't want to marry the prince. I think she's here because she's trying to escape the wedding," replied Jacqueline in a low voice.

"She doesn't want to marry the rich, handsome man who fell in love with her and turned the whole country upside down trying to fit her foot into the glass slipper?" said Nadine.

"All those women, lining up and trying to fudge their way into marrying a prince," said Suzette in disgust. "I don't blame Cindy at all, to be honest. Men are *not* Disney princes. Even princes aren't Disney princes."

"With Prince Charles being the perfect example," said Nadine grimly.

"You know in the original Grimms' fairy tale, each stepsister cut off part of her foot so she could fit in the slipper," said Jacqueline. "It was the blood leaking from the shoe that gave them away."

"Eww," replied Nadine. "And quit trying to ruin my fairy tales—both of you!"

"Well, you married a rich and handsome man, and look how it turned out for you," Suzette said, referring to her friend's neurosurgeon ex-husband.

"Ugh," replied Nadine. "Just like Princess Diana."

"Speaking of which, I've got something to tell you," Jacqueline said grimly, thinking of Amanda Gauthier and what she'd said about wise woman websites and all. "In a sec. Cinderella, I've got Dodger's trousers." She hurried down the hall to meet Cinderella, who still carried the pickpocket's coat.

"Thank you. It'll only take a moment. Mrs. Danvers showed me where to find needles and thread," said Cinderella. She glanced curiously at Suzette and Nadine, but made no comment. "And that woman who was at the back door—well, she's gone now. I suppose she'll probably come back if it was important."

"Okay, good. Thank you." Jacqueline handed her the trousers. "Um...take your time, Cinderella," she added, thinking yet again about the wisdom of having a pickpocket make his way through what she hoped would be a crowd of people. Should she just keep Dodger locked away until after the party?

"What did you have to tell us?" asked Suzette.

"It'll have to wait—it's almost three o'clock!" said Nadine suddenly. "Time to open the doors!"

Oh God. Jacqueline's stomach clenched, but she moved to the front door and took down the sign, then unlocked it.

"There are already people out there," said Suzette. "This is going to be a *huge* success!"

Jacqueline's nerves jumped again, but she pushed the anxiety aside.

"I'll get the back door," said Nadine, giving Jacqueline a supportive pat on the arm. "You greet your guests!"

The first person Jacqueline saw was Wendy with her fabulous buttery-leather pink purse. She went to Jacqueline immediately and said, "I'm so sorry about yesterday. I don't know what happened to me. I just turned into a blubbering mess."

"Hormones, probably," said Jacqueline, giving her a smile.

"You're being kind, and I appreciate it. I do want to talk to you, though," Wendy said with a firm grip on Jacqueline's arm. "Not now, of course, but later?"

"Yes, that's fine," Jacqueline said, just as she caught sight of a head of close-cropped strawberry-blond-going-white hair in the back of the small surge of people. Her stomach jumped, and, mortifyingly, she felt her cheeks heat as the broad shoulders below came into view.

Detective Miles Massermey caught her eye through the cluster of people, and he smiled as he trailed the others inside.

She'd met the detective the day after arriving here at Three Tomes, when a man's body was found in the apartment upstairs. Massermey was a sturdy, still mostly muscular man who had a definite Leif Erikson-in-a-suit vibe with his ruddy, freckled face and still-bright-red beard and mustache. Though his hairline was starting to recede and his middle beginning to thicken—and whose wasn't?—he was definitely a man who pushed her hormonal buttons in a major way. He was also named after Miles Messervy, aka "M," from the James Bond books, which warmed her librarian's heart.

Most importantly, he hadn't arrested her two weeks ago when she broke into a crocodile pen at the zoo.

"Hello," he said when she had the chance to greet him. "Looks like you're going to have your hands full for a while." The corners of his eyes crinkled with a smile.

"Hello, Detective," she said. She felt a little awkward calling him Miles, especially in public, even though he'd told her she should do so. "It looks that way," she added, looking around at how crowded the front of the shop had become in the last few minutes. People were picking up books and leafing through them, talking, and flowing down the hall into the genre rooms. And there were already three people in line to pay. She was so happy she could burst.

"Congratulations," he said. "I'm very happy for you *and* for Button Cove. There's nothing like a small-town bookshop."

"Thank you," she said, feeling a renewed rush of pleasure. "There's food upstairs in the tea room," she told him as he began to ease away so she could speak to a customer.

Massermey paused, then leaned close enough for her to get a good whiff of him—*yum*—and murmured, "But is there coffee?"

She laughed and murmured back, "Don't tell Mrs. Hudson, but I sneaked in a carafe of hazelnut roast in the sci-fi/fantasy room. There are cups, too."

"Thanks be," he said with a gusty laugh, and winked as he slipped away—heading for the room with all the Frank Herberts, J. R. R. Tolkiens, Piers Anthonys, and Patricia Briggses.

"Who was *that* nice, cool drink of water?" said a familiar voice in her ear.

Jacqueline turned to Wendy, who apparently had been hovering. "He's a detective on the police force here in town." She kept her voice casual because, after all, there was nothing more between her and Miles Massermey than a mutual adoration for coffee. So far, anyway.

"A detective?" Wendy seemed taken aback. "What's he doing here?"

"Probably looking for a book," Jacqueline retorted a little frostily. "Or simply supporting a small business."

Her friend was beginning to rub her the wrong way, and she wasn't sure why. "Like everyone else, I assume. Or maybe they're here for the food; who knows," she added with a laugh. "Speaking of books, was there something you're in the mood for, Wendy? I can point you in the right direction." She managed a bright smile. "The rooms of the shop just kind of go on and on, leading into each other like a labyrinth of cubbies and bookshelves. A person can get lost in there—not that that's a bad thing."

"That's not a bad thing at all," said Wendy with a shared laugh, which made Jacqueline feel bad about her moment of irritation. "I'll just go browse in the romance section—you do have one, don't you?"

"Of course," Jacqueline replied. Knowing how brisk the circulation was at the library for romance novels, she'd turned over one of the largest rooms solely for that genre. "And the section is quite robust. Second room on the left. There's a really fun and sexy series I just started carrying by Liz Kelly."

"I'll check it out."

Jacqueline plunged back into greeting newcomers as they came in. She noted with mild trepidation that Mrs. Danvers had taken over at the cash register, but the dour expression on the housekeeper's face had settled into something less than terrifying and merely cool. The customers didn't seem to notice, and Jacqueline thought she saw an actual uptick at the corners of Danvers's mouth at one point.

But she still wondered if the woman had something up her sleeve.

"Are you the new owner?" said a voice behind her.

Jacqueline turned to see a young woman, probably around fifteen, standing there. She wore glasses that even the most forgiving of people wouldn't consider stylish, and her stick-straight dark blond hair was cut in such a way that it was clear whoever had wielded the scissors had neither a mirror nor a clue. The ends were choppy and uneven, and the face frame was crooked. Her nose was a little too small and pointy for her face, and her cheeks were covered with freckles, along with a bit of acne on her chin and forehead. She wore baggy clothing that completely hid the shape of her body, but behind the glasses, her large, almond-shaped eyes were a stunning chocolate color, framed by long lashes in a pale face that made her freckles stand out.

"Yes, I'm Jacqueline Finch," Jacqueline replied, remembering the days of cutting her own hair and failing miserably. Of course, back then there hadn't been YouTube videos or TikTok to help guide a person through the process, just *Tiger Beat* magazine for inspiration. She smiled. "What can I help you with?"

The girl leaned a little closer, and Jacqueline caught a whiff of something floral and feminine that was probably her deodorant working overtime. "I...I need some help." She looked around furtively, then gestured with fingernails painted a chalky white for Jacqueline to follow her to the edge of the room, away from people.

Jacqueline complied, but she felt a little surge of nerves. "Are you looking for a book?" she asked, hoping her anxiety was unnecessary.

The girl shook her head, those pretty chocolate eyes focused on Jacqueline and magnified by the glasses she wore. "No, but I do like to read. I'll buy a book if I need to," she said earnestly.

Jacqueline sighed internally. "We have an extensive young adult section," she said brightly. "It's in the room with the lavender and blue walls." Walls she'd painted with great pleasure only a week ago before adding a collection of Bohemian-patterned floor poufs. There was a bright-colored rug on the floor and on the walls and ends of the bookshelves, she'd hung movie posters for the adaptations of popular teen novels like *Twilight*, *The Hate U Give*, and, of course, *Harry Potter*. The look of that room had become one of her favorites.

"I'm not really here for a book," said the girl. "To be honest. I need a...a..."—her voice dropped so as to be nearly inaudible—"a love potion."

No way. No way.

Jacqueline barely contained her vehement response. After all, she had been asked for very strange things at the library. Once someone had actually asked for a BDSM for Dummies kind of book.

Instead, she merely smiled warmly and kept any hint of condescension from her voice (she hoped) as she replied, "I don't have any love potions. Or any kinds of potions. I do have some very nice teas in the café, however, and also some beautiful essential oil blends in the New Age room upstairs, along with some incense. Maybe something like that would, uh, help your situation."

The girl's expression tightened into one of determination, and her cheeks flushed. "Look, I know you have to say that. But I can pay. I have money. Lots of it, Miss Finch." She patted the cross-shoulder bag that hung in front of her torso. *"Please."*

"I'm sorry—I really don't have any sorts of potions here at all," Jacqueline replied in her firm librarian's voice. "No matter how much money you have."

"But I *know* you help people here," the girl said. Her eyes were bright with sudden, unshed tears. "You know...in a *special* way."

Jacqueline opened her mouth to reply, then closed it. What the *hell* was she going to do? Just then, she caught sight of a tall, elegant figure from the corner of her eye. It was Zwyla, dressed in a silky aubergine top, accompanied by Pietra and Andromeda.

If there was anyone who could help—either by defusing the situation or, heaven forbid, by producing some sort of love potion—it would be the ZAP Ladies. "What's your name?" she asked the girl.

"Kara." Those brown eyes were filled with hope.

"Come with me, please, Kara," Jacqueline said, and began to thread her way to the trio of women who were standing at the base of the stairs leading to the tea room. "Hello, ladies," she said as she approached.

"What a wonderful turnout!" said Andromeda, beaming as she surged into hugging Jacqueline. "I'm so happy for you."

"This is *phenomenal*," cried Pietra, clapping her hands together, making the clutter of bracelets she wore sparkle and clink.

"Thank you," Jacqueline replied, then gestured for the girl to step forward. "This is Kara," she said, keeping her voice pitched so that only the three older ladies could hear. "And she has come in here to Three Tomes looking for a *love. Potion*." Jacqueline's voice became a little steely, and she looked at each of the women meaningfully.

Pietra's eyes widened. "Oh," she said, her mouth and eyes perfect circles. The bracelets slid into silence. "Well, I—"

"As I'm a little busy at the moment," Jacqueline said, still holding on to that steely tone, "I thought you might be able to talk with her." She felt quite certain her meaning and intention would be very clear, especially to Zwyla, who was looking at Kara with cool, calm eyes.

"A love potion," said the tall woman.

Kara, who seemed a little taken aback at being foisted off on the ZAP Ladies, swallowed hard and nodded. She gave Jacqueline a desperate look, but Jacqueline ignored the plea in her eyes and said to the ladies, "I've got to visit with my guests. Perhaps you can give Kara some tea and find out more about her situation."

"But..."

Jacqueline swept off without a backward glance, wondering when she'd developed such a spine. Of course it was probably simply because there was no possible way she could provide a love potion to Kara —and even if she could, she wouldn't for very obvious reasons. She'd read enough books to know such a thing was a recipe (ha ha) for disaster.

As she plunged back into the party, Jacqueline focused on working the room, so to speak: introducing herself to everyone, and always asking what they liked to read as a conversation starter. She pointed out the tea room upstairs, gave directions to the different genre rooms, introduced Sebastian (Max was nowhere to be found; she suspected he wasn't one for social frivolities), and explained why a particular vintage edition of *Animal Farm* was priced at four hundred dollars. She spotted Cinderella making her way through the small throng with Dodger's coat and trousers over her arm, and she was just about to navigate over to thank her when a man stepped in her path.

She looked up into the craggy but somehow handsome face of a man in his late thirties and smiled as she offered her hand to shake his. "Hello. I'm Jacqueline Finch, the proprietress here at Three Tomes. Can I help you find something to read? Or would you

prefer to sample some of the scones and pizza puffs
we have upstairs?"

Just as she finished this smooth greeting, she noticed the woman standing right next to him...Amanda
Gauthier.

7

Amanda's eyes were wide with something like desperation or warning, and Jacqueline swallowed hard as she shook hands with the man she knew must be Kenneth Gauthier.

"Nice little shop you have here," he said as he released her hand. "I'm Kenneth Gauthier of Big Bay Winery. This is my wife, Amanda." He smiled down at her, and Jacqueline got the impression of big, wolflike teeth so purely white it had to be unnatural, considering the fact that he probably drank a lot of red wine.

Along with his craggy face, Kenneth Gauthier was a man of average height and build. But the sharp suit he wore and the way he carried himself gave him a very attractive edge. No doubt about it: he and Amanda were a stylish, good-looking couple. "We were already upstairs and saw the spread of refreshments—everything looked and tasted wonderful. The only thing it's missing is a little Big Bay vino, right, Mandy?" He gave his wife a gentle nudge as he continued to smile.

"Every party needs lots of wine," Amanda replied in a casual voice. "You have some great pours up there, but next time, feel free to contact us if you want to spotlight a local vintage. We'll give you a good deal, won't we, darling?" She glanced up at him, then offered Jacqueline a business card with a professional smile.

"Amanda's the one to talk to about all of that," said Kenneth, giving his wife a proud smile. "She's the VP of sales and marketing for Big Bay. I understand you're new here, Ms. Finch, so if you want to come up for a tasting and to check out the winery, let us know." His smile remained bright and friendly. "Mandy will take care of you, I promise."

"I'd love to take you up on that," Jacqueline said, wishing she'd thought to offer a local wine. She winced inwardly at her rookie mistake as she noticed the way Kenneth's hand was curled around Amanda's arm. It was wrinkling the dusky rose sweater she wore. "I hardly ever say no to wine."

"We happen to believe one never should," he replied with a chuckle.

Feeling around for a topic of conversation, Jacqueline said, "I just love the color of your nail polish, Amanda."

"Oh, thank you," Amanda replied, fanning her fingers in front of her. "I actually have the bottle in my purse—I had to do some repair the other day. Let me see if I can dig it out and give you the name."

"That would be great."

Amanda dug in her purse. "It's called Magenta Marvel," she said, her voice a little muffled as she looked down inside the large leather tote. "Hmm. I don't seem to be able to find it. Maybe when you come up for the tasting, I can show you."

"That would be perfect," Jacqueline said. Then she turned to Kenneth. "Now that we've got the beauty talk out of the way...is there something I can help you find? Or did you just want to browse?"

"Oh, I'm fine with browsing. Where's the business section? I don't read a lot of fiction," said Kenneth apologetically. "I'll just go off and see what's there, and I'll catch up with you in a few, Mandy."

Jacqueline gave him directions to the business section and he went off.

"Thanks," said Amanda ruefully in a low voice. "I mentioned coming here for the event today, and he decided it would make sense to meet another business owner—for obvious reasons. That's why I was in such a rush this morning; I wanted to talk to you before we got here together. Anyway...?" Her voice trailed off expectantly.

"As you can imagine, I've been too busy to give your situation much more thought today," Jacqueline told her, though, to be honest, she'd hardly been able to *not* think about the implications of Amanda's first visit. "If I come up to the winery tomorrow, is there a place we can talk? I wasn't kidding when I said I hardly ever say no to wine." And, in spite of herself, she was curious about the road where the car had nearly run Amanda down.

But...ugh...she really shouldn't be getting involved —so why was she stepping a foot into the pool?

It was just a wine tasting, she told herself. And local businesses supported local businesses.

"That would be perfect. You can text me at the number on my card and let me know what time is good for you. I'm flexible." Amanda smiled. "Thank you."

"Sure," Jacqueline replied faintly, realizing she'd just dug herself in deeper. "Why don't we just say one o'clock tomorrow?"

"Perfect. The address is on my card."

Jacqueline sighed as Amanda slipped off into the crowd. She really needed to talk to the ZAP Ladies about all of this. There was no way she was going to get dragged into the problems of random women who walked in the door of Three Tomes. She simply wasn't equipped on any level to deal with it.

"Are you the new owner?" said a voice behind her.

Jacqueline turned. The speaker was a tall woman dressed in jeans, a casual plaid button-down shirt, and a pair of fabulous cowboy boots in cream with pale blue stitching. Her face was devoid of makeup—a bravery Jacqueline envied, herself being the age of forty-eight and possessing numerous fine lines around eyes, nose, and mouth—and her hair was a stream of long, frizzy dishwater-blond curls. The woman looked like she was in her early forties.

"Yes, I'm Jacqueline Finch. And I *love* your boots," Jacqueline said with a gesture toward said footwear.

"Oh, thank you. My wife got them for me from Sundance catalog—a big splurge for my fiftieth birthday on top of the huge party she threw for me," replied the woman. "I told her it was too much, but she wouldn't listen. She spoils me."

Fifty? *Damn.* And hardly a wrinkle or sag in sight with not a stitch of makeup on.

"Great gift," Jacqueline replied. "Thank you for coming. Is there something I can help you find? Did you make your way up to the tea room yet? There's food and drink up there."

"Not yet...I wanted to talk to you," the woman replied. "I'm Elizabeth Rocco, and I was hoping you could help me."

Jacqueline's stomach clenched. "What sort of book

are you looking for?" she replied, forcing brightness into her voice.

"I'm not looking for a book," Elizabeth replied, leaning closer and dropping her voice. "I need your help...you know what I mean." She winked and gave an encouraging nod, and Jacqueline's heart plummeted to her feet.

Ugh.

~

"THAT'S HIM," hissed Nadine in Jacqueline's ear. "Suzette's possible hookup. He's not what I expected at all, but go, Suze!"

It was just before six o'clock, when the grand re-opening was supposed to end and the shop closed. The flow of people had remained steady for the entire three hours, and business had been so brisk that Jacqueline had had to excuse herself from Elizabeth Rocco and the two other women who approached her for some "help" in order to man the second cash register. Thank goodness she'd been able to get away before they dumped their problems on her.

"He looks nice," Jacqueline said, eyeing the tall, spindly man with sparse blond hair. He had a long face to go with his well-above-six-foot height, and there were deep, pleasant grooves in his tanned face and beside his prominent nose. "Did you meet him?"

"Briefly. His name is Wes, and he's an architect." Nadine, who wasn't shy about her interest in meeting a man to date, didn't have even a hint of envy in her voice. "I hope things work out for them. It's so hard to find a guy our age who isn't a dick, but has a working one. You know?"

Jacqueline spluttered a laugh. "We're only in our

late forties, Nadine...that doesn't really start to be a problem till they're older—fifties, sixties, and more."

Nadine grimaced, shaking her head. "Can't tell from my experience, though. My good old ex Noah started taking Viagra when he was forty-eight. Not that I've had any *recent* experience."

At that moment, Suzette looked over and caught them gawking at her and Wes. Even from across the front room, Jacqueline saw her friend's cheeks flush—she probably guessed what they were talking about—and Jacqueline hid a smile. Instead, she just waved and turned back to Nadine. "Stop staring. You're going to give her a complex."

"Right, right, I'll—"

"I can't find my wallet," said a man, rushing up to the counter. "Did anyone turn in a wallet they found?"

"No," replied Jacqueline, her heart sinking.

"I just had it, and now it's gone. I must have dropped it," he said, running a hand over his bald head as he looked out into the shop. "It's black leather with a braided trim... I'll have to retrace my steps..." He turned and started off.

"I'll help you look," said Jacqueline, slipping out from behind the counter.

And she knew *exactly* where she was going to start.

Furious, she fairly jogged up the steps to the tea room. She found the little café still filled with people, sitting around at tables or on the three stools at the counter. The fire blazed merrily in the huge fireplace, and a group of five women in their twenties were sitting in the sofas arranged there. They all looked at Jacqueline with interest as she appeared, then leaned close into each other and whispered, still gawking at her. When it seemed as if one of them was about to wave her over, Jacqueline quickly averted her eyes.

Those women looked *exactly* like the kind of group who would descend upon her asking for "help" with all of their problems. *Five* of them. At once! And in their twenties? Whatever their problems were, surely they would be horrific.

As Dodger would say, *Oi!*

Speaking of Dodger...

"Jack Dawkins," said Jacqueline from between clenched teeth as she marched across the room.

He was behind the counter, drying cups as Mrs. Hudson bustled about, refilling hot water in teapots and informing people of the type of tea vintage they should be drinking.

"No, ma'am, we don't serve coffee here," Mrs. Hudson was saying in a tone filled with soothing kindness and only a whiff of condescension for the customer's misguided question. "This is purely a tea shop. Now then, I expect you'll be wanting an Indian blend, won't ye? A Darjeeling, with a wee bit of honey and a splash of milk, and you'll be right as rain. Right, then —and you won't have none of that coffee breath to put someone off ye, then, now will ye?" she added, nodding meaningfully at the man who accompanied the customer and appeared to be her date.

"Yes, mu'um?" Dodger looked up at Jacqueline, innocence plastered all over his face. He'd replaced his lapel flower with a rose, probably pilfered from one of the bouquets for the party decorations.

"Give me that man's wallet *immediately*," Jacqueline hissed.

"What is it yer sayin' now, mu'um?" His blue eyes widened with practiced guile, but Jacqueline was having none of it. "A wallet's gone missing?"

"*The wallet. Now.* And anything else you might have slipped into your pockets," she said, holding out her hand. "This is not Mayfair or Kensington or any-where in Her Majesty's London, and Fagin is nowhere but between the pages of a book." She bared her teeth at him in a furious growl. "And even if he *were* here..."

"Awright, awright," he said with a wounded air. "It's just, a bloke's gotta take care o' 'imself, don't he? Ain't no one gonna give 'im a 'andout, are they now? Asides, me fingers was getting itchy to practice, now, weren't they?" He put down the towel and cup and came out from behind the counter. As Jacqueline followed him to the small pantry next to the unobtrusive elevator, she noticed that his trousers were no longer sagging or trailing, and the cuffs of his jacket ended just at his wrists. Cinderella had done a great job without even taking his measurements.

But that brief moment of satisfaction evaporated when she saw the size of Dodger's stash.

"What in the *hell* have you been doing?" she exploded, grateful she was facing away from the tea room and that her exclamation was muddled by the distance and dull roar of conversation and laughter from the tables behind them. "You *cannot* steal from my customers!" Her vision was tinged with red, even as her stomach surged and pitched with nausea.

He'd stowed at least six wallets (including a black one with braid trim), two small purses, and a fanny pack in a cardboard box that had held supplies. Beneath them, she spotted three wristwatches—one of them was a Shinola!—two silk scarves, and a pile of glinting gold and silver that were probably bracelets and necklaces. Her customers—or, more likely, *former* customers—were going to be very upset.

Dodger must have realized how furious she was, for he shrank back a little under the weight of her glare. "Oi, then, mu'um, I won't be doin' that again, awright now? It's just I ain't used ter bein'—"

"Enough. I don't want to hear it. Keep your hands out of other people's pockets," she said, gathering up the box of contraband. "Stay away from the customers or I'll—I'll—" She seethed, feeling the sudden fury blazing from her eyes and a sharp tingle of energy surging to her fingertips. For a horrible moment, she wondered if her witchy relatives *had* given her some of their enchanting powers.

"Awright, awright, mu'um!" Dodger held up his hands as if to ward her off. His green eyes were wide with terror. "I promise!"

Jacqueline didn't believe him for one minute, but she didn't have any more time to read him the riot act. She had to find the owners of all of these items before they left. Hurrying down the stairs with the box, Jacqueline looked around at the people still milling about the front room of the shop.

She spotted the bald man who'd alerted her to the problem. "Sir, I found your wallet upstairs," she said, setting the box on the front counter. She fished out the black, braid-trimmed leather folder. "It was in our lost and found."

"Oh, thank heavens," he said, taking it with obvious relief. "I can't imagine how I dropped it. I never even took it out of my pocket." He opened it up, and Jacqueline held her breath as he flipped through the cash inside. "Yep, all there." He closed the wallet and gave her a sheepish smile. "Sorry about that, but thank you for finding it. I'm not sure who turned it in, but whoever it was is a very honest person."

Jacqueline smothered a snort, nodding instead. "Thank you again for coming."

"Oh, I've got some things to buy—that's how I real-ized my wallet was gone. I'll be right back."

Jacqueline felt her own wave of relief that he wasn't going to storm out of the shop and complain about pickpockets. But what was she going to do with the other things Dodger had lifted?

"Excuse me, everyone," she said after a moment, raising her voice to be heard over the low buzz of con-versation and in the other rooms. "We've collected quite a few things in our lost and found today...if you're missing anything, you can come up and take a peek in the box."

Danvers, who'd been standing next to Jacqueline behind the counter during this entire debacle, gave a sniff of definite condescension. "Doing it that way, you'll have people just taking whatever they want," she muttered to Jacqueline. "Whether it's theirs or not."

Jacqueline gave her a frosty look. "Then I'll put you in charge of it. Here." She shoved the box toward Danvers. "No one will dare try to pull one over on you."

"Pull one over, ma'am?"

But Jacqueline had already stalked off. She was fed up with book characters coming out of their damned stories, and women wanting her help for things she couldn't do. A *love potion*?

Why didn't people just look for their answers in books? Or at least distract themselves from their prob-lems by reading? Both tactics had always worked for Jacqueline.

She sighed and wondered how she could politely encourage everyone to leave now that the party was over and the shop was due to close, for it was after six. She needed time to think, and she definitely wanted to corner Zwyla, Andromeda, and Pietra and ask them what the hell she was supposed to do.

"You look stressed," said a deep voice behind her.

Jacqueline turned to find Detective Massermey standing there. He was holding a cup of coffee, which he offered to her.

"Oh, God, thank you," she said, taking the mug gratefully. "Yes, I am stressed. I don't know that adding caffeine into the mix is going to help, but I don't care." She took a large gulp and sighed as the elixir of life settled in her belly and flowed through her limbs.

"Is there anything I can do to help said stress?" said the detective.

"No," Jacqueline said quickly. There was definitely nothing a cop could do about her thieving sort-of-employee—who wasn't really a person anyway...was he? And certainly she didn't need Massermey meddling in all of the "wise woman" problems. "But thanks. It's just been a long day—a successful one," she added with a genuine smile. "Very successful. And I'm very grateful."

"I'll say. Congratulations." He smiled. "When things settle down, maybe we can go somewhere where Mrs. Hudson won't be and get coffee. There's a nice little shop over on Front Street."

"That would be nice," Jacqueline replied, feeling her cheeks warm. It sounded like a date, which was something she hadn't had in a while—unless you counted Lester back in Chicago: a sort of friend-with-very-occasional-benefits and who acted as her on-call plus-one. A date wasn't such a bad idea. Especially with someone as nice as Massermey, who, bonus, reminded her of her obsession with Vikings, which had begun in middle school.

"I'll be in touch," he said, brushing her arm lightly in farewell. "Goodbye, Jacqueline."

"Mmm-hmm," said a low, chortling voice in her ear. "Did that Detective Put-His-Massive-Hands-On-Me just ask you out, Jacqueline, dear?"

She turned to see Andromeda wearing a catlike grin. "We're going to get coffee sometime," Jacqueline replied, cursing the fair skin that went along with her red hair and displayed even the slightest of flushes... including the one she was wearing now. "I need to talk to you and the others," she said before Andromeda could slip away again. "As soon as I close up."

Andromeda lifted a finely plucked eyebrow. "Sounds urgent."

"It is urgent."

"We can meet upstairs if you like," she replied. "In the apartment."

"Oh," Jacqueline said, suddenly remembering she was in the middle of moving flux. And that the ZAP Ladies were supposed to be moving some of her furniture over. But she hadn't seen or heard any sounds or activity that would have indicated it actually happened, even when the shop was closed for those couple of hours. "It's just a mess up there, with no furniture and—"

Andromeda was shaking her head with an affectionate smile. "No it's not."

Jacqueline stilled. "Do you mean you and Zwyla got my sofa and bed up there? When? I didn't hear or see anything?"

"Oh ye of little faith. We'll see you up there as soon as you close, all right?" Andromeda patted Jacqueline on the arm. "We'll get some tea ready."

Oh joy.

"I'll be up there as soon as I can," Jacqueline

replied, already going to the front door to flip the sign to CLOSED. There were still some customers in line to pay, so she stepped behind the counter to help Danvers.

To her relief, she saw that the contents of the lost-and-found box had dwindled significantly, with only a wristwatch (not the Shinola) and a small clutch purse remaining, along with small jumble of jewelry and a little metal wingnut. Mortification, relief, and fury warred inside her at the realization that so many people had been robbed in her store. She needed to send Dodger back into his book *right away*.

At least...after he helped clean up the tea shop.

Jacqueline rang up the last customer, giving her a pleasant smile and feeling grateful the customer hadn't asked for her help. Nadine and Suzette had been collecting stray plates, cups, and books and putting them where they belonged. Someone had locked the back door, and the shop was empty.

Except for Wendy.

"Oh, I didn't realize you were still here," Jacqueline said when she found her in the romance room.

"I just love what you've done in here," said Wendy, who was sitting in a plush armchair of siren red that should have been too large for the space...but somehow wasn't. "It's just the perfect room."

The exterior wall, which boasted two large windows, had been papered with a pattern of splashy cabbage roses in all shades of pink and red. The other walls had been painted with a pearlescent glaze. There was the large, plush red chair, and two smaller green ones tucked in the corner. This room didn't have a fireplace, but that was all right because there were more shelves to hold books.

Jacqueline smiled and ran the toe of her shoe over

the throw rug in front of Wendy's chair. "I couldn't re-sist this fluffy white rug, even though it collects dried leaves and debris like a lint roller! It just gives the room a luxurious and sensual air...which is what ro-mance novels are all about, aren't they?"

"Exactly. Look, I really need to talk to you," Wendy said, rising. She put down the copy of *Mr. Wright Now* she'd been paging through and picked up her purse, then rose from the chair.

Jacqueline held back a sigh. The ZAP Ladies were upstairs waiting for her, and Suzette and Nadine were also in the front room, likely wanting to talk to her about the success of the party. And, frankly, she would rather be with any of them than Wendy at the mo-ment. She sensed it was going to be too much work to have whatever conversation Wendy thought they needed to have, and she had other problems that were more urgent. Like love potions. "How long are you in town? Can we talk tomorrow? I'm going to be tied up here for a while. Cleanup and stuff."

"Oh." Wendy's face fell. "I see. Well, yes, I'll still be here tomorrow."

Jacqueline resisted the latent guilt-ridden urge to change her mind and say, "That's okay, we can talk now." Instead, she smiled and said, "Great. Tomor-row's Monday and the shop opens at ten. I could meet you here at nine."

"All right. Yes, that's fine. That'll work." Wendy picked up the book she'd been perusing. It had a sexy man in a suit on the front cover. "I guess it's too late to pay for this now, isn't it?"

"Not at all," Jacqueline said. "I haven't closed down the register yet." She noticed the shock on her friend's face.

Had Wendy thought she'd not expect her to pay?

Jacqueline frowned, then pushed away the thought. She was reading too much into things. She was tired and flush with the success of today, and she had a lot on her mind.

"See you tomorrow morning," she told Wendy, who carried her officially purchased book, as Jacqueline unlocked the door for her to leave.

The front room was empty, but she could hear sounds from upstairs in the tea room. Nadine, Suzette, Mrs. Hudson, Cinderella, Dodger, and even Mrs. Danvers were up there. Everything seemed to have been put away already, and Dodger was mopping the floor as well as he could while eyeing Cinderella, who was replacing the last few washed teacups on the shelf.

"Here," said Nadine, shoving a large glass of wine at Jacqueline. "Drink up and bask in your moment of glory! The party was a huge success. Congratulations."

"Thank you." Jacqueline sipped the wine, which was a robust zinfandel that had a jammy finish. She savored the flavors, then sighed with gusto. "I needed that. Thank you all for your help. I think we did pretty well with sales today."

"There was always a line, downstairs and up here," said Suzette. "You cleaned up."

"You look exhausted," said Nadine, patting Jacqueline's hand. "We decided we're going to do pizza at my place anyway, but if you want to beg off, we totally understand. That just means more of Suzette's pizza for me."

"Didn't you get your pizza fix with all those pizza rolls?" replied Suzette.

"Never," replied Nadine.

"I'll probably be over in a little bit," Jacqueline said, smiling. "Depends how tired I am." And how long she had to talk to the ZAP Ladies.

Nadine and Suzette left, debating pizza topping options as they went down the sweep of stairs. Jacqueline turned from saying goodbye to them to discover that the book characters were gone. The tea room sparkled and smelled like lemon polish, the lights were turned off, the chairs, tables, and everything were orderly, and even the fire had settled into a mere glow of orange embers.

She sighed and took another sip of wine.

All she really wanted to do was sit down in front of that glowing fire and read a few chapters of something delicious and comforting.

Instead, she had to go upstairs and deal with *stuff.*

8

W hen Jacqueline stepped off the elevator into her apartment, she gasped and stared.

The elevator was tucked behind the kitchen, next to the pantry and a stacked washer and dryer, but she could see through the kitchen and its open counter space into the living room...which was furnished.

Her beloved cobalt velvet sofa was in place in front of the fireplace, along with the low coffee table made from distressed, recycled wood. Jacqueline hurried through the kitchen, still staring, seeing her charming IKEA dinette set tucked in the perfect place against the wall, the books on the shelves, the two armchairs flanking the sofa...even the rustic blue and green rug on which she'd splurged, and which looked fantastic below the painting of the cedar tree over the mantel.

There were potted plants on the sills of the two tall windows that faced east. She recognized one as lavender and another as a Zanzibar gem plant. The third was a heart-shaped ivy that spilled out from the pot and trailed halfway along the sill, already giving an indication that it meant to spread. The pothos.

Zwyla, Andromeda, and Pietra were arranged on the sofa and chairs, enjoying a roaring fire in the grate that shot blue and yellow flames. A squat, cream-colored pot of forced daffodils Jacqueline had never seen before sat on one of the side tables, and a tray with a teapot and four cups rested on the coffee table.

"Wow," she breathed, still gawking. "How did you do all of this?" She walked over to the built-in bookshelves that lined one of the interior walls and then extended down the hall. She saw that all of her books were in place...organized just as she would have done. How was that possible? Even the photograph of her parents, who were retired and living in Tampa, was in its regular place next to some vintage Georgette Heyers and her Amelia Peabody collection. "How did you know..."

"Come, sit down now," said Pietra kindly. "You've been on your feet all day. Andromeda has brewed a lovely floral tea with lavender and marigold to help you relax."

"I spiked it with whisky." Andromeda set a delicate china cup in front of her before Jacqueline could decline. "And some of our honey. Consider it an herbal hot toddy."

"In that case..." Jacqueline replied with a smile, and sank onto the blue sofa she'd bought twenty years ago and refused to part with. Even the throw pillows—all in different shades and patterns of white, cream, and sage—were in place, although one of them she'd never seen before. Another housewarming gift? "I just... Wow. Thank you so much."

"We weren't sure where to put your bed," said Zwyla, digging in her massive purse. She pulled out an array of dollhouse furniture, including bed, dresser, mirror, side tables, and lamps, setting them on the table.

Jacqueline glanced at them, then did a double take

when she realized they were perfect models of her own bedroom furniture—even down to the quirky, asymmetrical zebra lampshades and bedding of watercolor roses in black, gray, white, and pink. The decorative throw pillows were even there. She looked at Zwyla, who merely shrugged.

"Makes it much easier to move and arrange when they're this size," Zwyla said. "Just put them where you want them and let me know."

Jacqueline had no words. But she did have the glass of wine in one hand and the whisky-spiked floral tea on the table and decided she was going to drink all of both of them. *My life is so weird right now.*

"All right, what did you need to talk to us about?" said Pietra.

Jacqueline swallowed a big gulp of wine. "First— love potions? Seriously?" She looked bug-eyed at each of the three ladies in turn.

"Oh, that." Andromeda flapped her hand carelessly. "Every teenage girl wants one."

"Well, what am I supposed to tell her—and any other teenage girl, or adult girl—that might come in here asking for one?" replied Jacqueline.

The three crones looked at each other. None of them appeared concerned or even the least bit taken aback by Jacqueline's frustrated speech.

Finally, with a quiet smile, Zwyla said, "I'm sure you'll figure it out. Usually," she went on, raising her voice a tad as Jacqueline began to huff out a response, "once the person is distracted or otherwise re-engaged, they realize a love potion isn't the answer."

Jacqueline goggled at her. "Right. Of course. Sounds like a plan." She wondered if they recognized the heavy sarcasm in her voice. "Distract and re-engage. Sure. No problem. Because teenage girls are so easily distracted from the boys they have crushes on." Damn—she was so upset that she was leaving her prepositions dangling. Which wasn't *actually* a grammar felony, but it always bothered her. "I mean, the boys on whom they have crushes."

Pietra cleared her throat. "I—we—have all the confidence in the world in you, Jacqueline," she said. "But life is always a learning curve and a complicated, exciting journey. Everyone should always be learning, and as long as you're open to growing, you'll figure it out." Her round cheeks flushed with earnestness.

"Right," Jacqueline said wearily. Why couldn't they ever give her a straight answer? She felt like the lead character in a teen novel, where everyone knew all the bad stuff and secrets in her life, but refused to tell her about them...just so she could make mistakes and muddle her way through life-and-death situations. "Well, what did you tell Kara?"

"I told her that love potions take a long time to make because they have to ferment," said Andromeda. "Which isn't *exactly* a lie, because they do have to ferment, and left to their own devices, it would take months for a love potion to be ready. That is, *if* one left it to its own devices." She winked.

"We never lie in these situations, Jacqueline," explained Pietra primly. "If you do, it taints the energy, and it can really backfire on you."

"I see." Jacqueline did not, in fact, see. "Love potions notwithstanding, I just—what?"

"Notwithstanding?" Pietra was beaming as she poked Andromeda. "She said 'notwithstanding.' Isn't that quaint and amazing? No one ever says notwithst—"

Jacqueline must not have completely smothered

her guttural scream, for Pietra cut herself off and clamped her lips closed.

Zwyla cleared her throat and gave Pietra a quelling look. "Yes, Petey, that was a unique word choice—but not really a surprise, coming from a lifelong reader, researcher, and book lover. But I think that's beside the point of what Jacqueline wanted to say, wasn't it, Jacqueline?"

"Yes," Jacqueline replied in a very, *very* calm voice. "Thank you. As I was saying, love potions notwithstanding, I don't know what to do about all of these women coming to me for help. This isn't what I do here! I own a bookshop. I'm not, you know, Dear Abby or—or Dr. Ruth, or *any* kind of therapist or detective or anything like that. Good grief, did you know that Three Tomes Bookshop is even listed on some *website* for wise women resources or something like that? Like a—a directory of witches?"

"A directory of witches instead of a *Discovery of Witches*." Pietra giggled. "That's funny."

"You're on a website? Really?" said Andromeda. "That's amazing! Which one?" She pulled out her smartphone and looked up expectantly, her slender, gnarled fingers poised to tap in the address. "Do we need to do some blogs? Or whatever that Insta thing is?"

Jacqueline gusted out an annoyed breath. "I don't know. I don't really care—except to get the listing taken off the website." She looked at the three women as the beginnings of tears stung her eyes. "I'm not equipped to handle this, ladies. I'm just a bookseller."

Zwyla tilted her head. "What on earth makes you think you're *just* a bookseller?" she said quietly. "And why a bookseller is *just* anything ever, anyway?"

"All I've ever done is love books. That's all I know."

Jacqueline felt a little tremor of something as the older woman continued to gaze at her, dark eyes delving into hers. "I...I don't know what to do about all of this. There's a woman whose husband is trying to kill her —at least, it seems that way—and she's coming to me for help! And there were at least two other women who wanted me to help them too..." This time, her speech was calmer, though no less impassioned.

"And what's so awful about that?" Andromeda's voice was quiet as well.

Jacqueline just shook her head mutely. Apparently, nothing she said was going to make a difference to them.

"You'll figure out what to do," said Pietra, who was comfortably sitting in one of the chairs and didn't have droves of women showing up at her place of business wanting love potions or protection from murderous husbands.

"The thing is, Jacqueline," Zwyla said, "we three can't change anything even if we wanted to. Three Tomes was built with good, deliberate intentions on a piece of sacred, energized earth. Its sanctity has to be protected...and its power should be respected and carefully and lovingly exercised as appropriate. And you'll eventually learn how to do that, in your own way and your own style. Now," she said, rising, "let's put your bedroom in order, shall we? I have a feeling you could use a solid night's sleep. Things will look much better in the morning, after a good sleep in your own bed and in your own space. You're still getting used to your new life."

Jacqueline allowed herself to be distracted by setting up her bedroom. It was a cozy space with three tall windows, one of them opening up onto a generous ledge that reminded her of a small widow's walk. A large wardrobe was built into one wall, and a full bath adjoined, but the fireplace was currently inoperable. Still, Jacqueline knew she would sleep as well as her perimenopausal hormones would allow her to in this room, and eventually she'd try to get the fireplace fixed.

Once the dollhouse-sized furniture was arranged where Jacqueline wanted it, Zwyla ushered her and the other ladies out of the room. "It's like making sausage," she said, stepping into the hall and closing the bedroom door behind her. "You don't really want to watch."

Though Jacqueline was wildly curious, she went back into the living room to sit with the older women. But to her surprise, they were gathering up their things—bags, shawls, tea set—to leave.

"Enjoy a quiet evening," said Andromeda. "Sleep well—snip a bit of that lavender and tuck it under your pillow. It'll help. Tomorrow you'll feel better about things. Oh, and I had some blackberries I thought you might want." She gestured to a vase on the counter that contained leafy stems laden with blackberries.

"Thank you," Jacqueline said, eyeing the unusual arrangement.

"You can go into your bedroom in about thirty minutes," Zwyla told her.

"Good night!" said Pietra, throwing her arms around Jacqueline in a joyful embrace. "It was a beautiful party!"

Once the three crones were gone, Jacqueline plonked onto the sofa to finish her wine. Andromeda had left the cup with her hot toddy, and she lifted the delicate china vessel to drink. It was delicious—floral, as promised, but with a spicy kick that was more than just the whisky. Maybe the marigolds? The honey gave it a sweetness, and the entire concoction sent warmth and relaxation flowing through her. She actually kind of liked it.

She sat on the sofa and looked around her apartment. Her new space. At first, she'd been adamant about not living above her workplace...but it just made so much more sense. And now that her things were all here, mostly settled in place, she realized there hadn't been any other option. This was where she belonged. The place felt *right*.

As she finished the last sip of the hot toddy, she found her attention settling on the cedar tree painting. She frowned, though, because she thought the painting was of the daytime—set deep in a forest, but with a stream of sunshine pouring into a distant glen and light filtering down between leaves, needles, and branches. But now that she looked at it again, she saw that it was set at dusk, just moving into a delicate gloaming.

As she sat just below and across, gazing at the painting, Jacqueline noticed more and more fine details. The image seemed to shimmer and shiver with energy. The tree's fernlike needles on their slender, delicate, gnarled branches bounced almost imperceptibly in an invisible breeze. Hints of other life—birds, butterflies, bees, dragonflies, and more—moved within the painting as if the fine brush strokes had come alive.

Jacqueline knew she was imagining the life in the painting, but the experience made her calm and meditative, and she just let it go and gazed. Nadine would be proud, she thought with a smile, and sipped.

She watched the painting for a long time, feeling it drawing her in as if she were in a soft, calm cocoon.

The night in the painting was soft and comforting, and there were twinkles from stars above and fireflies below.

People were there in the forest, near the sheltering cedar and beyond. Some of them Jacqueline recognized—Kara, the teenager who wanted the love potion; Elizabeth Rocco, the woman with the fabulous cowboy boots who'd never had the chance to tell Jacqueline what she needed help with; and to her amusement, Cinderella was there too, and so was Suzette...and then there were others, shadowy figures whose features Jacqueline couldn't discern but who nonetheless didn't seem threatening. A butterfly came to sit on her arm, and she felt the prickles on her hair as it walked daintily over her skin. An eagle flitted through the dark sky above, elegant, graceful, powerful, its white head glowing in the darkness. She smelled the cedar, reached to touch the tiny ice-blue berries, and heard, in a distance, the soft burble of running water.

All at once, Jacqueline opened her eyes. She hadn't realized she'd fallen asleep—or whatever had happened. Her wine was gone, the painting seemed still again, and the fire in the grate had died into bright orange coals. The room was dark and the microwave clock said nine thirty.

It was time for bed. She looked at her phone and saw that Nadine and Suzette had texted asking if she was going to join them for pizza. The last message in their thread was from Nadine, and included a row of heart emojis and glasses of wine, and the words: *You must be out for the night. Totally understand. See you tomorrow. Will save you a piece of pizza.*

Jacqueline smiled and texted back a heart emoji, ridiculously pleased that Nadine didn't use textspeak spelling when she typed. This was a woman she could really get along with—especially since she was going to save her a piece of pizza...and that she understood that Jacqueline hadn't blown them off, just needed some downtime. Someone like Wendy probably wouldn't have been so understanding, she thought sadly.

For a moment, Jacqueline considered going over there anyway—it was only across the street—but she decided she'd rather curl up in bed with a book (but which one? She had seemingly infinite options to choose from below!) and read for a while.

She had a feeling tomorrow was going to be an interesting day.

WHEN JACQUELINE CAME DOWNSTAIRS the next morning, she was in a great mood because she'd slept so well in her new apartment in her cozy room. It helped that the early May sun was bright, streaming through the windows from all directions.

As Jacqueline descended the back stairs from apartment to second floor, she realized how convenient it was to live above her shop *and* to have the likes of Mrs. Hudson already up and heating hot water— even if it was for tea, not coffee.

She wondered if the woman ever slept—literally. Did these book characters need to eat, sleep, urinate, etc.? Did they ever get a cold or a stomachache? Could they be injured or killed?

Jacqueline was one of those people who, when reading novels—thrillers, especially—got very concerned when the people on the run or in the plots didn't seem to have the chance to do any of those practical things, but still had the energy to fight off danger, have sex, or do other physical things. Everyone needed downtime, and she appreciated authors like TJ Mack who actually wrote in mealtimes, sleeping, and at least alluded to other such requirements.

Eating and sleeping were one thing...but what would happen if a character like Danvers or Cinderella was killed here, in real life? Would that affect the book they'd come out of? The story?

Fascinating and compelling questions. She'd like some answers.

"Good morning," Jacqueline said as she came into the tea room. "You're up early," she added, hoping to get some sort of confirmation from the landlady about how she spent her nights.

"Oh, yes, there's always plenty to do," replied Mrs. Hudson. "I've got your cuppa ready here. I've made you a red oolong this morning. Looks a bit strange in color, but don't be letting that put you off. Now, sit yourself down and drink up, luv, before it gets cold."

As she slid onto one of the stools, Jacqueline made a mental note to make coffee upstairs before coming down from now on. Of course, she'd have to locate her coffee maker first...

"Thank you," she said, taking the tea, which was an interesting dark red color. She drowned it with sugar and milk and sipped, while staunchly averting her eyes from the tempting display of cranberry scones from Sweet Devotion. "So, uh, where did Cinderella and Dodger go last night?"

Mrs. Hudson was energetically wiping off the pristine counter, and she glanced up. "Why, the same place they go every night, of course."

"The same place you go every night?" Jacqueline asked. It was time she got some answers.

"Of course," replied Mrs. Hudson.

"And where is that?" Jacqueline asked.

Mrs. Hudson didn't pause in her scrubbing. "So nosy this morning, aren't you, luv," she said briskly.

"Where do you go every night?" Jacqueline pressed.

Mrs. Hudson slammed her hands down onto the counter, making Jacqueline jump a little. "And what business is it of yours, then, missy? You might own the shop, but that don't mean you've got the right to be poking and prying about people's personal lives now, does it?"

Jacqueline blinked. "It's not as if I'm asking who you're having sex with— Oh, never mind." She frowned down at her tea, then lifted her gaze back to Mrs. Hudson. "I want to know about how this all works for you all—you know, those of you who come out of books."

The older woman tilted her head. "Come out of books? Doesn't everyone come out of a book?"

"Absolutely not," Jacqueline replied. "I didn't."

"Are you certain about that?" Mrs. Hudson asked. Her arch expression was so confident that Jacqueline's sense of reality shimmered for a moment.

"Of course I'm certain," she retorted...yet she still felt a little unsettled. What if she was...

No.

That was ridiculous. Of course she hadn't come out of a book, and it was—

"Miss Jacqueline! There you are!"

Cinderella dashed up the stairs, and to Jacqueline's envy, when she got all the way up, she wasn't the least bit out of breath. On her heels was Jack Dawkins.

"Yes?" Jacqueline said. "Is everything all right?"

"Oh, yes, but that woman has returned. The one

who wanted to come in yesterday when the shop was closed. She's at the back door again." Cinderella was carrying a broom and dustpan, and Dodger, who was eyeing her like a besotted puppy, toted a pail with a mop jutting from it. He was paying no mind to the fact that the water in the pail was sloshing wildly. Today, Cinderella wasn't wearing a kerchief over her light brown hair, and instead had it pinned up in a neat coronet of braids. Her dress was also slightly more modern: a loose cotton shift with lace along the hem and sleeve edges. She looked lovely.

"It's not even nine o'clock," Jacqueline said. "And we open at ten." She sighed and slid off the barstool. "I suppose I'd best see what this is all about, since she was so insistent yesterday." And then she remembered that Wendy was supposed to meet her at nine anyway, so she had no time to dawdle.

She hurried down the stairs, happy to leave her half-finished cup of red tea and the three book characters behind. Customers, even demanding ones, she could handle. Figments of authors' imaginations combined with a lack of coffee she could not.

When she started down the hall to the back, Jacqueline saw the figure at the back door. The window was made from mottled glass, so she couldn't make out any definite features of the woman standing there, but whoever it was must have seen Jacqueline's shadow, for she knocked again. Rather peremptorily, in Jacqueline's opinion.

"All right, all right, what's the big hurry...I'm coming," she muttered. Whoever it was, they were certainly determined to speak to her—a thought that filled her with some dread—but the fact that they hadn't come to the open house yesterday was surprising.

Jacqueline opened the door. "Oh, Wendy! It's you." She looked around outside. "Was there anyone else here with you?"

Wendy gave her a curious look. "No. It's just me. You said nine o'clock."

"Right. Come on in," Jacqueline said. Had Wendy been the insistent woman who'd been trying to get in while the shop was closed? If so, why hadn't she said anything yesterday during the party?

It didn't really matter, though.

"I hope I'm not interrupting anything," Wendy said as she followed Jacqueline into the store. There was a hint of sarcasm in her tone, leaving Jacqueline to roll her eyes unseen.

"No," she replied. "The shop doesn't open for another hour, so there's nothing else demanding my attention. Let's sit down in here—oh, I see the fire's already going." She gestured into the mystery and thriller room.

Once they were seated, Jacqueline turned to Wendy and said in a very businesslike voice, "Now, please tell me what's on your mind."

Wendy drew in a deep breath as she clutched her purse to her belly and said in a rush, "I've been cursed."

"Cursed?" Jacqueline's insides turned to ice. "Surely you don't mean literally..."

"Yes, I mean literally," Wendy snapped. "And now I know who did it. And why."

"Wh-who?" said Jacqueline.

"You did," replied Wendy. "*You* cursed me, and I want you to take it off!"

9

J acqueline gaped at her friend. Had Wendy
gone mad?

"You think *I* cursed you?" she exclaimed. "Me?
How? Why? When? And, again, *how*?"

"I don't know *how* you did it," Wendy said. "But obviously it was you. It all started after you left Chicago,
and now you're here—at this store with all its mystical,
weird stuff."

Jacqueline's cheeks were hot with fury. She even
felt a trickle of sweat running down her spine. "I did
not curse you," she replied flatly. "That's ridiculous.
Even if I had the faintest idea *how* to curse someone, I
wouldn't ever do it—especially to a friend."

Although, as she said those words, she wondered
if Wendy really *was* her friend.

She drew in a deep breath and noticed that Cinderella was hovering in the hallway just outside the
room where they were sitting. Well, if she wanted to
come in and brush the ashes from the hearth or stoke
the fire, she was going to have to wait until Jacqueline
set Wendy Tract straight.

"All right, look...maybe you should start from the
beginning," Jacqueline said, quelling her righteous

fury. "And tell me why you think you've been cursed—"

"Oh, there's no doubt I've been cursed. It's been confirmed," said Wendy. Although her voice wasn't quite as strident and accusatory as it had been.

"Confirmed? By whom?"

Wendy shrugged. "This woman...she has a strange name. It doesn't matter, because I know why you did it and I sort of can understand it—"

"*Excuse* me?" Jacqueline's cheeks were fiery once again, and she felt a tingling in her fingertips. Uh-oh. "I'm going to ask you to leave if you continue those accusations."

Wendy blinked. Perhaps she wasn't used to Jacqueline being so direct.

Jacqueline wasn't used to being so direct. But it felt good to stand up for herself. She was incensed. "Who told you that you were cursed?"

"I told you—it was this woman. I met her yesterday. I was knocking at the back door of the store, but you were closed."

"Getting ready for the party," Jacqueline reminded her.

"Yes, but I really wanted to talk to you. And that young woman wouldn't let me in. I'm—I'm scared, Jacqueline." Wendy's voice quavered.

"I would be scared, too, if I thought I was cursed," Jacqueline replied. "But I wouldn't accuse my friend of doing it."

Wendy's cheeks turned a little pink. "Anyway, as I was leaving—because I was *turned away*," she added so passive-aggressively that Jacqueline did a double take, "a woman came up to me. She'd been sitting in the little courtyard next to the back door—the one that's walled in with the big tree?"

The cedar tree. A little prickle rushed over Jacqueline's shoulders.

"And she asked me what was wrong, and I told her I'd been trying to talk to my friend who owned the shop, but that I'd been turned away," Wendy went on. "She seemed very nice, and so we sat in the courtyard and I kind of told her what was going on—"

"What *is* going on? Why do you think you're cursed?"

"Because everything in my life is going wrong. There's—there's a rumor at the library about me... and..." Wendy pursed her lips and looked away.

"About you and whom?" Jacqueline asked.

"About me and Desmond Triplett," Wendy said in a rush. She was still looking down.

It took every bit of self-control for Jacqueline not to laugh bitterly. Oh so bitterly. "Just like there was a rumor—an *untrue* rumor—about me and Desmond. A rumor that you believed. And now you're saying the same thing has happened to you?"

"Yes." It sounded as if Wendy could barely ground out the syllable.

"Notice that my first reaction isn't to believe the rumor," Jacqueline said dryly.

"Probably because you caused it," Wendy shot back. Her cheeks were flushed dark red and her head of curls trembled. "And I've just been advised that my position is being eliminated. I've got two months to find a new job."

Not here in Button Cove, Jacqueline thought immediately...then was ashamed for it.

"The same sort of thing happened to *you* three weeks ago. It can't be a coincidence. It just can't be."

"It's probably not a coincidence," Jacqueline admitted. "But I didn't have anything to do with it. Don't forget, *I* was cursed first—if you can call it being cursed. But I lost my home too, so—"

"*And* you inherited *this*, so, yeah, things worked out just fine for you," retorted Wendy. "Look, I just want this curse or hex *gone*, all right? And that woman I talked to—I can't remember her name; it was something like Medala or Endala or—"

Oh. Shit. Jacqueline's heart sank. "*Egala?*"

"Yes, that was it, I think."

"Lady in her late fifties, maybe, a little bit of a Professor Umbridge vibe? Same hair?" *Crap, crap, crap.*

"Yes—like Queen Elizabeth hair. Like she just had it washed and set at the salon," Wendy said. "Dishwater blondish. You know her?"

"Distant relation. She thought she should have been the one to inherit the bookshop," Jacqueline said. "Instead of me."

Wendy merely quirked a brow. as if to say, *Well, maybe that would have been better.*

"So Egala is the one who told you I cursed you," Jacqueline said. "And you believed this strange woman over someone you've known for more than ten years."

"Well, she had a sort of way about her," Wendy replied. "Like...I don't know. Mystical. Like she *knows* stuff."

"She's a witch," Jacqueline told her.

"I'm not surprised," Wendy replied, shocking Jacqueline with her acceptance of the fact. "I suspected it. But she told me I had to insist that you remove the curse. I didn't realize it was *you* who'd caused it until I talked to her. I just thought...well, I just thought my life was going downhill and you might be able to give me some encouragement after everything that happened to you."

Jacqueline realized her fingers had been digging

into her palms. Probably better than raking them across her so-called friend's face. "I see. So I have to remove the curse because I'm the one who put it in place."

"That's what she said."

"And if I do, what happens? The rumor just goes *poof!* and is gone? Your job isn't eliminated? What does Robert think of all this?"

Robert was Wendy's husband of thirty-plus years.

Wendy's eyes filled with tears. "That's the worst part. He told me he wants a divorce."

"Because of the rumor about you and Desmond?" Jacqueline was shocked. Robert Tract was an easygoing, vanilla sort of guy who had always seemed to avoid rocking the boat. Not that infidelity—or the suspicion of it—wasn't a good reason to rock said boat.

"No...he told me before the rumor started," Wendy said. "I didn't believe him at first—I told him I wanted to try to work things out—but he's not interested. It's like...he just turned off, you know? Like he just decided he was done with the marriage."

Jacqueline didn't understand why Wendy hadn't *led* with the divorce request when listing off the reasons she thought she was cursed. Maybe because it was the most painful part for her?

"All right." Jacqueline wasn't sure how to proceed, but she expected her next step would be to talk to the ZAP Ladies. Unless she could hunt down Egala and have a little face-to-face with her.

"All right, what?" said Wendy.

"I'm going to have to do some research," Jacqueline said. "About what you're saying—to see if it's true and to find out what to do about it. It might just be a string of bad luck," she said. "You know...karma can be a real bitch." She eyed Wendy meaningfully. "What goes around comes around."

Wendy flattened her lips. "Just get this damned curse off me. I want my normal life back."

"I'll do my be—"

"If you don't, I'll do everything I can to ruin this place," Wendy added, gesturing to the shop. "And you know there's a lot I can do." Her eyes narrowed with malice.

Jacqueline felt a little frisson of nervousness. Wendy did have a lot of connections: she was the president of the regional American Library Association and knew many people at the national level; she was also very tied in to the indie bookstore association in the greater Midwest, and she had a fairly well-read book blog, where she posted reviews of reads, indie bookstores, and tea shops.

And if Wendy had somehow been befriended by Egala, Jacqueline knew that would just make everything worse. It was in Egala's best interest for the bookshop to fail—then she'd have the chance to take it over.

And that was something Jacqueline was not about to let happen.

~

JACQUELINE WAS STILL SHAKING with fury when she closed the door behind Wendy. It was nine forty-five, so she had fifteen minutes to collect herself before she had to open up.

What had happened to her good friend? How could Wendy even think such a thing about Jacqueline? The accusations, the snideness...that wasn't the sort of personality she was used to from Wendy. Her friend had always been mild-mannered, if a little judgmental, but never confrontational like this.

Maybe she really *was* cursed.

A rattle at the front door of the shop attracted Jacqueline's attention, and she looked over to see who was demanding entrance ten minutes before opening.

Her heart skipped a beat when she recognized the man standing there, peering into the shop.

Kenneth Gauthier.

What was he doing here?

When he realized she'd seen him, he waved energetically and smiled, nodding, as if to say, "Please open up."

Ignoring the jumpiness in her belly, Jacqueline went over and unlocked the door. "Good morning, Mr. Gauthier," she said, standing in the narrow opening. "We're not open for another ten minutes, and I'm afraid I'm in the middle of something right now."

"Oh, geez, I'm so sorry," he said, looking abashed. "I didn't mean to bother you—I just wanted to drop off a few samples."

He raised his arm, and that was when she saw he was holding a bag weighted down by four bottles of wine.

"Oh, wow," Jacqueline replied, feeling a little ashamed for being such a stickler. After all, it was only eight minutes or so until ten. Small business owners could—and should—be flexible, she decided. "That's so nice of you. Thank you."

She opened the door and stepped back, inviting him to enter.

"I don't want to keep you," said Kenneth, looking around the shop as if trying to identify what he was keeping her from. "I really just wanted to drop these off, and to tell you thank you for reopening the bookstore. Amanda was very worried when the previous owner died. She was afraid the shop wouldn't open again." He set the bag of bottles on the counter with a satisfying clink and gave a little laugh. "She's such a book lover—always has a book or her tablet in her hands, reading." His bright smile faltered a little.

"She was very interested in the shop," Jacqueline said. "I hope she'll come back. Is everything all right?" she asked, noticing that his smile had all but disintegrated.

"Oh...yes. Yes, everything's fine." But his expression and tone indicated just the opposite.

"Amanda mentioned she has severe asthma," Jacqueline said. "I hope she's feeling all right."

Kenneth sighed and scrubbed a hand over his forehead. "She's fine. There was a bad scare last week —a really bad one; she could even have died—but she's fine now. She's *fine*."

Jacqueline got the impression he was trying to convince himself of the fact.

To convince himself Amanda was still alive and healthy, despite his attempts to the contrary?

Jacqueline stifled a shiver and looked down the hall to see if anyone else was around. She wasn't thrilled about the idea of being alone with a possible murderer. Or attempted murderer. Even if he did come loaded with wine.

"Well, thank you so much for bringing the wine out for me," she said, hoping he'd get the hint and leave. "I'm definitely going to enjoy it, I promise."

"I do hope you'll schedule a tasting up at the winery, though," he said. "We'd love to have you, and..." He hesitated, then went on in a little rush, "I don't think Amanda is all that happy right now. She seems... well, I think she could use some friends. We—uh—

haven't been married that long—only three years—and she moved up here from Chicago when we got married. I think she misses the city and her friends, and..." He heaved a sigh. "I don't know why I'm telling you all of this. It's not like you're a bartender." He gave a little laugh.

Jacqueline chuckled in return. "No, but I'm a librarian. I'm used to listening to people's problems too —just different kinds." She realized as she spoke that it was shockingly true. As a reference librarian, she helped people find answers to the most obscure questions. She also helped readers find the perfect book—or books—to feed their souls.

"Well, that's kind of you," Kenneth said, still looking around as if he were unsettled.

"I am going up to the winery this afternoon," Jacqueline said. "Amanda and I have an appointment at one."

"Oh!" He looked surprised but pleased. "I'm glad to hear it."

"I guess you didn't need to make a special trip to drop these off," Jacqueline said with a smile, indicating the bag of wine.

"It was my pleasure. Really. I have a meeting in town with my banker this morning anyway."

"Oh, that's convenient," Jacqueline replied, wondering if the meeting had anything to do with the inn Amanda said her husband wanted to build. The inn that would be financed by her life insurance policy...

Jacqueline gave herself a mental shake. She had no idea whether Amanda Gauthier was paranoid, or was correct about her husband.

"Can I treat you to a cup of tea and a scone as a thanks for the wine?" Jacqueline asked.

"That would be so nice of you," he replied with a

surprised look. "Thank you. I'm normally a coffee drinker, but that woman upstairs yesterday really sold me on a London Fog."

"There's nothing better than Earl Grey with steamed milk. I tend to add too much sugar for most people, though," Jacqueline told him as they climbed the stairs.

Dodger was sweeping the floor and Mrs. Hudson was bustling about behind the counter as usual. Cinderella was nowhere in sight, which could have accounted for Dodger's woebegone expression.

"Mrs. Hudson, would you please make Mr. Gauthier a London Fog and give him whatever pastry he'd like? He brought me some wine from his vineyard, and I wanted to say thank you," said Jacqueline.

Kenneth slid onto one of the counter stools and flashed Jacqueline a smile. He was a very attractive guy, she thought, despite not being traditionally handsome. It was a shame he was trying to kill his wife.

Might be trying to kill his wife, she reminded herself. She didn't really get any sort of danger or even an icky vibe from him, but that didn't mean squat. It wasn't like Jacqueline was used to interacting with potential killers.

When she looked at the clock and realized it was ten, she excused herself and went back downstairs to open up the shop. A few moments later, Kenneth came downstairs, carrying a to-go cup and a small pastry bag.

"Well," he said, flashing a pleasantly crooked smile, "I suppose I'd best be off. I hope you enjoy the wine. Thank you for the treats." He gestured with the cup and bag. "And thanks for—uh—for meeting with Amanda. It'll be nice for her to get to know more people in town."

Jacqueline said goodbye and watched him walk to the door, mulling over what he'd said about Amanda not really knowing many people in town. It seemed odd that she would be the VP of sales and marketing for a local winery and not know many people.

Wasn't that the definition of sales and marketing— networking, interacting, schmoozing? And if Amanda had been here three years and still didn't know many people, what did that say about her?

Shaking her head, Jacqueline tucked away the thought. Maybe she'd find out more when she met with Amanda this afternoon.

Not that she was getting involved.

She wasn't. She really wasn't.

JACQUELINE SPENT the rest of the morning helping the few customers that came in and packaging up some online orders, including the surprise sale on eBay of a signed first edition of Julia Child's *The Way to Cook*. It went for a tidy sum, and that made Jacqueline smile as she carefully swathed the book in bubble wrap, then closed the flap of the box with a Three Tomes sticker.

Mrs. Danvers was in and out of the front room and the genre rooms, muttering to herself. Jacqueline felt a little guilty that though she had expected some machinations from Danvers at the party yesterday, nothing had happened. Instead, the woman had been useful and almost polite.

It was nearly noon when Suzette came in through the front door with a jingle of the bells. Danvers was behind the counter, ringing up an order with a sour smile, and Jacqueline was unboxing an order from Penguin Random House.

Jacqueline greeted her friend with enthusiasm and an apology. "I'm sorry I flaked out on you two last night," she said. "I had to talk to the ZAP Ladies, and by the time they left, I realized I didn't have the brain-power to walk across the street—even for pizza."

"No worries at all," Suzette replied, handing her a foil-wrapped packet. "Nadine and I saved you a couple of pieces. I totally understand. After my grand opening, I soaked in the tub for an hour, had two huge negronis, then went to bed and slept till noon the next day. Thank goodness the bakery is closed on Mondays! Anyway, I can hardly believe you're here and working."

Jacqueline peeked inside the foil packet and was assaulted by the scent of homemade pizza. "I might have to eat this now," she said, suddenly starving. "Want to go up to the café with me while I do? I'll treat you to a tea or whatever you want. I have to leave in about an hour anyway."

"Sure."

"And you can tell me all about Wes," added Jacqueline with a grin.

"Oh," said Suzette, her angular cheeks turning pink. "There's nothing really to tell. We're just—as the twenty-somethings say—talking."

"With talking being the precursor for sex?" asked Jacqueline.

"Ha! No, with talking being the precursor for dating," Suzette told her. "Of course, at our age, maybe we should just jump to the sex part. That's what Nadine said."

Jacqueline laughed. "That girl obviously needs to get laid. She's got sex on the brain."

"Nothing wrong with that," said Suzette as they reached the top of the steps to the café.

"No, indeed," said Jacqueline as Miles Massermey's face popped into her mind. She felt her cheeks warm. That was jumping the gun a little, she told herself. He'd only asked her for coffee, and she wasn't even certain she was interested.

Oh, hell. Of course she was at least *interested*.

She'd be a fool not to be. But before she dove in, Jacqueline figured she'd better learn a little more about the guy. Like, was he a player? Did he always go after the new gal in town? And why hadn't Nadine or Suzette gone for him?

Or had they?

At forty-eight, Jacqueline was suspicious and gun-shy when it came to men. She'd never married (although she'd come close until she learned that Josh had been bonking one of her friends), and hadn't had many relationships that lasted for more than a few months. She liked her single life, liked not being responsible for anyone but herself.

Now, though, she was not only responsible for herself, a bookshop, and two cats...it also seemed half the female population of Button Cove was trying to get her to take care of them too.

She and Suzette sat at a table near the fireplace, which wasn't lit today, since the weather was relatively warm and sunny.

"So, tell me about Wes," Jacqueline said. "While I eat."

"Don't you want to heat that up?" asked Suzette, eyeing the cold pizza.

"No need. Cold Italian food is one of my favorites," Jacqueline said with a sigh of pleasure. "So...Wes."

"He's a nice guy. Divorced ten years. Two kids, both in college. He's an architect, is a partner in a small firm, and works out of a gorgeous office that overlooks the bay. He's not super outgoing, but he's got a dry sense of humor. One big snafu, though—he doesn't eat carbs." Suzette's eyes crinkled with humor. "Kind of funny for a baker to maybe be dating someone who doesn't eat carbs."

"He doesn't eat any carbs?" Jacqueline asked, so very sad for the man. "At all?"

"Very few. So I don't know how that's going to work out," Suzette replied with a shrug. "I mean, I can't imagine being involved with someone who won't taste my bread or cupcakes."

"Well, you always have me and Nadine," Jacqueline said with a laugh. "Does he do commercial or residential work?"

"Mostly commercial. He's done quite a bit of work for some of the distilleries and wineries around here," replied Suzette. "He doesn't do the flashy, sleek sort of modern-day buildings, so his style fits in well here in Button Cove."

"Hmm," said Jacqueline. "Do you happen to know if he's done anything for Big Bay Winery?"

"I don't know. We haven't gotten into that much detail. So far we've just covered the basics on employment, kids, current favorite streaming shows—I didn't mention *Fleabag*, though because he's Catholic and there's that hot priest thing in season two—and we've agreed that *Star Wars* is better than *Star Trek* and that there should never have been three *Hobbit* movies." Suzette's smile seemed genuine, and Jacqueline felt a surge of happiness for her. "I'm going to try to get him to watch *The Great British Baking Show*, but he might nix that because of his carb avoidance. So, why were you asking about Big Bay?"

Jacqueline leaned closer across the table even though no one was around but Mrs. Hudson—behind the counter—and Dodger, playing with the elevator. "Okay, you won't believe this, but...yesterday the wife of the owner came in here and told me she thought her husband was trying to kill her." She sat back in her seat as her friend reacted with appropriate shock and awe.

"What?" Suzette's eyes goggled and her jaw fell open. She stayed that way for a full minute as Jacqueline just nodded grimly. Finally, Suzette shook her head and said, "I have so many questions, I don't know where to begin."

"Right?" said Jacqueline. "Have you met either of them before? The Gauthiers—Amanda and Kenneth."

"I've met someone from Big Bay. Older guy. Maybe sixty? He seemed like a decent guy. Dressed nicely, was courteous and respectful to me. It was a business networking thing, and you know how men—especially older ones—can sometimes be condescending to women business owners. So...he's trying to kill his wife?"

Jacqueline shook her head. "Not the same guy. Kenneth Gauthier is in his early thirties, so maybe that's the father you met. Amanda—that's the woman who asked me for help—told me his family owns the winery."

"What makes her think that he's trying to kill her? And more importantly, why is she telling *you* about this and not Detective Massermey?"

Jaqueline heaved a sigh. "You won't believe it." She hesitated, trying to figure out how to explain the situation. At last, she decided to just say it. "Apparently, Amanda Gauthier thinks I run some sort of...I don't even know how to describe it...service to help women, here at the bookshop. Like a witchy-magical sort of helping service."

This time, Suzette's reaction was even better. She dropped her cup onto its saucer with an ugly clatter and burst out laughing, even as her eyes widened with horror. "You...have...*got*...to...be *kidding*...me," she gasped between hoots, dabbing at the sloshed tea with her napkin. "What in the *hell*?"

"I *know*. And here's the best—or worst—part," Jacqueline said with a roll of her eyes. "She's not the only one. Two other people—women—approached me at the party yesterday and asked for my wink-wink-nudge-nudge help." She gave her own exaggerated winks.

Suzette settled back in her chair. "Holy shit."

"Yeah." Jacqueline had a sudden thought. "So, you've been around here for a while. On Camellia Court, I mean. Have you ever heard any rumblings about it? You know, that Three Tomes is the place to go if you need—I guess I'll call it wise woman help?"

Suzette didn't respond immediately, but she didn't hesitate long. When she spoke, it was thoughtful. "Not *really*. But there's always been a little buzz about the ZAP Ladies. And *maybe* a little hint that Cuddy Stone was a unique individual and the crystals and runes and tarot cards she sold here at Three Tomes were all sort of special and unique. But nothing as blatant as 'Help me because my husband is trying to kill me,' or—"

"Or 'I need a love potion,'" Jacqueline said dryly. "As someone requested yesterday."

"*No*." Suzette's expression was comical.

"Yes. That was an ask from a fifteen-year-old girl." Jacqueline went on to explain about her conversation with Kara, and then how she'd tried to foist her off on the ZAP Ladies. "They basically told me to figure it out," she said in conclusion. "And, oh, by the way, that love potions need to ferment for months before they're ready." She rolled her eyes really hard.

"Wait until Nadine hears about this," Suzette said between uncontrollable giggles. Jacqueline was pretty sure she was laughing at her situation, not what Nadine's reaction was going to be when she found out that women were coming into the shop and asking for witchery help. "So what are you going to do?"

"I'm going to Big Bay Winery at one—crap, I have to leave in about ten minutes—to have a private wine tasting with Amanda." Jacqueline shrugged when Suzette gaped at her. "I'm mostly going for business networking, but I guess I'll see if I can find out anything else. I don't really know what Amanda wants me to do for her—"

"Why, she'll be wanting a protection charm, then, won't she, dearie?"

Jacqueline had been so intent on her conversation with Suzette that she hadn't realized Mrs. Hudson was nearby and, obviously, listening as she fluttered a feather duster about. "What?" Jacqueline said, shocked.

"I said, a protection charm—or an amulet— should do the trick," replied Mrs. Hudson as if she were suggesting a sencha blend instead of English breakfast.

"Now, Mrs. Hudson, what would Mr. Holmes say if he heard you spouting such nonsense?" Jacqueline said with a little snort of laughter. "You know he's very practical and science-based."

Mrs. Hudson sniffed as she danced the duster over the top of a framed blow-up of a *The Hound of the Baskervilles* cover hanging on the wall. "That's because he's a man," she retorted. "Men don't believe in such things."

"I'm not sure *I* do," muttered Suzette.

"Tsk, tsk, ma'am...if you'll pardon me for saying, it's the likes o' you who should be the first to believe," said Mrs. Hudson. "Being a woman of a certain age."

Jacqueline and Suzette exchanged glances, then Jacqueline decided she might as well poke the bear a little more. "So how does one go about getting a protection amulet, then, Mrs. Hudson?" she asked brightly.

The landlady paused and skewered her with a very pointed look—as if she knew Jacqueline was pushing her buttons and maybe even condescending to her. Which of course she was. "Now, that's not right you making fun, luv. Women've been protecting and helping women for centuries, you know. Why, even that Miss Adler—"

Mrs. Hudson clamped her lips shut and turned away suddenly. The feather duster began to whisk energetically along the top of *The Crucible*.

"Wait, wait, wait," Jacqueline said, reaching out to touch Mrs. Hudson's arm so she'd turn back. "Just one minute here."

"Yes?" Mrs. Hudson's tone was haughty, but Jacqueline caught a hint of chagrin in her eyes.

"Did you know Irene Adler? The only woman who outsmarted Sherlock Holmes?" Jacqueline was fascinated in spite of herself.

Mrs. Hudson scoffed. "The only woman he *knew* about that outsmarted him," she said. "You think I rented a flat to that bloke for years and never had one over on him? Pish. The man was so enamored with his own intellect he missed half the things going on. Why, I can't tell you how many times I had the best of him when it came to— Well, never you mind." She shook her head, a small smile playing at the corners of her mouth.

"Well, that's quite enlightening, Mrs. Hudson," said Jacqueline, determined to get details from her later. "Tell us about Irene Adler. Did you help her put one over on Sherlock?"

Mrs. Hudson clamped her lips closed and shook her head. Yet the gleam in her eyes gave a clear indication that Jacqueline was on the right track.

"You'd best be getting on your way, dearie, if you're going to make your appointment on time," the landlady said.

Jacqueline looked at her phone and saw the time. "You're right. But don't think this conversation is over, Mrs. Hudson," she added.

The landlady said, "Pish," then moved on to dusting the frame of *The Bluest Eye*.

"Let me know how it goes," Suzette told Jacqueline as she pushed her chair in at the table and gathered up her cup and napkin. "I want all the details."

"I'm sure the only thing I'll have to report is whether I like their Chardonnay or not," replied Jacqueline. "But I'm going to have to break it to Amanda that there's nothing I can do to help her. She really should talk to Massermey."

"Speaking of our favorite detective," said Suzette as they walked down the steps together. "You two looked pretty cozy talking in the corner yesterday. Are you going to go out with him?"

"He did ask me for coffee," Jacqueline replied. "And I'll probably go—"

"Probably?"

"Well, I want to know more about him, I guess. I mean, I'm new in town. Does he always go for the new girl? The fresh blood? If he's so eligible and fantastic—"

"Not to mention good-looking and nice," Suzette added.

"Right. If he's all that and a bag of chips, why is he single?" asked Jacqueline.

"Have no idea. But I can tell you two things. One, he's never showed any interest in me other than just pleasantries, and I was the new girl about a year ago. And two, I think he was involved with someone from down in Wicks Hollow for a while after his divorce, but apparently that didn't work out. So, no, it's not that you're the new girl or fresh blood or anything like that. I think he just *likes* you. Or is at least intrigued by you. Nothing wrong with that," Suzette said, giving Jacqueline an affectionate jab with her elbow.

"Thanks for the info. All right—I'm off to meet with Amanda Gauthier."

"Are you sure you don't want to bring a protection charm with you?" teased Suzette.

Jacqueline rolled her eyes. "No."

10

It was a lovely drive up to Big Bay Winery. Having been in Button Cove for less than a month, and working hard to get the shop ready and her flat painted, Jacqueline hadn't been able to spend much time exploring the area.

Now she found that the "pinkie" region of Michigan—a slender peninsula jutting northerly into Lake Michigan—was stunning country, filled with lush, rolling hills, thick, verdant forests, shimmering lakes large and small, cherry and peach orchards, and vineyards. Even now, before all of the leaves had fully popped and the fruit trees were just starting to think about blossoming, the views were breathtaking. The indigenous peoples who settled here had called the area "Land of Delight" for obvious reasons.

Jacqueline's trusty Subaru Outback trundled along the sweep of a two-lane highway that curved along the grand Lake Michigan bay, a hairsbreadth outside of town and where the Button Cove Zoo sat right next to the public beach. Jacqueline grimaced when she recalled the night a few weeks ago when she'd risked her life to climb into the herpetarium in order to acquire a crocodile tooth.

She'd been trying to save the ZAP Ladies from a curse Egala had put on them, and the tooth was one of the ingredients needed for the antidote that she had somehow been induced to make. Her heart sank as she navigated along the bay and out of town to the northwest. Did this mean she was going to have to do something just as dangerous in order to remove the curse on Wendy? A curse she had definitely not put on her but was somehow taking the blame for?

So *not fair!*

Following the GPS's directions, she drove out of town, then turned west to follow a curving road that led up a long, rolling hill. It was paved, but when she reached the sign for Big Bay Winery, the turnoff was a wide gravel road that continued winding up the small mountain.

This must be the road Amanda had mentioned she walked on, and where she believed Kenneth had tried to run her down in his Tesla. Trees and brush grew thickly along either side, and butted up close to the edge of the S-curve road. When the trees were in full leaf, their arching branches would make a low, thick tunnel of green over the road. Jacqueline wondered where the vineyards were if there was so much forest.

She drove for about a mile before the forest opened up into a pretty glen nestled at the base of three large hills. She drew in her breath at the beautiful sight before her: the pristine white buildings cupped in the palmlike valley, and grapevines growing in rows upon rows upon rows, up and along the rolling hills that surrounded the cluster of buildings. Each plant looked like hardly more than a gnarled brown tree, perhaps chest-high if she stood next to them, and trained to grow along rows of fencing. They looked like spindly, skeletal soldiers lined up in infinite troop formation over the mounding hills.

There was ample room for a small inn on the property, Jacqueline noted as she navigated the Outback left at the fork in the road, following the signs for *Office* instead of *Tasting Room: Welcome!* Two cars were parked in the tasting room lot, which was more than she'd expected for a Monday afternoon before Memorial Day.

The office building was adjacent to a long, large building made from brick. The bigger structure looked like a huge barn at least three stories high, and Jacqueline suspected that was where the wine was made. Large, mysterious pieces of machinery that looked like they belonged on a farm were parked outside the barn, with great vats attached to them. Two men were standing nearby, talking while gesturing to the machines.

A few cars were parked in the lot by the office building, and she noticed one of them was a silver Tesla. Shockingly, it didn't sport a vanity license plate.

After sliding her own trusty vehicle into a spot next to the Tesla, she climbed out and glanced inside the car that presumably belonged to Kenneth Gauthier. The interior was neat as a pin, with nothing to indicate the identity of its owner. Not even a pair of sunglasses.

Wondering whether Kenneth was going to join them for her meeting, Jacqueline slung her purse over her shoulder and headed for the main door.

The office building looked like it might have been a cottage or gatehouse at one time. It was larger than a bungalow, but still compact, with only two stories and a square footprint. Painted white with forest-green trim, the combination echoed in the Big Bay logo, the structure was quiet and welcoming, with two barrels of splashy red geraniums flanking the steps onto the porch. Jacqueline raised her brows at the optimism of placing geraniums outside before Memorial Day, but she supposed they would just replace the flowers if they got caught in a frost—or cover them.

Obviously, being farmers and vintners, the Gauthiers would pay very close attention to the weather and frost warnings.

Jacqueline stepped inside the office building and was surprised to discover there was no receptionist on duty. The main desk where one would work was clean and empty other than a dark computer and landline telephone. However, someone had given the place attention, for a vase of fresh flowers sat on the desk, and next to it was a small sign that read: *Welcome to Big Bay Winery!*

Jacqueline looked around for a moment. Amanda was expecting her, so should she wait for her to appear, or make her way to Amanda's office, wherever that was?

The small building had only one hall that led from the entrance, and she could see that it ended at another perpendicular hall. But there was no sign of life, nor any voices to indicate whether she should wait or not. A set of steps led to the second floor, but Jacqueline didn't know whether Amanda's office was up there or not.

With a sigh, she started down the hall. There were three doors—two were restrooms and the third was labeled *Conference Room*. At the end of the hall, she had the choice of going right or left down another, very short corridor. The right side ended in a door to the exterior, while the left ended with a door.

Jacqueline went left, and was satisfied when she

saw the door at the end of the hall had a nameplate that read *Amanda Gauthier*.

She knocked on the closed door and waited. A quick check on her phone told her she was now two minutes late for their one o'clock appointment, so Amanda should be expecting her. She listened, and there were still no sounds from behind the door or from anywhere else in the building.

That seemed odd, but then again, it wasn't high season, so she didn't expect the office to be exactly bustling. It was just past the lunch hour, so maybe everyone was out to lunch...or maybe they'd tasted too much wine during a meeting and were all napping. Jacqueline smiled to herself. Naps were one of her favorite things; she thought everyone should take a nap whenever possible.

She knocked a second time, louder, and called, "Amanda? It's Jacqueline Finch for our one o'clock."

Still no answer. She thought she heard something from the other side of the door, so she knocked again. "Amanda?"

Still no response. Frowning, she was just about to walk away when she smelled something.

Gas.

It seemed to be coming from nearby—

I have a gas fireplace in my office, Amanda had said yesterday.

Jacqueline's heart surged into her throat, and, despite feeling a little odd, she crouched near the floor to sniff.

Gas. Stronger now, coming from beneath the door.

Holy shit.

Feeling as if her heart was choking her, Jacqueline tried the doorknob. Fortunately, it turned, and she flung the door wide. A strong waft of gas assailed her.

"Amanda!" she cried when she saw the woman crumpled on the floor.

Jacqueline dashed into the office, leaving the door wide open. Amanda was on the floor near her desk. The smell of gas was strong, but there were no flames in the firebox.

"Help!" cried Jacqueline as she knelt by Amanda, trying not to inhale too much gas herself. "Amanda!"

Amanda moaned and shifted slightly, sending a wild wave of relief through Jacqueline.

"Help!" she cried again, as loudly as possible.

Feeling a little lightheaded herself, Jacqueline surged to her feet and stumbled over to the French doors that led to the outside. She whipped them open and gulped in fresh air, then turned back to Amanda as she pulled out her phone.

"Amanda?" she said, kneeling next to her. "Can you hear me?" She wanted to get her up and over to a source of fresh air as soon as possible. Taking Amanda by the arm, she dragged her across the floor toward the open French doors, also grateful for another surge of fresh air.

Once she got Amanda close to the opening, she dialed 911. When the operator came on, Jacqueline explained as quickly as she could. She could still smell the gas, and knew there had to be a way to turn off the fireplace—if that was what was causing it.

"EMTs are on their way," said the operator. "Is the victim conscious?"

"She's moaning a little, but doesn't seem to be lucid," said Jacqueline. "Can you also notify Detective Massermey of the Button Cove Police Department?" she said as she looked at the fireplace, trying to figure out how to turn it on or off. The smell was much stronger next to it, and she could hear the hiss of gas spewing into the air. Fortunately, having the door to the office open and the French doors as well was causing a decent draft. "Ask him to come." She gave her name and added, "He knows me. Please let him know I think he should come."

She was feeling lightheaded again, and she went back to the French doors to gulp more fresh air. Amanda's eyelids fluttered, and Jacqueline felt another rush of gratitude even though Amanda's eyes settled closed again. If Jacqueline hadn't gotten to the appointment on time... If she hadn't been persistent in knocking and trying to keep her appointment... She didn't like to think what would have happened. Especially since no one had responded to her cries for help.

After another few breaths of fresh air, Jacqueline went back over to the fireplace. She needed to turn off the gas flow. It took her a minute, but she finally found the round black knob nestled near the front of the hearth. She turned it, and the soft hiss of gas ceased.

Finally.

Shaky now that things were as under control as they could be, Jacqueline went back over by Amanda, who was stirring more stridently now.

"Amanda?" Jacqueline said, kneeling next to her and facing the open doors. "Can you hear me?"

Amanda moaned, and her eyes fluttered open and stayed open this time. "What...what happened?"

"There was a gas leak," Jacqueline said. "I think you passed out. The EMTs are on their way."

"A...gas leak?" Amanda's eyes flew open wide. "What do you mean?"

"I don't know," Jacqueline replied. "There's the strong smell of gas, and I think it was coming from your fireplace. I arrived for our appointment, and you didn't answer the door, so..." She shrugged.

At that moment, she heard the sounds of sirens in the distance. That was faster than she had expected, considering the smallish town and its hilly, rural roads.

"How could there be a gas leak?" said Amanda groggily. She struggled upright into a sitting position, leaning against one of the open French doors. "From where?"

"The fireplace," Jacqueline told her as the sirens screamed closer.

"But I use that fireplace every...day." Amanda's eyes were wide and bloodshot. "Oh my God. Oh my God! I told you! He tried again, didn't he?" Her voice rose, scratchy from the gas, as a shaking hand went to cover her mouth.

Jacqueline was saved from having to reply by the sounds of running feet and a shout. "I'd better go out and meet the paramedics," she said.

She hadn't even gotten to the door when Kenneth Gauthier burst in. "What is going on here? What's happened? Amanda! Are you all right? Who called the ambulance? Ms. Finch? Are you all right?" He went directly to his wife, who still leaned wearily against the open door. "I smell gas! What happened?"

Jacqueline noticed how Amanda edged slightly away from Kenneth, giving Jacqueline a pleading look from over his shoulder. "I'm all right," she said. "It appears the fireplace was leaking gas."

Kenneth, who'd been crouched next to his wife with her hand in his, surged to his feet. "The fireplace? Leaking gas? But it's been fine..."

The rest of his words were indiscernible to Jacqueline, for she had gone down the hall to guide the paramedics to Amanda. She'd just pointed the pair of them down the hallway when an SUV pulled into the parking lot and parked next to the ambulance.

Jacqueline was relieved to see Detective Massermey emerge from the vehicle. His strawberry-blond-turning-white hair glinted in the sunlight, and she noticed with approval the way his dress shirt fit over broad shoulders as he pulled on the suit coat he'd left hanging in the back of the SUV.

"Jacqueline," he said as she approached. "What's going on? Are you all right?"

"I'm fine, but Amanda Gauthier could have died." Jacqueline found herself squinting in the sunlight as she looked up at him.

"Gauthier. The wife of which Gauthier—David or Kenneth?" Massermey asked, confirming what Jacqueline had suspected: in the relatively small community of Button Cove and its environs, most everyone had at least heard of most everyone else. Especially law enforcement.

"Kenneth. The younger one," Jacqueline replied.

"All right," replied Massermey. He didn't seem agitated about being called in, nor did he seem impatient to learn why she'd done so. She liked that he didn't swoop in and demand details or give orders. "What happened?"

Jacqueline gave a brief description of why she was here and how she'd found Amanda. When she was finished, he lifted a brow and said mildly, "I know you didn't call me here over an accidental gas leak."

"No." Jacqueline hesitated. Was she going to be breaking a confidence by telling him what Amanda had told her?

But Amanda hadn't impressed upon her about keeping it a secret, and besides, Jacqueline had nearly found a dead body instead of an unconscious one. She had her own traumatic story to tell, and that was her right. "So...Amanda thinks someone has been trying to kill her. And this seems to me like another incident that could fall under that umbrella. She uses that fireplace almost every day, she said. So I thought you should look around...just in case. And, you know, get the incident put on record."

"All right," he replied with a nod. "I'll see what I can find out."

"Um...Detective," Jacqueline said, catching him before he started off into the building. "Don't say anything in front of the husband about what I told you."

He paused, his light blue eyes settling onto hers. They'd gone from mild to very sharp in an instant. "She thinks it's him."

Jacqueline nodded.

"All right. I'll take that under advisement."

"Thanks. I'm...um... I think I'd best get back to the shop," Jacqueline said. "There's nothing else I can do here. I'm happy to give a formal statement if you need one."

"Sounds good. Thanks." He gave her a smile that was definitely more personal than professional, then strode into the building.

Jacqueline didn't see any reason for her to go back inside and get in everyone's way. Amanda was probably going to be taken to the hospital anyway, so they wouldn't have time to talk. They'd catch up later.

But, really, it wasn't Jacqueline's problem. It was Detective Massermey's investigation now. She'd done the responsible thing and alerted the authorities and called for medical help. There was nothing else she needed to do.

After all, she wasn't Nancy Drew, or even Miss

Marple. Jacqueline winced when she realized she was getting closer in age and personality to Agatha Christie's elderly detective than to the young, titian-haired sleuth. Ugh.

Regardless, she had no interest in getting involved with a potential murder investigation. Unlike every character in every cozy mystery she'd ever read, Jacqueline had absolutely no desire to poke her nose into other people's business, hunt down clues—which meant talking to people about something other than books—or put herself in danger from a killer.

Thus, it was with a clear conscience that she drove down the hilly, winding road where Amanda Gauthier had nearly been run over, and back toward Great Bay and Button Cove.

My work here is done, she told herself with a satisfied smile.

Back at Three Tomes, Jacqueline parked in the rear of the shop and let herself in through the back door. To her pleasure, she saw a few customers browsing in various rooms as she made her way to the front to check on Mrs. Danvers.

Not that Mrs. Danvers needed checking on. The idea was ludicrous. But as owner and manager, Jacqueline felt obligated to do so.

When she passed by the young adult room, she glanced inside and saw someone sitting on one of the big Bohemian-style poufs in the corner. Jacqueline's step faltered when she recognized the girl as Kara.

Unfortunately, the girl must have seen her from the corner of her eye, and she surged to her feet. "Miss Finch!" she said, setting down the book she'd been reading. "You're back."

"So I am," replied Jacqueline, unable to hide her

lack of enthusiasm. Kara must have come here right after school.

"Are you going to help me?"

One thing about the girl—she got right to the point. Jacqueline heaved a sigh. She struggled for a minute, then gave in to the hopeful look in Kara's eyes. She walked into the room and sat down on a wrought-iron cushioned bench in front of the window. The floor cushions were fine for agile youngsters; she'd stick with hip-height seats, thank you very much.

"So you want a love potion," she said.

"Yes, please," replied Kara eagerly, plopping back down on her pouf.

Today she was wearing a Michigan hoodie and jeans. Her hair was pulled back in a ponytail, and she'd pushed her eyeglasses up onto her head— maybe because she didn't need them to read. Jacqueline thought again how pretty her big, dark eyes were. Right now, they sparkled with excitement.

"Tell me more," Jacqueline said, hoping that if the girl talked, she'd be able to figure out how to help her —or, more accurately, how to dissuade her.

"Well, it's..." Kara looked around as if to ensure no one was listening. But it was just the two of them in the room, so she went on. "There's a guy. At school. He's really nice and cute and...well, he doesn't really notice me except because we're lab partners in chem."

Oh great. Was this going to be one of those situations where the geeky, nerdy girl gets the football player because she helps him with his homework and he realizes there's more to her than the pretty, popular cheerleader he's dating? Jacqueline quelled her reaction to such a cliched setup and merely nodded encouragingly for Kara to continue.

"His name is Bryson, and...I just want him to notice me," Kara said. "I want him to like me and to ask me out. I want him to *love* me."

"So," said Jacqueline, shuddering internally at the teen's desperation. But what girl hadn't been there, at age fifteen or sixteen—desperate to be noticed and liked by someone?

Heaven knew she'd been there herself, seriously crushing on Carl Dudek, who'd been a basketball player—a guy who never looked at the girl with bright red hair who was waaay too smart for him. "When you think about a love potion, what exactly does that mean? How does it work?"

Kara seemed surprised by the question, but to her credit, she paused to think before answering. "So, well, it's something you drink and it makes the person fall in love with someone. I guess... Well, I think most of the time, it's the first person they see after they drink it, right? That's the person they fall for? Unless... maybe it's like those polyjuice potions in Harry Potter, where you have to include something from the person who you want them to love, you know, in the potion? Like a piece of hair or something? So it makes the connection."

"And so they drink this potion and then...what happens? They see the person—you—and suddenly are head over heels in love with them?"

"Right," replied Kara, her eyes gleaming with hope. "Exactly."

"So, does this person—the one who drank the potion—realize what is happening? Do they feel any different? Do they *wonder* why they suddenly love this person whom they've never noticed before?"

"Um...I don't really know. Why are you asking me

all these questions?" Kara sounded frustrated and confused.

Jacqueline hoped she was getting to her. Getting her to *think*. "Well, if you want a love potion, it's best to figure out exactly what your expectations are first. Don't you agree?"

"Oh, right. I guess. Sure. I mean, I figured *you'd* just tell me how it works, since you're the one making it."

Jacqueline stifled an outraged laugh. "So if Bryson" —why would anyone give their kid a name that rhymed with a vacuum cleaner? She could hear it now: "Bryson, Bryson, sucks like a Dyson!"—"were to drink this potion and fall for you...well, what if he *didn't* want to fall for you? What if there was someone else he liked? What if he's gay and likes guys? But he drank the potion and liked you anyway."

"That would be okay," Kara said. "Because he would be *happy*. See?"

"How do you know he'd be happy?"

"Because I'd be the best girlfriend ever. I'd *make* him happy. And that's what love potions do, right? They make you fall in love, and you're automatically happy when you're in love."

Oh man. There were so many things wrong with being fifteen or sixteen...

Jacqueline kept her expression blank. She supposed at this point she could just tell Kara no, tell her that she didn't make love potions, tell her that it wasn't *right* to take someone's free will away from them or to make someone love you artificially...but she found herself wanting to fix the problem rather than sending it away.

Dammit. What was wrong with her?

This isn't my problem.

But Jacqueline didn't like to make waves, and she

was inclined to try to help someone who needed help —as Kara clearly did in this case. And she was afraid of what else Kara might do if she turned her away. What if she went and found Egala and induced *her* to make a love potion?

Jacqueline shuddered at the thought.

"I'd make him happy, and he wouldn't even care that he hadn't noticed me before," Kara said. There was an element of urgency in her voice. "Besides, he isn't gay. He had a girlfriend."

Not that having a girlfriend—especially as a teen —precluded a man from being gay, but Jacqueline decided not to mention that at the moment. "Tell me more about Bryson," she said, knowing it was a prevarication, a stalling tactic—but she was still clutching at straws, trying to find a way out of this predicament.

"He plays bassoon in the marching band and he's got curly, dark hair. He's tall and kind of skinny, but I don't care because he has this really great smile," Kara said, her eyes going dreamy. "We laugh a lot in chem because neither of us really know what we're doing. I mean, usually it's good to have a lab partner who has a clue, but neither of us do. We just kind of stumble along. We'll be lucky if we get a B-minus in lab."

"I see." Jacqueline was mildly surprised that Kara wasn't the brainy girl paired up with the jock...but she guessed that only happened in books or movies.

"At least we haven't blown up the place," Kara said with a laugh. She had a really pretty smile, Jacqueline thought. She wondered if Bryson had noticed that— and her big, expressive eyes.

"He sounds nice," Jacqueline said. "I wonder what he would say if he knew you wanted to give him a love potion."

Kara's expression froze. "You're not going to tell

him!"

"Of course not," Jacqueline replied. "This is between us women."

"Okay. Whew. You freaked me out for a minute."

"But what would he say, do you think?" Jacqueline asked. "If he knew you were going to basically force him to love you?"

Kara frowned. "Force? I wouldn't force him. I'd just...help him. You know. Make him see me in a different way so he'll like me."

A-ha. Maybe Jacqueline was getting somewhere. "Well, giving someone a love potion without their knowledge is basically forcing them to do something they may or may not want to do."

"I don't agree," replied Kara stubbornly. "I mean... isn't it like hypnotism a little? You know, when you're hypnotized, you don't do anything you actually, really don't want to do, like, you know, deep down inside. So if he had a love potion but didn't really want to love me, then he wouldn't..." She trailed off, looking a little confused.

Jacqueline remained silent throughout that convoluted argument. She hoped Kara would begin to listen to herself and start to rethink her plan.

"It's fine. It'll be fine. Why wouldn't he want to love me? I just want to help him see me—you know, really *see* me—in a way he hasn't before."

"That is an excellent point. Why *wouldn't* he want to date you?" Jacqueline said. The germ of an idea was beginning to formulate in her mind. "All right...well, before we can proceed, there are a few things you'll have to do to help prepare."

Kara jolted upright, her shoulders going back and her chin going up. "I'll do whatever I need to do. Do you need me to get a piece of his hair or something?"

"No, no, nothing like that," replied Jacqueline quickly. "The first thing I need you to do is to bring him something to drink one day in class. Do you know what he likes to drink? Coffee? A latte? Mountain Dew? Gatorade?"

"Why do I— *Oh!* I get it," Kara interrupted herself. Her eyes widened. "So that he gets used to me giving him something to drink so I can slip in the love potion in the future. That's *brilliant*, Miss Finch."

Yeah, right. Jacqueline set her teeth and made a neutral sound. She was being very careful not to actually commit to anything. "It's the first thing. So do that, and—this is important—when you give him the drink, you need to...um...ask him three questions." Jacqueline was just making up stuff as she went, hoping that something would make sense at some point.

"Three questions. Okay. What are they?" Kara whipped out her smartphone and tapped on it, then looked up eagerly at Jacqueline, whose brain had just misfired into blankness.

Out of the corner of her eye, Jacqueline caught a movement at the doorway. It was Cinderella. She'd been mopping the hallway, and now she stood there, unabashedly listening to the conversation. Jacqueline didn't mind—it was a weird conversation, and she'd want to listen in too if she'd been walking by.

"What do I ask him?" Kara said.

"Um...you need to ask him any three questions you can think of that will get him to talk to you about something other than chemistry lab." Lame. Lame, lame, *lame*.

Kara frowned. She apparently agreed with Jacqueline's internal voice. "Like...why?"

Why, indeed. Jacqueline fumbled for an answer.

Coming up short on reasons, she merely smiled and said, "You came to me for help, didn't you?"

Kara nodded. "Right. All right." She heaved a sigh. "It's just so hard to talk to him. I get so nervous and—and you know."

"That's why you ask him the questions and let *him* talk. People love to answer questions, especially ones about themselves. Now, don't worry if you can't do everything right away, if it doesn't work out or you can't figure out what drink to bring him immediately. You've got time."

"But I don't, really. I want him to take me to prom. It's in two weeks," said Kara in a rush. "And he needs to have time to do a prom-posal, and to order a tux, and—"

"A prom-posal?"

"Yeah, you know—it's when the guy sets up a really cool way to ask his date to prom. Like a surprise thing that's really special. Sometimes people will do it, like, during a sports event at school—but that's kind of lame. Or they get some friends to come and play music on your front yard while he sings a song asking you to go. That kind of thing. People post videos of prom-posals on Insta and TikTok if they go well."

You don't ask for much, do you? Jacqueline thought. "Didn't Andromeda and Zwyla tell you it takes time for a love potion to be ready?"

"Who? Oh, you mean those old ladies? They don't know anything about it, I'm sure. I think they were just trying to put me off. I know *you* know what you're doing," Kara said. "Because you own the store."

Just kill me now.

"Well, I've got work to do," said Jacqueline, rising from the bench. "Stop back into the shop after you've done those first two steps and we'll go from there."

She wasn't ashamed that she fairly fled the teen fiction room before Kara could ask her any more questions. It was all about self-preservation.

Fortunately, there was a customer in the front room who took Jacqueline's attention right away. By the time she finished helping the woman find a copy of *The Grapes of Wrath* and then a second customer locate *Pat the Bunny* and *Goodnight Moon*, Kara had gone.

Jacqueline sank onto the stool behind the sales counter and expelled a long breath. Dodged two bullets today—so far, anyway. Amanda Gauthier's problem had been foisted off on Detective Massermey —who was wildly more equipped to help than Jacqueline—and Kara (*Prom-posals? Good grief...*) would be distracted for at least a day or two. She hoped.

Distraction. That was what the ZAP Ladies had told her to do, wasn't it? Fancy that, as Elizabeth Bennet might say. Maybe they had been helpful after all.

The door rattled, clunked, and then swung inward with a sharp jangle of the bell, heralding the arrival of none other than Andromeda, Zwyla, and Pietra.

It was as if they knew *precisely* when Jacqueline didn't particularly want to talk to anyone, let alone three interfering, nosy women. But there they were, looking bright-eyed and cheerful and delighted to see her—even Zwyla.

"Well? How did everything go today?" said Pietra.

"And last night, in your new place?" added Andromeda.

"I trust the furniture behaved itself," Zwyla said, lifting her brows.

"Everything's fine," Jacqueline said. "Sort of. The apartment is great. Thank you for all of your help. It would have taken me another week or two to get it all settled without you." She lapsed into silence, waiting to see if they would divulge a reason for coming, or if they were just being nosy.

"I'm so glad," said Zwyla warmly. "We just wanted you to know we thought yesterday went very well."

"The place was packed," said Pietra. "And nothing went wrong."

Jacqueline zeroed in on that comment. "Were you expecting something to go wrong?"

"Oh, no, not at all." Pietra back-pedaled verbally as well as literally. She bumped into Zwyla, who caught her before she stumbled into the round table of books.

"Well, there was always the possibility that Egala might show up," said Andromeda, who already had Sebastian draped over her shoulders. The tawny-haired cat purred louder than a motor, and his tail made a sweet little circle around the corner of her shoulder. "But she didn't, so—"

"*Actually*," said Jacqueline, "she did show up. She just didn't come inside." How could she have forgotten about Wendy and her accusations? That was something she definitely needed to talk to the three crones about—and here they were.

"She did?" Pietra's eyes were wide. "Oh dear. What happened? Did she throw books around again? How did we miss her? We were all watching for her, just in case she showed up in—well, in disguise."

"In disguise?"

"She means with an altered appearance," Andromeda explained.

"Like...how altered?" Jacqueline asked.

"Very," said Zwyla. "Completely different nose, mouth, hair, face shape—you know. The whole nine yards. But we would have recognized her. The eyes don't change."

"Oh. The *eyes* don't change," Jacqueline said. "Thank heavens for that. The eyes. Don't. Change." She caught herself before the hysterical laughter took over.

It was just a little too much.

"Egala was here? But we didn't see her," said Andromeda, placing her hand on Jacqueline's arm. Immediately, a gentle, tingling warmth swept through Jacqueline, and the edge of hysteria waned. "Was it after the party?"

"She told a friend of mine—an ex-friend, I mean, from back in Chicago—that I cursed her. The friend. Wendy." Jacqueline sighed—too many pronouns. She gathered her thoughts and tried again. "Wendy— who's here in Button Cove—thinks I cursed her."

"Oh dear," said Pietra. "That's not very nice. Not very nice at all! And here I thought Egala would just go away now that it was *obvious* you belong here. Especially since you basically saved her from Crusilla."

"No one ever thought Egala would just go away," said Andromeda, giving Pietra an eye-roll. "And now she's here, stirring up trouble."

"She certainly is. Wendy is furious with me, and I haven't done a thing! She blames me for everything." Jacqueline felt the sting of tears in her eyes and furiously blinked them back. There'd been a whole crapload of stuff going on in her life over the past twenty-four hours, but she didn't need to cry about it.

"She had the pink purse," said Zwyla suddenly, capturing Jacqueline's attention.

"Yes. How did you know?"

Zwyla gave her a pitying glance. "The purse is cursed."

11

"**O**h, that's *brilliant*," said Pietra, her eyes wide and her cheeks flushed with admiration. "Give a woman a spectacular purse that's hexed, and you've got it made. She's under your spell, so to speak, because she's never letting that bag out of her sight. Wish I'd thought of it. It gets boring doing charms and hexes on baked goods. One bite, and they're gone. *Poof!*"

"Wait—charms and hexes on baked goods? Like blueberry scones?" Jacqueline was outraged. "Have you ever—"

"Of course not," Pietra replied, highly offended. "Not to *you*." She flattened her lips and gave Jacqueline a quelling look.

"I did notice the purse," said Andromeda thoughtfully. "But I missed the hex part. What gave it away, Z?"

"You were too busy sipping wine and flirting with that bald man with the dark beard—it was obviously dyed—to notice," Zwyla told her. "He was a little young for you, don't you think?"

"Well, at least I wasn't hiding from Paul Bunyan," retorted Andromeda. "Sneaking around the romance shelves, peering around the mysteries, darting behind the Harry Potters—"

"Oh, for the Good Mother's sake, Andi, you don't need to bring that up again," Zwyla said with a huff. "He wasn't even there, so your point is irrelevant—and besides, I was paying very close attention because I expected something to happen. As we all did. *None* of us thought Egala would go gently into that good night." She gave Pietra a meaningful look.

"Wait...*what*? Paul Bunyan?" Jacqueline interrupted. "He was here again?" Had Mrs. Danvers picked up another fallen book after Jacqueline specifically told her *not* to? And how on earth could she have missed seeing Paul Bunyan?

"Again?" said Pietra.

"He was here a week or so ago, but I thought he left. Yesterday—at the party—was he here? I didn't see him. Why were you hiding from him?" Jacqueline asked Zwyla.

"Good old Paul—and talk about *massive hands*! That guy's got *winners*," Andromeda said with a mischievous chuckle. "Anyway, Paulie's got a thing for our Miss Z here," she went on with a sly smile. "But he wasn't here yesterday. He's hard to miss."

"He certainly is," said Zwyla grimly. "How many times does a man have to hit his head on the door header before he learns to duck? The whole building shudders every time he does."

"Well, if he wouldn't wear his hair in a man-bun —" Andromeda began.

"Paul Bunyan likes you?" Jacqueline said to Zwyla, still trying to keep up with the bouncing conversation.

"Oh, he's got it *bad*," said Pietra with great relish. "The poor guy lumbers out of his book—ha, ha, *lum-*

bers; did you see what I did there?—whenever he can, hoping to catch a glimpse of Z."

Well, that explained why he'd sat in the chair and stared out the window in the direction of Camellia House for two days.

"Just be glad he wasn't here with Babe," said Andromeda, stroking the fluffy, tawny-haired Sebastian, who remained in his stole-like position over her shoulders and accepted her attention as if it was his due. "That beast's shit is the size of bricks...and I mean cinder blocks."

As fascinating as the conversation was, Jacqueline decided it was time to rein in the old ladies. "Let's back up here so I understand. Paul Bunyan has a thing for Zwyla, and Wendy is in possession of a cursed purse? Is that what's making her act the way she is? She started off kind of apologetic when she first showed up, but by the time she left this morning, she was not only accusing me of cursing her, but threatening to ruin my shop. It was like she was...well, cursed or possessed or something."

"She probably is. And that has Egala stamped all over it," said Andromeda. "She's just feeding the fire."

"So what do I do? Please tell me nothing," said Jacqueline.

It was so much easier to just do *nothing*.

But she didn't think that was the answer, for the three crones were looking at her with varying degrees of disappointment and exasperation.

"I suppose you *could* do nothing," said Andromeda in a kind voice. "But then that just gives Egala all the power. She can stir things up even more by giving out more purses, you know. To more people."

"More purses?" Jacqueline didn't like that idea at all.

Pietra shook her head sadly. "Next thing you know, you'll have men in here with cursed wallets and brief-cases and—and hexed condoms and—"

"No one is going to hex a man's condom," said Zwyla. "Even Egala."

"Well, why not? They carry them in their wallets all the time, and it's just as difficult to part them from their condoms, because just in case, right? Unless they're using them, of course; then it's a free-for-all. Anyway, it's just as difficult as getting a woman away from her purse—"

"*Petey*," Andromeda said with an exhausted sigh. Pietra lapsed into silence, but from the rosy flush on her cheeks, Jacqueline suspected she was still thinking about men and their condoms.

Good grief. Petey and Nadine ought to get together.

"You could do nothing, of course," Andromeda told Jacqueline, "but then you still have the problem."

"I knew you were going to say that." Jacqueline sighed. "I suppose I've somehow got to get the purse away from Wendy—would that fix it?" That seemed reasonably easy compared to stealing a crocodile tooth.

The crones exchanged glances.

"Good question," replied Zwyla. "It could be the purse itself; it could be something inside it. But sepa-rating her from it would be a good start."

Jacqueline remembered the way Wendy was al-ways clutching the handbag to her middle and won-dered how she was going to manage extricating it from her. "All right. So what do I do once I get the purse?"

"Bring it to us," said Andromeda.

Jacqueline nodded. She'd be more than happy to foist the cursed purse off on the crones. But getting it away from Wendy was going to be a challenge. Especially since she was furious with Jacqueline.

Just then, she heard the sounds of someone descending the stairs from the tea room. It was the Artful Dodger, and although he was as neat and groomed as she'd ever seen him, his expression was filled with gloom.

"She won't let me ride in th'el'vator no more," he said, casting a dour look upstairs toward the unseen Mrs. Hudson. "Says it de-stracts me."

Jacqueline looked at him and realized the answer to her quandary had just presented itself. What better use of a pickpocket than to have him steal a cursed purse?

"Never mind that, Jack. I've got a job for you," she said.

~

THE BOOKSHOP'S official closing time during the week was eight o'clock, but if there were customers or people walking along Camellia Court, Jacqueline had taken to moving those hours later. She did so by propping the front door open to the balmy spring evening.

It was even easier to stay open late now that she only had to climb two flights of stairs to be home...in her own cozy apartment instead of a rented room at the inn.

The time was after eight o'clock, however, and since there weren't any other people in the store, Jacqueline went to flip the sign to CLOSED.

She had just done so when a figure appeared in front of the window.

"Amanda!" Jacqueline opened the door and let the young woman inside. She glanced down the street to make certain there was no one else around and was just in time to see the hearse pull away from the curb.

Apparently, the only rideshare option in Button Cove was that dingy black hearse. She shook her head as she locked the door behind her. Just another strange factor of living on Camellia Court.

"I wanted to come by and thank you for what you did today," said Amanda. She was pacing the floor, wringing her hands. "If you hadn't shown up when you did..." She looked at Jacqueline with dark, worried eyes.

"I'm so glad I was there," Jacqueline said. "Are you feeling all right? Did you go to the hospital and get checked out?"

Amanda nodded. "Yes. They said no residual effects...but now I'm really scared. He almost succeeded this time!" Her voice rose a little.

"Did you talk to Detective Massermey about what's been going on?"

"Yes. I told him everything. He seemed to take me seriously, but there's not really anything he can do without proof. You know? If we could just find my inhalers—he probably stashed them somewhere—or even figure out what happened to the fireplace. That *wasn't* an accident. Someone did something to the gas valve and made it leak when I turned it on. He must have removed a nut or a bolt or something that made it leak," she said, still pacing.

"It is very concerning," Jacqueline agreed.

"I really do need your help," said Amanda. She reached out and grabbed Jacqueline's hand, clasping it tightly. "Please. Isn't there something you can do? Like a—a—"

"A protection amulet is what you're wanting, dearie."

Jacqueline suppressed a sigh as they both turned to see Mrs. Hudson making her way down the stairs. Damn. She thought the older woman had gone away to wherever for the night.

"Oh, yes!" cried Amanda, spinning back to Jacqueline again. "A protection amulet is just the thing! Something to keep me safe from anyone who is trying to—to hurt me or do something awful to me. Or take me away or whatever." She was grabbing at Jacqueline's hands again. "Can you help me? Can you protect me?"

Jacqueline, of course, had no idea how or where to get a protection amulet. But she couldn't deny the fact that Amanda clearly needed something to keep her safe—at least until Massermey figured everything out.

But couldn't Amanda just stay somewhere for a while? Why did it need to be an *amulet*?

"Of course she'll help ye," said Mrs. Hudson, looking at Jacqueline meaningfully. "Now, you just come on upstairs with Mrs. H, and we'll get you a bracing cuppa whilst *she* sees to your protection, then, dearie."

"But..." Jacqueline let her voice trail off under the dark side-eye Mrs. Hudson was giving her.

Sherlock's landlady gave an annoyed sniff, curled her arm protectively around Amanda's waist, and directed her toward the stairs. She cast a pointed look at Jacqueline from over her shoulder as they began to ascend, leaving Jacqueline to stand there helplessly.

What the hell was she going to do about a protection amulet? Maybe she could just give Amanda a little medallion or some crystal from the New Age room upstairs and tell her that was what it was. A placebo sort of thing.

A movement in the shadows caught her attention,

and Jacqueline turned to find Mrs. Danvers standing there, looking more than ever like an irritated crow.

"Well?" demanded the housekeeper.

"What?" Jacqueline responded.

"You'd best get to it," said Danvers, lifting her long, slender nose as if she smelled something unpleasant. "Ma'am," she added as if under duress to be deferential. "Else that woman will just keep coming back and nagging at you."

Jacqueline found herself agreeing with Danvers for probably the first time ever. But that didn't make her task any easier.

"The problem is, I don't have the first idea how to make or acquire a protection amulet," she confessed—then immediately regretted acknowledging her weakness to the likes of Danvers. "And I don't expect you do either," she added with a little bit of spite. After all, there hadn't been a hint of witchcraft or magic in *Rebecca.*

Darkness and malice, yes. Murder too. But not magic.

Danvers looked down her long nose at Jacqueline. "Look around you. Ma'am." With a disgusted sigh, she directed her gaze to the locked cabinets under the stairs where all of the vintage and first-edition books were kept.

Jacqueline felt her cheeks warm. Well, of course she was in a bookshop, but it wasn't like she had books about charms and potions and that sort of thing here...

Did she?

There was a Wiccan collection in the religion section, but anyone could buy those books and use them. She had no idea of the efficacy of what was in them.

Yet...

Jacqueline found her feet carrying her over to the locked cabinets. She'd looked through them, of course —even taken out several beautiful books and sighed over them. They were filled with smooth blue Nancy Drews with orange printing (not the tweed ones; those weren't worth much at all), first editions by Agatha Christie, Dorothy L. Sayers, Conan Doyle, Heyer, Twain, Cather, Poe, O. Henry, Morrison, and more, and signed copies by deceased authors such as Elizabeth Peters, Julia Child, Anne Rice, du Maurier, and others.

And down in the corner, in a special locked section she'd hardly noticed, there were several very ratty old volumes with titles that had become nearly obliterated over the years. Thick ones the size of the OED, tall, slender ones with narrow spines, small, hand-stitched ones the size of her hand, and more. Most bound in leather in every shade of brown or weathered gray. Some with stamped titles on the spines, some with no markings at all.

Next to them, there was one book facing out. A book she'd devoured as a child. She shivered, and her belly did a freaky little flop when she brushed her fingers over the cover of *What the Witch Left*.

Well, then, she thought. *Not very subtle, are you, Cuddy?*

But it wasn't that book she reached for. It was the big, fat volume that was so thick it was nearly a cube. And it looked *old*. Old and mysterious.

If there was ever the perfect example of what a spell book would look like, this had to be it.

The great tome was heavy and its cover was scarred. The pages and binding smelled of must along with another, more pleasant and intriguing scent she couldn't identify. The edges of the pages had been hand-cut, so they were uneven and jagged as well as tattered from time and use. Jacqueline looked around and saw that Danvers had disappeared. She decided to take the book into the sci-fi and fantasy room. It just seemed appropriate.

There was a small corner fireplace in that space—a chamber where she'd painted the walls a dark cobalt blue but left white trim around the windows, fireplace, and along the floor and ceiling to keep the room from being too dark. As in every genre room, there were chairs arranged by the fireplace and also a bench beneath a window. A fire crackled happily in the grate, and Jacqueline suspected she knew who had arranged for that.

It was creepy the way Danvers seemed to anticipate her.

What was even creepier was the cup of hot tea—steam rolling from it—sitting on the table next to the chair...as if it had been waiting for her.

Eyeing the teacup suspiciously, Jacqueline sank into the one-and-a-half-person chair upholstered in rich forest-green velvet studded with satin-covered green buttons. She wasn't certain she was going to drink it, but the gesture was...nice.

When she opened the book, Jacqueline fancied she heard a sort of sigh emitting from the pages. A waft of scent—age, must, and something else, something that made her skin tingle pleasantly—came from within.

The pages crackled beneath her fingers, and Jacqueline was almost afraid to look through them, for fear they would crumble away. But she took care as she turned each page, and realized the papers were less fragile than they appeared. The print was old and irregular, as if the type had been laid out by hand and with different blocks. There were numerous notes in a variety of inks, styles, and discernibility on the pages, giving her the impression that many different people had written, collated, and experimented with the recipes within.

She couldn't quite get herself to think the word "spells," even though that was surely what they were.

Jacqueline thumbed through carefully until she found the section she was looking for.

Protection.

A little shiver of awareness prickled over her shoulders, lifting the hair at the nape of her neck in a chill like the Gardella Venators might experience in the presence of an undead. But there were no vampires around—at least, as far as Jacqueline knew. She grimaced and looked around warily, then returned to the book.

Jacqueline had reached for the cup of tea and was bringing it to her lips to sip before she realized what she was doing. The tea was not the same floral infusion that Andromeda had served her last night after the party. This one tasted vibrant, with mint and lemon and licorice.

Despite the fact she didn't care for tea, Jacqueline sipped as she lightly brushed her forefinger over the page and read.

And read.

Read some more.

After a few minutes, turning several pages, absorbing, thinking, she looked up. Her teacup was empty. The essence of lemon and licorice hovered on her tongue with the scent of mint lingering in her nose.

She knew what to do. At least, what the book told her to do.

And somehow she knew that was right.

She looked back at the page with one particular recipe and reviewed the items she'd need.

Onyx or black quartz—crystals she could find in the New Age room behind the tea room. How handy was that?

The rest of the items were upstairs in her newly furnished apartment:

Black pepper.

Cloves.

Lavender.

Blackberries and blackberry leaves.

Blackberries, which Andromeda had brought to her yesterday, still clinging to their leafy branches.

Had she known?

Jacqueline shook her head. It didn't really matter whether the crones had anticipated her situation, she told herself as she rose from the chair. She had work to do—strange, unfamiliar, and yet interesting work.

At first she thought she'd make the protection amulet in the kitchen of her flat, as most of the ingredients were up there.

But then she realized there was a better place: the cellar, where all of the energy was concentrated and there was a spot of bare earth, sacred and waiting.

Jacqueline took a deep breath and squared her shoulders as she walked out of the room, tucking the heavy tome beneath one arm.

This was gonna be different.

12

Jacqueline didn't want to make a fire on the floor in the cellar, for obvious reasons. Instead, she found a large three-wick candle scented with lavender (which was one of the ingredients for the protection amulet, and she thought it would only enhance the process), along with a little, short-legged bowl that would fit over it without snuffing out the flames.

Hopefully that would be enough to warm the ingredients so she could put the black onyx in it to steep, because that was, apparently, how you made a protection amulet.

Jacqueline's insides were very squiggly when she gathered all of the ingredients and set them up on the bare earth floor. The quiet tinkle of running water should have been calming, but there wasn't much that would ease the nervousness she was feeling.

"I just hope everything doesn't go, you know, *poof!*" she said. Chemistry had not been her favorite subject.

Or maybe she *did* want things to go poof. The directions didn't actually say...

Jacqueline sighed, pushed away the wild, tangled thoughts about whether she was messing with things she didn't understand and why she had to do this in the first place and maybe she *should* go back to Chicago and what would happen if she accidentally set the damned house on fire—all those beautiful books!—and got to work, kneeling next to the patch of exposed dirt.

Before she began collating the ingredients, she closed her eyes and set the intention by speaking it out loud in a way that sounded a little clumsy to her ears.

"Allow only good to come from this. I create this amulet not for me, but for a woman who needs protection. Please let it be so."

She hesitated using the witchy phrase "so mote it be," and hoped her paraphrased words would work.

The little bowl fit over the candle jar, but the vessel's little legs kept it from cutting off the oxygen, and moments after she set it in place, Jacqueline touched the bowl to see whether it was getting warm. It was— enough to have her yanking back her finger and frowning at how hot it had become so quickly. Seemed like those three little flames had a lot more energy than she'd imagined and had worked very quickly.

She supposed that was a good sign.

The recipe required water in which to steep the ingredients, so she ladled it from the tiny trickle that wound pleasantly through her basement floor. She figured: sacred earth, sacred water.

And then she began to add the other items: black peppercorns, fresh lavender needles (from the plant Andromeda had conveniently put on her windowsill), cloves, and the blackberries and their leaves. But the recipe didn't give actual measurements. Instead, it was more proportional: three parts clove, two parts peppercorns, and so on. Was she supposed to use a spoon or something consistent to measure out the ingredients (one part being a teaspoon or tablespoon or a cup?), or was one part of a clove simply one dried clove head, whereas one part of black peppercorn was one tiny berry?

Why hadn't whoever written this book been more explicit? Or, at least, whoever made the notes in the margins—couldn't they have clarified?

Jacqueline hesitated and dithered for far too long before she decided to just measure out the ingredients with the same spoon (one part) and hope for the best.

After she added the last ingredient—two spoonfuls of blackberries and their leaves—she gave everything six counterclockwise stirs, as per the directions. She nearly had a heart attack when a feisty little *pop!* of smoke and scent came from the small bowl.

Holy shit. It's working.

She stared at the little bowl, then remembered the onyx. Once more setting her own private intention ("*allow only good to come from this*"), she lowered the cherry-sized stone into the bubbling contents of the small bowl and said the words written in the book: "*I ask you, Great Mother, to infuse this stone with protection from all evil and malice, keeping danger from Amanda Gauthier.*"

When the stone slid into the infusion, Jacqueline heard a quiet sizzle, followed by a few tiny sparks. She stared down into the bowl, somehow both delighted and terrified.

She'd done it.

Or, at least, she'd done *something*.

~

"KEEP it with you at all times," Jacqueline told Amanda when presenting her with the onyx.

The young woman's eyes were wide and her movements reverent as she held out her hand for the stone. "Will it really work?" she asked.

"Yes," Jacqueline said with confidence she didn't really have. But when she let the stone tumble into Amanda's hand, the Amanda jolted and gasped.

"It's— Why, I can *feel* it," Amanda said, staring down at the faceted black crystal. "It's... It feels *alive*."

"Yes," Jacqueline said, more with relief than actual belief.

"Thank you! I can't thank you enough!"

Jacqueline stepped back before Amanda could throw herself at her in an embrace. "Yes, of course. But please remember: nothing is completely foolproof. So be careful. Keep an eye out. And let Detective Massermey know if anything bad happens, all right?"

"I will. I will!" Amanda started to go, then spun around. "Oh my gosh, I almost left without—without paying. What do I owe you?"

"Oh." Jacqueline hadn't thought about that at all. It seemed somehow crass to take payment for something like this. It might even be illegal. She looked around as if to ask someone for help, but no one was there except Max, who eyed her balefully from his lofty perch. Even Sebastian was absent. "Um...how about a case of Big Bay wine?"

"*Done!*" Amanda said, then giggled. "I thought you were going to ask for my firstborn child or something like that."

Jacqueline laughed uncomfortably. "No, no, nothing like that." That would be Rumpelstiltskin, she thought, then clamped off the idea before the creepy little man took form.

Just then, Dodger appeared from somewhere in the back of the bookshop—or maybe the back door. His eyes were wide and he looked as if he was about to explode with information or exclamation, but Jacqueline cut him off. She didn't want Amanda to hear whatever he had to say...especially since she'd sent him off to try to nab someone's purse. As he wasn't holding a pink purse, however, she could only assume something had gone wrong.

"Just a minute, Jack," she said, holding up a hand. "All right, then, Amanda. Good luck. Keep that with you. And, uh, keep me posted," she felt obliged to add. Even though she really didn't want to be involved any more than she already was.

"I will!" Amanda sailed out of the shop, and Jacqueline locked the door behind her.

A glance at the clock told her it was going on ten p.m.—goodness, had it taken nearly two hours to make the protection amulet?

"What is it, Jack?" she said, turning to Dodger at last. "Did you get the purse?"

"It's 'at girl, mu'um," he said, his words tumbling out like gaming dice. "She's gone!"

"The one with the purse I wanted you to snatch?" Jacqueline said, although she didn't think of Wendy as a "girl" and couldn't imagine anyone else who could. "Did you find her?"

"No, mu'um, not 'er—it's the one what wanted the love potion!" His eyes were about to burst out of their sockets. "Blimey, she's gone off w'me love! Me *Cinderella!*" He was clutching his top hat so hard it was nothing more than a crumpled wad.

"All right, all right, slow down," said Jacqueline. "You're saying that Kara—the girl who wants a love potion—and Cinderella are together." She didn't see any immediate reason to be freaked out, but apparently Dodger did. They were girls about the same age, after all. And both had love problems.

Heck, maybe Kara had realized she liked girls instead of guys—or maybe Cinderella had realized she liked girls, and that was why she didn't want to marry the prince—and Dodger was afraid he was going to lose his chance with Cindy.

Not that he had a chance with Cinderella anyway, Jacqueline reminded herself. They were from completely different stories...

Or maybe Kara and Cinderella had just gone off shopping to find some more comfortable shoes. Glass slippers had to be horrid to wear.

"Do you know where they went?" Jacqueline asked as Dodger hopped from foot to foot as if his pants were on fire—or as if he expected her to do something.

As if.

"O' course I do! They went to the *ball*, they did! They can't do that, can they?"

Jacqueline stared at him, squinting a little as the words sank in. "What do you mean, the ball? Which ball?"

"*The ball!*" He was still dancing from one foot to the other, his eyes goggling and his freckles bright in his pale face. He'd dropped his hat, and it was being crushed beneath his boots. "Blimey, mu'um, it's the ball where Cinderella meets Prince Anton!"

"What are you talking about?" Jacqueline said, still staring as the floor seemed to melt away from her feet, leaving her stranded in the middle of some crazy world. "Are you saying that both Kara *and* Cinderella went into the book?"

"Aye, mu'um!"

Now the ground beneath her seemed to spin and there was a wild roaring in her ears. "But..."

Kara was inside Grimms' Fairy Tales?

Impossible.

"Come on, mu'um," he said, grabbing her by the arm. "We hafta go! We can't let 'em stay! We *got* to bring 'er back, mu'um!"

He gave a good yank that at any other time would have resulted in a strong reprimand, but at the moment, Jacqueline couldn't fault him for his desperation. How in the hell was she going to get Kara back out into reality?

"We got to find 'er!"

Despite the fact that Jacqueline suspected the "her" Dodger was talking about differed from the "her" *she* was worried about, she allowed him to pull her down the hall, dragging her by the wrist.

Sure enough, there on the floor of the sci-fi and fantasy room was the tattered old Grimms' that had fallen two nights ago.

Before Jacqueline had the chance to grab for it, or even speak, Dodger was jumping onto the open book —and pulling her with him.

The next thing she knew, she was falling.

13

Jacqueline screamed.

She knew she was the one screaming because as she hit the ground—somewhere hard, somewhere shadowy—her breath got knocked out of her and the screaming stopped in a sort of weird strangle.

"Hush up, there, mu'um," said Dodger, clapping an impertinent hand over her mouth. "Someone'll 'ear ye."

Jacqueline's eyes gaped wide and she snatched his hand away as she stared at the place where they'd... landed, she supposed was the word. Landed.

Landed inside a book.

Good grief, how many times over her lifetime had she wished she could go into a book? Live inside a story? *Be* Elizabeth Bennet or Jo March?

What the *hell* had she been thinking?

She felt faint, and she was pretty sure it wasn't just due to falling and landing... Oh, God, how was it possible that she was *in a book*?

She was on the verge of becoming hysterical, with her fast, shallow panting and the *impossibility* of what had happened. Her head felt like it was about to float away from the rest of her body, and there were red and pink spots dancing before her eyes...

"It's allays like 'at at first when ye come in, mu'um. Just ye breathe easy and slow and it'll come around and yer 'ead'll settle."

Jacqueline managed to keep from shouting at Dodger, but just barely. Instead, she did as he suggested—began to breathe easily; at least, as easily as she could—while she looked around and tried not to freak out.

Stone floors, stone walls, high ceiling...dark, cool... but in the distance, the sounds of revelry: music, conversation, laughter...

Dammit. They were definitely at Cinderella's frigging ball.

She guessed that was better than being at the old witch's house in "Hansel and Gretel," but she would have preferred to just stay home, thank you very much.

"How—" she began, but stopped herself. It didn't matter *how*—at least right now; later, she could pick it all apart. What mattered was finding Kara and figuring out how to get them back to Three Tomes. Not that she was responsible for the teen's actions, but, hell, she *was* responsible. After all, she owned the weird-ass bookshop. Jacqueline blew out a frustrated sigh.

"Are ye feelin' better yet, mu'um?" said Dodger, looking around uncertainly. "*Gor...* I ain't never been in someone else's story afore. I didn't even know I could. Sure is a lot o' toffs down there with 'eavy pockets..."

Jacqueline resisted the urge to throttle him— mainly because she still needed him to get her back to wherever. If he could. Her breath seized up again, and she felt her chest tighten at the thought of being stuck here in *Grimms'* forever.

Instead of allowing the panic to take control, she drew in a few calming breaths and pointed toward the spill of light beyond a stone archway. "We've got to find Kara and get her out of here—back to the bookstore. Right away. You know how to do that, right?"

"Aye, mu'um, and Cinderella too," said Dodger, alleviating one concern and creating another at the same time. "We can't be leaving'er 'ere."

"Oh yes we can," Jacqueline said flatly. "This is her story, not yours—and definitely not mine and Kara's. Now let's go." She marched to the entrance of the fortunately empty chamber in which they'd landed, and peeked out.

They were on some sort of ledge or balcony that created a gallery overlooking the great hall. Fortunately, everyone else in the entire story was apparently down below, for it was—as Elizabeth Bennet would say—quite the crush. The dance floor was so crowded, it seemed impossible for people to move about, but somehow they were dancing, mostly in line dances that allowed a lot of partner changes.

The women were dressed in bright colors with lots of lace, feathers, ribbons, and jewels, while the men wore, as usual, drab clothing in blacks, dark blues, browns, and grays. There was an occasional bright sash on one of the men—royal blue, red, gold.

A large clock hung at one end of the vast chamber, positioned above the dual-sided, sweeping, grand staircase that looked *exactly* like Jacqueline had always imagined it would. Behind the staircase landing was a massive double wooden door—obviously through which Cinderella would enter during the ball...which clearly she hadn't done yet, since it would be obvious. And besides, Jacqueline had spotted the prince, who was in the center of the crush with a kaleidoscope of colorful gowns moving about him.

He was a handsome devil, Jacqueline decided. Even from up here, she could see his thick gilt hair and broad shoulders. A flash of his face as he spun a bridal candidate in the dance revealed a strong chin, dark brows, and chiseled features.

"We've got to find Kara. Cinderella's going to be making her grand entrance anytime," said Jacqueline, eyeing the clock. It was nearly ten, and she figured a two-hour slot was enough time for the prince to fall for the belle of the ball.

The question was, why had Cinderella brought Kara here? Had Kara insisted on coming, or had the fairytale character brought her—either willingly or unwillingly?

She turned to Dodger, pushing him back into the chamber. "What happened? Why did Kara come with Cinderella? I didn't even know Kara had come back to the store."

"Aye, she came when you's in the cellar doing whatever it was you was doin," Dodger told her. "Miz 'Udson said as 'ow I could be done w' me work so she could give a cuppa to that other lady—the one wot with the husband come to the party yestiddy. So I come down the stairs—she still won't let me take th'elevator, th'old crank—and there they was, sitting in the room, Cinderella and the girl—talking.

"They was talking about *love potions*, and me Cinderella was telling 'er all as 'ow they didn't work for real, true love, and 'ow they weren't fair to the person givin' it to, and the girl was arguing about it, and next thing ye know, Cinderella says, 'I'll show ye!' And she takes her by the hand, pulls down the book, and jumps in!" Dodger's eyes were wide. "I didn't know ye could *do* 'at—take someone wi' ye, 'hoo ain't in the story!"

"That makes two of us," said Jacqueline grimly. "But that doesn't help me figure out where Kara might be. And there are no love potions in Cinderella, so I don't even know what she was thinking, dragging Kara in here."

"Blimey, Kara's gotta be with Cinderella, don't she? And I'm wantin' to find me Cinderella before she sees that prince again." Dodger frowned. "Gonna talk some sense into 'er."

Jacqueline had started to walk out of the chamber again, but she stopped and whirled on him. "Jack, you *can't* keep Cinderella from finding her prince," she said fiercely. "And you can't talk any sense into her. That isn't going to work. She's got to stay in her story, and you've got to stay in yours. And you can't go messing with the plot lines." She bored her nitpick-y librarian's stare into his eyes. He took a step back.

"Don't 'afta get yer knickers all twisted up," he said sullenly.

"Just so long as you understand: Kara comes with us and Cinderella stays."

Dodger muttered something but then gave a reluctant nod.

"All right, let's go," Jacqueline said, leading the way out of the chamber and back onto the gallery that ran around the edge of the great hall, more than ten feet above the ground. The walkway was wide enough for them to make their way along the wall while remaining unseen by the people below. That was good, because Jacqueline was still dressed in the twenty-first-century fashion of jeans and a tunic-style shirt, and would surely stand out and attract attention if she was seen.

But how the hell was she going to find Kara? The castle was not only huge, it was crowded with people. Not only partygoers, but servants. Everywhere.

Just then, a sort of hush filled the space below. Jacqueline felt a prickle over the backs of her shoulders, and she rushed to the edge of the stone railing.

She knew what was about to happen, and dammit, the fairytale lover and young girl in her wanted to see it for herself: the Cinderella Moment.

The massive wooden doors had just closed behind a woman dressed in the most incandescent, sparkling, *incredible* silvery-white dress Jacqueline had ever seen —and she was a big fan of the Met Gala and Oscar red carpets. The gown shimmered; it glowed; it was blushing pearlescent one moment and cool, moonbeam-like the next. It floated and swirled and twinkled as if it had a life of its own. Whatever fabric created the wide, flowing skirts had to be some sort of magic.

More sparkles glinted in the girl's dark blond hair, which was piled high at the top of her head. She wore long gloves that appeared as gossamer as a spider's web, and that sparkled like one sprinkled with the morning dew.

The hush covered the crowd like a blanket as everyone turned to look at the figure standing alone on the landing, looking down and out over the ballroom. It was impossible to look away; it was as if the silvery dress and the woman in it were the most powerful magnets in the world.

As Jacqueline watched, the woman lifted her head

as if to survey the lay of the land, and Jacqueline gasped when she got a good look at her face.

That wasn't Cinderella.

That was Kara.

In Cinderella's dress.

14

"**W**here the bloody 'ell is me Cinderella?"
exclaimed Dodger.

Despite her shock, Jacqueline had the presence of
mind to shove Dodger away from the edge of the
gallery before someone heard or looked up and saw
them.

No, no, no!

This can't be right. This can't be happening.

Kara had taken Cinderella's place? How?

She edged forward again and looked down in time
to see Prince Anton making his way to the steps
through the spontaneously parting crowd. He wore a
trim white coat with epaulets and a diagonal purple
sash edged with gold fringe over dark pants. His eyes
were as fixated on Kara/Cinderella as everyone else's
were, and he held out his gloved hand—as gallantly
and elegantly as Jacqueline had always imagined the
prince would do—to help her down the steps.

She caught a glimpse of a glass-slippered toe as Kara
lifted the magical, frothy, starry-sky skirts she'd somehow
been bequeathed and glided down to the dance floor.

A sigh rippled through the crowd as Prince Anton

bowed to Kara, then drew her into his arms. A waltz began to play and the couple eased into the *one*-two-three, *one*-two-three box steps, spinning about as if they'd danced together a hundred times.

Which, considering how many versions there were of the story and the number of times it had been told or read, was a vast understatement.

But what did this mean? Kara wasn't Cinderella... but she'd stepped into the role as if it was made for her. And the prince seemed to have fallen for her as easily as he had done the real Cinderella.

Or, at least, been attracted to her enough to ask her to dance.

What would happen afterward? Since Kara wasn't Cinderella, would the prince discard her and dance with others until he found the real Cinderella—or...what?

Jacqueline's head hurt, and she felt like she was going to throw up. How in the hell was she going to fix this? What if the Grimms' tale was irrevocably altered because of Kara and Cinderella?

Was that even possible?

And why the hell did *Jacqueline* have to be the one to fix it, anyway? She hadn't caused any of this.

"At least me Cinderella ain't dancing with the prince," Dodger said with a complacent nod. "She's likely waitin' around fer me to fetch her, now, ain't she?" He brushed at his coat and straightened his cuffs. "Now all we gots to do is find 'er."

He started off, but Jacqueline yanked him back by the collar of his coat. "Oh no you don't," she said. "Don't you dare go off without me. We stick together, understand?"

"Awright, awright," he said, rubbing the back of his

neck as he gave her a scowl. "But we got to get down 'ere. Me fingers is itchin'."

"Keep your itchy fingers in your pockets," Jacqueline told him. "The last thing we need to do is to attract attention."

"But—"

She growled wordlessly at him, and he sighed unhappily.

"Fine," he grumbled. "Stay wi' ye and keep me fingers in me pockets. Don't know wot's the point o' bein' at a party with so many toffs if a bloke can't 'elp 'isself ta their 'eavy pockets."

"I thought you were going straight," Jacqueline said, easing out on to the balcony again.

She couldn't take her eyes from the bird's-eye view of Kara as Cinderella waltzing so gracefully with Prince Anton. As much as she knew no man was a Disney prince, there was something about seeing the fairy tale come to life—to *real*, palpable life—that compelled her to watch. And, it seemed, the prince was just as enthralled with the woman in his arms as everyone else was.

"Why you sighing like that, mu'um?" said Dodger in her ear. "And why you *cryin'*?"

Jacqueline ignored his obviously masculine perspective and tried to tell herself she needed to start looking for the real Cinderella. But everything was just so pretty down there, so magical and beautiful and *romantic*...

Suddenly Dodger crowed, breaking into Jacqueline's reverie. "There she is!" He was leaning over the railing, goggling and waving. She yanked him back before he fell down into the crowd—which seemed mesmerized, but would probably notice a body falling amongst them. Dodger didn't seem to mind, though, as he was smiling with obvious relief.

Somehow, he had managed to pick out Cinderella from the packed throng of people below. *Love looks not with the eyes but with the heart,* Jacqueline thought in the common misquote of Shakespeare. In this case, she thought the misquote was more apt.

Even after Dodger pointed to where Cinderella was sitting and she'd had Lasik to fix her nearsightedness, it took Jacqueline a moment to see the fairytale character. The young woman was in a corner on a cushioned bench, mostly out of sight of the dance floor. She appeared calm and relaxed—even amused —as she happily popped grapes into her mouth, munching them around a smile as she watched her story unfold without her.

Despite this brief distraction, Jacqueline's attention was immediately regained by the same tableau that captured Cinderella's gaze: Kara waltzing about with Prince Anton.

Jacqueline and Dodger needed to make their way down to the main floor to Cinderella, but Jacqueline found she simply couldn't pull herself away from the story unfolding below. Nor did the other partygoers seem to be able to do so. Everyone watched Kara and her flowing, shimmering gown, as starstruck as the prince himself.

Jacqueline lost track of time, gazing down at the beautiful couple as they spun around the floor—almost as if she were hypnotized or bespelled, for the next thing she knew, the clock was striking.

Jacqueline gasped and came back to reality, looking immediately to the clock above the ballroom.

The two hands were nearly upright, and the *bongs*

reverberated throughout the hall, filling her ears and vibrating throughout her body.

It was midnight.

Midnight, and she'd done nothing but stand here and watch. For two hours! It *was* as if she'd been hypnotized.

She saw Cinderella—no, *Kara*—stiffen and pull away from Prince Anton, glancing up at the clock.

The prince reached for her, but Kara evaded him and, in true Cinderella form, hurried away, rushing up the steps toward the entrance.

Anton went after her, but the spell seemed to have been broken. The crowd surged around him, gowns of pink, gold, lavender, and all shades of blue and green, along with their ribbons, feathers, lace, and flounces, swallowing up the prince as he tried to get to Kara.

The girl stumbled on the stairs, then did what any woman in her right mind who was on the run would do: she paused to yank off her impractical and probably very uncomfortable heels. She left one on the top step, cuddling the other like a football as she dashed toward the doors...which opened as if on their own.

True fairytale magic, Jacqueline thought as she spurred herself into action far too late.

"We've got to get outside and find her before she drives off," she said, spinning toward her companion.

But Dodger was gone.

No!

Jacqueline's heart plummeted, and she actually thought she was going to faint. She spun, looking around, but the gallery was empty of everyone but herself.

Don't panic. Don't panic. Don't—

How the hell was she going to find Dodger, Cinderella, and Kara in this massive castle? Or outside of it—which was probably where Kara was by now, in the pumpkin-turned-coach.

Don't panic.

But she was panicking. She'd *told* Dodger not to leave her alone! Not to split up!

Desperate, Jacqueline leaned over the railing, looking for any sign of the pickpocket or Cinderella. Her fingers gripped the cool stone railing as her heart galloped in her chest and her stomach tightened around the heavy rock that had lodged there.

Cinderella was no longer in the corner where she'd been watching the ball, and Jacqueline couldn't see Dodger, despite his red hair. It was like *Where's Waldo?*, but a lot more desperate.

Tears of anger and frustration welled up, and she was just about to start shouting for Dodger—what the hell did she have to lose?—when she felt someone behind her.

She spun, and the tears turned to relief when she saw Dodger emerging from the shadows.

"Where the *hell*—"

"This way," he said, and, waving a hand for her to follow, he darted off down the gallery. Jacqueline hurried after him, well aware of the fact that she was more than twice his age and not in nearly as good of shape as she should be. At least she was wearing decent shoes.

Fortunately, she was able to mostly keep up as he bounded down the spiral of the narrow stone steps that led to the main floor. After that, Dodger lived up to his name and threaded his way along a different arched gallery that opened onto the dance floor on one side and more corridors on the other. Despite the way they cut through the crowd, no one seemed to notice them—mostly because the partygoers were standing around chattering and gossiping about the mysterious woman in the silvery dress.

At last, they reached a small wooden side door. Dodger opened it and peeked outside, then gestured for Jacqueline to follow. They found themselves, as expected, in the bailey—the walled-in yard around the castle building.

Dodger led the way toward the large opening out of the castle grounds, where a metal-toothed portcullis had been raised in order to facilitate easy coming and going for the ball. Again, no one seemed to notice them, and they hurried out of the massive opening.

The night was comfortably warm and topped by a starry sky. There was no moon, but torches along the battlements and walkway to the castle offered plenty of light. The long drive up to the entrance was clogged with carriages of all shapes and sizes, most of them parked, waiting for their owners. A forest sprawled to the right (Jacqueline had no idea what direction it was), and it was toward this dark expanse that Dodger dragged her—for, by now, he'd taken her by the wrist in order to help her keep up.

If I ever get back, I'm going to start doing cardio every day. Jacqueline pressed a hand over the stitch in her side as she gasped dry breaths and tried not to stumble over her own two feet.

She wasn't crazy about going into the dark forest without a light, and suddenly remembered her phone was in her pocket. She pulled away from Dodger's grip and leaned against a tree, panting, as she dug out the device and turned on the flashlight. Surely no one would think anything of it, even if they saw a light in the forest —they'd assume it was a torch or lantern on a carriage.

She hoped.

"Wot's 'at?" Dodger wasn't even out of breath, and she hated him for that.

"A light," she said, puffing. "Where are we— *Oh!*"

Cinderella had emerged from behind a large tree. With her was Kara, whose dress had, of course, disappeared on the last stroke of midnight. She was once again wearing twenty-first-century clothing, and her hair hung in lank swaths over her shoulders. Despite appearing a little shell-shocked, Kara seemed unharmed.

"Thank God!" Jacqueline cried, barely keeping herself from lunging at the teen and hugging her—or giving her a good shaking and talking-to. She'd do one or both of that later; now she wanted to go back to reality.

"Take us back now," she said to Dodger, turning off her phone's light. She shoved the device into her pocket, trying not to worry about whether they *could* go back.

After all, that was what happened in books, right? You thought you were all safe and sound, ready to heave a sigh of relief, when you found out, nope, it wasn't over, no, you couldn't go back, *oops*, you were stuck here or someone was going to keep you here because they were the villain and they had a dastardly reason—

Jacqueline tamped down the panic. "Jack Dawkins, I want you to take Kara and me back *now*."

"But mu'um—"

"*Now!*" Jacqueline didn't care that she was shrieking. She grabbed him by the arm and, with her other hand, took Kara's arm.

Cinderella—Jacqueline wasn't certain whether she

was the villain or not—started to speak, but Jacqueline ignored her and glared at Dodger.

He muttered something, moved in a funny, twisty sort of way, and then suddenly Jacqueline was falling.

Again.

15

Once again, a scream filled Jacqueline's ears. But this time, it wasn't her own.

She tumbled onto a wooden floor, with Kara's shriek still ringing at a high pitch, and landed on her knees. *Ouch*. Dodger and Kara bumped into her as they landed as well, with the pickpocket the only one making a perfect-ten landing, tumbling in a neat somersault and landing on his haunches.

Jacqueline groaned even as she confirmed, with wild—crazy-wild—relief that, yes, they were back at Three Tomes. She recognized the rug, the plank floor, the bookshelves...

And the shiny black shoe tapping in annoyance on the floor next to her fingers.

Jacqueline looked up to find Mrs. Hudson and Mrs. Danvers (whose shiny black shoe was expressing her extreme disappointment). It wasn't only the shoe. Both women wore very dark expressions as they looked down at her, hands on their respective hips.

In this situation, at least, the housekeeper and the landlady seemed to be in accord: furious.

"Wot in the bleedin' hell d'ye think yer doin'?"

Mrs. Hudson exploded, her Cockney accent far thicker than usual.

At first, Jacqueline thought she was shouting at her, but it was Dodger's ear that Mrs. Hudson had snagged. He gave a pitiful cry as she yanked him to his feet. "Wot were ye thinking?"

"Ow," he cried, rubbing at his abused ear. "Oi, ye don't need t' get all—"

"Ye have no business doing such a thing!" Mrs. Hudson went on, shaking her finger. "Mixing up stories! Traveling across books! What were you thinking?"

Relieved to not be in disgrace herself, Jacqueline pulled to her feet. But when she came upright, she found herself face to face with a thunderous-looking Mrs. Danvers.

"It wasn't me," Jacqueline said. "He dragged me into the story because Cinderella took *her* in!" She pointed a thumb at Kara.

Danvers gave her a look of clear disbelief laced with fury. "That is *forbidden*," she said in a deep, dark tone. "Who knows what damage you've done? Ma'am."

"I haven't done any— Look, forget it, all right? We're all here and Cinderella is back in her story, and — What's wrong?" Jacqueline's admittedly weak defense was interrupted by the sound of sobbing. "Kara, what is it?"

"It w-was awful...and m-magical at the same time," she said, her eyes glistening. "I'm so confused."

Jacqueline immediately turned her full attention to the teenager. Danvers and Hudson could suck it. She hadn't done anything wrong, but now she had to find out what had happened from Kara. Good grief, she hoped the girl's parents weren't wondering where she was! It had been almost ten o'clock when Dodger dragged her into the book. That was hours ago.

"Tell me what happened," Jacqueline said, urging Kara toward the two chairs. They were in the sci-fi and fantasy room, just as they had been when they left.

A quick look around told her the Grimms' book they'd presumably come back out of was gone (weirdly, she didn't remember seeing it or stepping on/out of it when they came back), and, she realized suddenly, also missing were Danvers, Hudson, and Dodger. Had the two women taken Dodger off to read him the riot act? And had they taken the book as well? Did that mean Cinderella wouldn't be able to come back?

These questions flitted quickly through Jacqueline's mind, but she didn't have time to mull them now.

"Sit down here, and let's talk about what happened," she said. "But first...maybe you should call your parents or someone to let them know you're all right."

Kara looked at her smartphone. "My mom thinks I'm babysitting, but I got off early tonight. She doesn't expect me till after eleven."

Jacqueline looked at her own phone and was shocked that it was just after ten o'clock. It was as if no time had passed from the moment they jumped into the book and the time they returned, à la *The Lion, the Witch and the Wardrobe*.

Well, that was convenient. At least she didn't have to worry about news headlines like *Teenage Girl Goes Missing from Bookshop*.

But now she wondered whether the same thing

happened on the book side—did the story stop until the character returned?

She gave her head a mental shake. Another question she could mull—and maybe get an answer to—later. "All right. Now tell me what happened."

Kara was just about to speak when she glanced up and caught her breath.

Jacqueline turned. Cinderella was standing there.

"You're back," Jacqueline said unnecessarily. And warily. She wasn't certain what to expect from the fairytale character.

"Yes," replied Cinderella in a quiet voice. "Are you all right?" she said, looking at Kara.

"Yes. I'm just... It was so weird," Kara said. She didn't seem to be afraid of or wary of Cinderella, but Jacqueline wasn't quite ready to relax. She didn't trust Cinderella's motives. "It was like I was myself, with my own thoughts and memories, but I was also *you*, you know, Cinderella—and I was doing things, like, automatically, you know?"

Jacqueline lost interest in Cinderella for the moment and turned her full attention to Kara. "So you were aware of what you were doing, but you knew what you had to do, and—"

"And I *had* to do it. It wasn't like, okay, I know the fairy tale so I knew what had to happen next, so I did it. It was like I was—you know—like that spell in Harry Potter where you make someone do something whether they want to or not. The Imperius Curse, I think it is.

"Like, I felt myself climbing down from the carriage and walking up the steps to the door, and I wanted to stop and, you know, take a breath, get ready before I walked in and maybe check my hair...but I couldn't. I just kept walking. And those *shoes!* Glass slippers are not even a little bit comfortable."

"They're awful," agreed Cinderella vehemently. "I've asked Godmother to change them to something else, but she won't. They're 'instrumental to the story,' she always says."

Kara shook her head sympathetically, then went on with her explanation. "Later, I wanted to stop dancing with the prince after about five spins around the room, and I just couldn't. It was *weird*. It was like someone else was controlling me."

"You wanted to stop dancing with the prince?" Jacqueline asked. "Oh, because of the shoes."

"Omigod, *yes*. The shoes *killed*. But not only that—he had the *worst breath*. It was *rank*, I'm so not kidding, and he was so *boring*. All he did was tell me how beautiful I was and about how he practices sword fighting every day in case he has to fight a *dragon*—as if I'd want to be with a gym rat." Kara grimaced, then her face softened. "I mean, it *was* pretty amazing at first. And lots of the time after that. I was *Cinderella*. You know, everyone was looking at me and talking about me—which was really cool, and made me feel like a princess—but also made me feel really strange. But the *dress* was, omigod, gorgeous! Like, it was magical." She stopped and looked at Cinderella. "But it was really magic, wasn't it?"

Cinderella nodded soberly.

Jacqueline felt like it was time for her to step in. She thought she might be starting to understand Cinderella's reasoning for bringing Kara into her story, forbidden as it was. "Magic...just like a love potion, right? Kara, don't you see? You were doing things you didn't want to do—being with a man you didn't really like, but you didn't have the choice."

"Well, yeah, but I *knew* it wasn't real." Kara shrugged. "A love potion is different because it makes you *love* the person. So you're happy. I didn't love the prince. At *all*." She made an "ew" face. "But it was really awesome being Cinderella for a little while."

Jacqueline exchanged glances with Cinderella, suddenly feeling sympathy for the fairytale character. "But a love potion—"

"What about Prince Anton?" said Cinderella. "How do you think he felt?"

"What do you mean?" replied Kara.

"Think about it," said Jacqueline, picking up the thread. "He fell for you in the same way he fell for Cinderella. You're not the same person. So how could that be? How could he so easily fall for someone completely different? The only thing that was the same was the dress and the environment—"

"*And* the perfume you were wearing," broke in Cinderella. "The *perfume*, which was a love potion."

Jacqueline did a double take and looked at Cinderella. "What? I never knew that." She wanted to say, "Are you sure?" but realized that was stupid. Of course Cinderella would know. It was *her* story.

Cinderella nodded. "That's right. It wasn't just the dress that caught Anton's attention. Or my entrance to the ball in that stunning gown. My Fairy Godmother gave me a perfume that was designed to make him fall for me. How else would you explain the way he immediately fell in love with me, and tore the kingdom apart to find me—after only a short time of dancing?"

"Well, there is such a thing as love at first sight," Jacqueline said weakly. She knew at least two happily married couples who could claim that was how they'd met.

"There might be, but I don't believe Anton really loves *me*. And I certainly don't love him. It's the perfume, you see. Anyone who wore it and the dress would capture his love. But neither of us have a choice, and—and..." A perfectly formed tear spilled out of one of Cinderella's blue eyes and rolled down her cheek like a stunning diamond. "I don't want to marry him."

"Well, *I* don't want to marry him," said Kara flatly.

"But you understand the point Cinderella is trying to make," Jacqueline said, turning to the girl. "Giving a love potion to someone doesn't make them *really* love you. It's just as fake and unfair as you having to go through the motions as Cinderella at the ball. You wanted to stop dancing with Prince Anton, but you couldn't because you were *compelled*. And maybe he wanted to stop dancing with you—deep inside—because he didn't really love you—because, after all, you aren't really Cinderella, are you? But he couldn't do what he wanted to do deep inside because of a love potion perfume."

She could, finally, see the dawning of comprehension in Kara's beautiful eyes. "But..." the teenager began. "I really, *really* like Bryson. Like, a *lot*."

Jacqueline took a deep breath and expelled it slowly. "All right. I get that. But you didn't like being forced to dance with the prince and his bad breath and workout stories; you have to see that it wouldn't be right to force Bryson to like you. *But* there is such a thing as a natural love potion," she went on briskly, forestalling the stubborn argument rising in Kara's eyes.

This was, Jacqueline reminded herself, one of the reasons she didn't regret not having children:

teenagers. She'd had plenty of experience dealing with them at the library, and while some of them were quite wonderful, she'd never been fond of the idea of having one of her own.

"A natural love potion? What does that mean?" Kara sounded intrigued and wary.

"It means using your own—um—*loveliness* to attract the attention of someone you're interested in. It's not a foolproof plan, but it works an awful lot of the time. It's the process I already started you on today," Jacqueline went on quickly, making shit up as she went along and hoping it made some sort of sense.

At this point, she just wanted to get rid of Kara and Cinderella and go upstairs and read with a cup of tea.

She stopped her thought right there. A cup of *tea*? Since when had she thought of tea as a comfort—

Jacqueline gave herself another mental shake and realized Kara was waiting for her to continue. "I told you to ask Bryson three questions. And to bring him something to drink. Both of those are ways to demonstrate your own 'loveliness': kindness—by offering him a gift—and interest, by asking him questions about himself and listening to him speak. Do you see?"

Kara frowned. "Maybe. But that sounds pretty weak. You said you'd work on the other, real love potion, though. The one that takes months to brew?"

"Right," Jacqueline said with a sigh. She clearly wasn't going to convince Kara of the error of her ways. At least not tonight. But she did have the buffer of a few weeks, at least, to help guide the girl through getting to know Bryson better and helping him to get to know her. Maybe by the time a few months were up, things would be happening. Or maybe Kara would have found someone else to moon over.

Or prom would be done.

Or school would be out.

"I'll keep working on brewing that," Jacqueline said. "But in the meantime, you still have things to do to prepare for its efficacy, all right?"

"Right. Bring him a drink. Ask him three questions. Then what?"

"Then report back to me and I'll tell you the next steps," Jacqueline said, doing her best to keep from sounding impatient. "And now," she said, rising from her chair, "it's time for me to close up the shop and send you on your way."

"All right." Kara heaved a great sigh. "Thank you, Miss Finch. And...thank you for a really weird time tonight," she added to Cinderella. "It was pretty cool."

Jacqueline let Kara out the back door, locking it behind her. Then, without a glance to see whether Cinderella was still around, she slipped into the back stairway and climbed up to her apartment.

Tomorrow morning would be soon enough to deal with everything else, including Wendy and her cursed purse.

Unsurprisingly, Jacqueline's dreams were filled with Cinderella ballroom scenes with her, Jacqueline, being spun around the room, mingled with purses with crazy eyes and ferocious teeth where the flaps usually were. Dancing through all of it were bottles of Big Bay wine, lavender and blackberry sprigs, and Amanda Gauthier's wide brown eyes.

When she peeled her own eyes open, Jacqueline wasn't certain whether it was a relief to be out of the dream and into reality or not. Part of her wanted to fling the covers over her head and read an old Georgette Heyer novel while ignoring the world for a day.

But she was an entrepreneur now, a business owner—and besides, Jacqueline suspected neither Danvers nor Hudson would allow her to hide away. Since they both knew where she lived, she might as well get up. The last thing she wanted was for them to find her in the ratty t-shirt and boxers in which she'd slept, with her newly curly hair a wild rat's nest.

Dutifully, she did her morning stretches, noticing a little soreness that was probably related to the extra activity (i.e., the running through the castle with Dodger) from last night. Sighing, she forced herself to do a few jumping jacks just so she could say she'd done some cardio.

She washed up, brushed her teeth, tamed her hair and dressed, then made herself some coffee for her insulated travel mug. Thus armed, she went downstairs to face the day.

To her surprise and pleasure, the shop was quiet and empty. Jacqueline took her time turning on the lights and booting up the computer, enjoying the moment alone with her books.

No hovering, tea-pushing Mrs. Hudson. No glowering, judging Mrs. Danvers. No disruptive Dodger. And no sad-eyed, brooding Cinderella.

Jacqueline felt a pang of sympathy for Cinderella, but she pushed it away sharply. The girl was a *fairytale character*, for Pete's sake! She was destined to marry the prince and live happily ever after.

Yet, as Jacqueline fussed with some of the book displays, moving the new Ian Rutledge mystery into a prime spot next to a gorgeous reissue of *Dune*, the new V. E. Schwab, and a stunningly photographed Mexican cookbook, she couldn't completely abolish the memory of Cinderella's woebegone expression.

Jacqueline tried to tell herself that arranged marriages had been *de rigueur* for most of history, but her pedantic librarian brain reminded her that: one, a fairy tale wasn't history, and two, by definition "Cinderella" wasn't an arranged marriage tale but one of supposedly true love or love at first sight.

Dammit.

There was nothing she could do about Cinderella's plight.

Because...what if she did? What if Cinderella never went back into *Grimms*?

What would happen?

Would anything happen?

Sebastian jumped lightly up onto the table next to *Dune* and gave Jacqueline a flirtatious side-eye. She reached over to pet him, letting her hand glide over his silky fur and feeling the rumble of his delighted purr.

"There's nothing to be done about it," she told him when he fixed his amber eyes on her. "She's from a book. She's not even real."

Sebastian turned around, presenting her with the tail end of his figure, and she scratched him lightly on the top of his rump at the base of his tail. He purred even more loudly and collapsed onto the table, rolling onto his back to give her access to scratch his belly. Jacqueline obliged, and noticed Max strolling into the room with his tail aloft and a sneer on his face.

Just then, both cats swiveled to look toward the front door, and Jacqueline turned just in time to see the three ZAP Ladies crowding at the window.

Jacqueline heaved a sigh. Would she ever have a morning without being visited by the three crones? Or without *anyone* peering through the window before the shop opened?

There was no sense in ignoring the ladies or trying to put them off. Her shoulders slumped in defeat, Jacqueline went to the door and unlocked it.

"You know the shop doesn't open until nine during the week," she said as she stepped back to let them in. "And it's barely past eight thirty."

"Well? How did it go?" said Zwyla without preamble as she swept in, the fringe of her poncho brushing her knees. "Did you get the purse?"

"We came to help you de-curse it," said Pietra. She was carrying a basket that was possibly filled with baked goods, but could also be holding whatever one needed to de-curse a purse.

"Oh, no," Jacqueline said, flustered. "I kind of forgot about it. I sent Dodger off to see if he could find Wendy and maybe, um, relieve her of the purse, but something else came up."

"You forgot about it?" said Andromeda, who'd already gathered up Sebastian and was cradling him like a baby. Today, her normally spiky hair was combed back from her elfin features and tucked behind her ears. It was also jet black tipped with pure white.

"What came up?" asked Pietra, rummaging through the basket. "Here you are, Max. Now, don't turn up your nose at me. I know you like my catnip-catmint treats. No one's going to judge you for taking the biggest one, you know," she added, crouching on the floor near the black cat.

"Oh...well, nothing, really," Jacqueline said, feeling her cheeks heat. She didn't know whether she should tell the crones what had happened. "I did make a protection amulet, though."

"You used the blackberries, then," said Andromeda with a smile. "I thought they'd come in handy."

"Clever of you," said Zwyla. She was speaking to Andromeda but looking thoughtfully at Jacqueline. "Something came up?"

Jacqueline shook her head and shrugged. "It was nothing really. It—"

"She went into a book."

Jacqueline gasped; she hadn't seen nor heard Mrs. Danvers approach. The housekeeper was wearing her normal expression of displeasure, but this time it was combined with accusation.

"You did *what*?" said Zwyla. Her almond-shaped eyes widened into circles.

"I didn't *mean* to," Jacqueline said, darting a furious glance at Danvers. "Dodger dragged me in."

"Dodger took you into *Oliver Twist*? I bet that was fun," said Andromeda. "Dirty, stinky, smoggy Victorian London would not be my idea of a—"

"No, he...um...took me into *Grimms' Fairy Tales*. Into 'Cinderella.'" Jacqueline felt like she was going to confession, and she wasn't even Catholic. "Because Cinderella took Kara into her book," she went on, raising her voice to be heard over the loud and shocked exclamations from her audience. "We had to get her back."

"Crones bones!" cried Zwyla. She appeared staggered by this information, the first time Jacqueline had ever seen her looking anything other than cool and controlled.

"I know, I know, it's forbidden—but I didn't know," Jacqueline said, glaring at Danvers, "and I didn't have a choice. He just grabbed me and in we went."

"'Cinderella'? You were in '*Cinderella*'?" said Pietra.

Her eyes had gone dreamy. "Which part? Were you at the ball or— No, no, tell me you were at the part where the Fairy Godmother dressed her with a *swoop* of her wand! I don't know why *we* don't have wands," she said, pouting a little. "It would be so convenient—"

"Never mind the wands," Zwyla said. "What happened, Jacqueline?"

Giving Danvers one more dark look, Jacqueline launched into a brief but thorough explanation. "So you see, everything turned out fine. We all got back safely, and I think Kara actually might get the point about how love potions aren't really the thing. I'm actually hopeful she'll give up on the idea—"

"Did anyone see you?" inquired Andromeda, still rocking Sebastian in her arms.

"No one saw us," Jacqueline said.

Zwyla seemed to relax a little. "All right, then. No one saw you, everyone is back...perhaps it won't be as tragic as I feared." She focused those dark eyes on Jacqueline. Two fine lines bracketing her mouth indicated her seriousness. "Understand that the wrong person going into a book can alter it irrevocably. It's like the idea of time travel," she went on. "Any interaction with the characters or the setting can change the storyline permanently. So *don't do it.*"

"I certainly don't intend to," Jacqueline replied, feeling chastened—which was totally unfair because she hadn't done anything wrong.

"Very well," said Zwyla. "Now, what about the purse?"

"I sent Dodger off to try to find Wendy last night and get the purse, but he either couldn't find her or didn't even go because of what happened with Cinderella and Kara. So maybe today..."

Jacqueline trailed off as a figure appeared at the window of the shop door. She didn't recognize the man who stood there.

Seeing her inside, he knocked gently on the glass and smiled, pointing at the door as if to ask her to open it.

Jacqueline hesitated, but she couldn't ignore him. She'd at least find out what he wanted.

When she opened the door, she noticed the black hearse parked on the street right in front of the shop. Even from here, she could see the interior was upholstered in dark purple. The car was still running, and it seemed obvious the man at the door had come from the vehicle.

She put him in his late fifties, maybe just sixty. He was a tall man with gangly limbs and an expressive face that was neither handsome nor homely. His brown hair was fighting with encroaching gray, and losing badly. It was pulled back into a short, low ponytail, which revealed a fairly good hairline around the temples. He had a closely trimmed beard and mustache that had completely lost the battle with gray and was now sporting some white parts as well. His denim shirt was buttoned all the way except for the top button, revealing a hint of black tee beneath it.

"Hi," said the man. "Sorry to bother you; I see you're not open yet, so thank you for letting me in. Someone left this in my car—I'm a rideshare driver— and I wasn't sure what else to do with it. I thought maybe you'd know who it belonged to."

He handed her a familiar brown paper bag that was stamped with the Three Tomes Bookshop logo.

"Oh, thank you," said Jacqueline, taking the bag, which held a single book. She pulled out a trade paperback of *Gone Girl.* "I'll check our records and try to find out who bought this."

"It was a coupla days ago," the man went on. "I kept it, figuring whoever it was would realize they must have left it in the car, but I haven't heard from anyone. I didn't see a receipt, either." He shrugged. "So, I thought the best thing to do would be to bring it here."

"I'm surprised whoever left it didn't realize they lost their book," said Jacqueline.

"People are always leaving items behind. You wouldn't believe some of the weird things that get forgotten on the floor. Sunglasses, hats, and scarves are big ones; gloves too. Medication, inhalers, syringes, batteries, lipstick, scissors...even a pair of slippers, a dozen eggs once, and another time, a whole box of Trojans. Unused," he added when Jacqueline's eyebrows shot up. "Sometimes I wonder if people leave things behind on purpose."

"That's kind of rude, if you ask me," she said, "leaving your unwanted things behind for someone else to clean up."

"Nature of the beast," he said with a shrug. "Believe me, I've seen worse, long before I started driving strangers around. But sometimes it's the things they *do* in the back seat, if you know what I mean, that's even worse than what they leave behind. Nice shop," he said suddenly, looking past her into the store.

"Thank you," replied Jacqueline. "Um...I have to ask...is that your hearse?"

He grinned, his wide, mobile mouth revealing a lot of teeth. "Yep. I'm the only rideshare driver in town, and most people get a kick out of riding in a hearse. It's got lots of room for luggage in the back. Of course,

I tell people they have to leave room for the ghosts to sit in the front with me." He chuckled.

"Well, it's certainly different," Jacqueline replied, thinking of the purple interior. The back was probably done in velvet, but she couldn't tell from here. She wondered if Nadine had spoken to the man. She'd seemed awfully interested in the hearse, and the driver was kind of cute, if a little quirky.

"I spent all my life trying to keep people from ending up in a hearse, and now all I want to do is get them into one," he said, still smiling. When Jacqueline lifted her brows and gave him a look, he explained, "Retired ER doc. Living the dream up here in Button Cove by driving people around."

She thought she detected a hint of irony in his voice, but it was difficult to tell with that smile of his.

"Ah," she said. "I get it." She smiled and offered her hand. "I'm Jacqueline Finch, by the way. Been here for less than a month. Nice to meet you. I've seen your —uh—hearse quite a bit over the last week."

"Gerry Dawdle," he replied, shaking her hand with a large, knobby one of his own. "Nice to meet you. Anyway, I've got to get on my way—I have a pickup at one of the B&Bs on the bay. I hope you can find the owner of that book."

"Thanks for dropping it off," she said, then closed the door behind him.

When she turned back to the three crones, she discovered them huddled together. Pietra looked over, her eyes bright, and said, "Well, what are you going to do now?"

Jacqueline eyed the three of them suspiciously, but she couldn't tell what they'd been talking about. And she wasn't sure she even wanted to know.

"I'm going to open my shop," she said breezily. "I'll

be sure to let you know when we get our hands on the cursed purse—or if anything else happens with Wendy. Thank you for coming by," she added meaningfully. That was as close as her people-pleaser self would allow her to get to actually asking them to leave.

They seemed to take the hint, for Andromeda unwound Sebastian from around her neck, and then they bade Jacqueline goodbye as she turned the front door sign to OPEN.

She went to the back door and did the same there, and on her way back up to the front, she glanced into the science fiction and fantasy room.

The thick, old Grimms' book was on the floor.

But it was closed. Not open.

Jacqueline eyed the tome suspiciously, then looked around the room. No sign of anyone around.

Usually the book was open when a character came out. And when they went back in for good, the book showed up on the front counter, closed.

Shrugging, she swooped down to pick it up just as the bell on the front door jingled. She was moving so hastily that she missed the book—a coordinated athlete, she was not—and she had to reach for it again. Her fingers brushed past it once more, and with a growl of frustration, Jacqueline slowed her movements, made them careful and deliberate, and finally closed her fingers around the book.

But it felt weird in her grip. Frowning again, she looked at the thick, raggedy volume of fairy tales she was holding.

The faded title imprinted on the front seemed blurry, and she realized it was because she didn't have her reading glasses. Even the edges of the book looked weird to her tired eyes—sort of indistinct.

The little bell on the front counter rang, its tinny chime reverberating through the store. A customer was waiting.

Jacqueline hurried to the front, carrying the book, and when she saw who was standing at the counter, she nearly dropped *Grimms'*.

It was Wendy. And she was carrying her rosy-pink purse.

16

"Hello, Wendy," Jacqueline said warily. She set *Grimms' Fairy Tales* on the shelf under the counter and tried to fix a welcoming smile on her face.

"Well?" demanded her former friend. "Are you going to remove the curse you put on me, or do I have to get nasty?" The dark circles under her eyes were emphasized even more by Wendy's red glasses. It reminded Jacqueline of graffiti drawn on a photograph: scarlet circles around the eyes to highlight them. "I've already begun to compose a few emails," she added snottily. "To several *select* people. All I have to do is hit send."

"I definitely want to remove the curse," Jacqueline said, eyeing the purse. She wondered what would happen if she asked Wendy to just give it to her.

Could it be that easy? After all, this was real life— such as it was—and not a book, where nothing was ever easy during a hero's journey or a heroine's quest.

But Jacqueline had already completed her own heroic journey, hadn't she? By coming here and embracing her new life as owner of Three Tomes, working with literary characters come to life, accepting that there were things in life she couldn't always explain, paranormal and supernatural and metaphysical things...right?

"I need your purse," she said firmly and clearly. "In order to dissolve the curse."

"Oh no you don't," Wendy said fiercely, hugging the purse close to her body.

Damn.

Of *course* wasn't going to be that easy.

"Egala told me you'd try to get it away from me. She told me not to give it to you," Wendy went on. Her eyes looked wild, and for the first time, Jacqueline noticed how frazzled Wendy appeared overall: her mouse-brown hair was frizzy, her eyeliner was crooked and her mascara smudged, and her blush wasn't blended at all—plus it was an unattractive orange shade. Her long shirt was misbuttoned, too.

"Wendy, if you don't give me the purse, I can't remove the curse. It's that simple. So it's your choice. But I can see the toll it's taking on you."

Jacqueline deliberately turned her back on Wendy and began to rearrange a display of middle-grade novels she'd added on a small table near the stairs to the tea room. Her fingers trembled a little, and her belly squished and moved alarmingly, but she wasn't about to let on to Wendy how nervous she was about her reaction. "It's making you feel out of sorts and tired and angry." She held off using the word "crazy," but it certainly sat topmost in her mind.

There was a long, tense silence, broken only by the soft shuffle of pages and quiet thump of books on wood as Jacqueline adjusted the table display.

The bell over the door jangled, and she looked over. Despite everything else going on, she couldn't contain a delighted smile. "Detective Massermey," she said. "How are you today?"

"I'm great," he replied, his eyes lingering on her just long enough that she got the message: he was great because he was seeing her. Jacqueline couldn't hold back a flush. Damn her red hair and fair skin! "Wanted to stop in and see about getting coffee," he went on. "Can you get away this afternoon? I should be free after three."

Jacqueline avoided looking at Wendy, who remained near the counter glowering like a malevolent toad, with her bulging, red-framed eyes, and frizzed-out hair, still holding the accursed purse. "I should be able to skip out for a while at three. Unless some big school system purchaser comes in and wants to order three cases of *Nineteen Eighty-Four* or *Cold Sassy Tree*... then I might be a little late."

The lines at the corners of his vibrant blue eyes crinkled. "Sounds good. Better Grounds—it's over on Front Street—a little after three, then?"

"I'll be there," Jacqueline said, willing her cheeks not to heat up any more.

"Have a great day. Sell lots of books," he said, then slipped out the door.

"Must be nice," said Wendy bitterly. "A big, good-looking man like that interested in you while your best friend's life is falling apart. Of course, you planned it that way, didn't you?" she sneered, her eyes flashing with an ugly light. "You *want* to destroy my life."

Jacqueline lost it. "*I did not curse you.* You're definitely under a curse, Wendy, but it's not from me. And if you don't let me help you..." She lunged, grabbing for the purse.

And screamed.

Snatching her hand back, Jacqueline looked at it,

her fingers shaking. Her palm and the insides of her fingers were bright red, and it freaking *hurt*.

"Serves you *right*," Wendy said, but she was eyeing Jacqueline warily as she continued to hug the purse against her belly. "What happened? You scrape yourself on the clasp?"

"No. The damned thing burned me. It's definitely hexed," Jacqueline replied angrily. "You need to get rid of it."

"What's going on down here?" Mrs. Hudson appeared from halfway down the stairs.

"I need some ice, please, Mrs. Hudson," Jacqueline said, wondering whether it would even work on a hand burned by a cursed purse. Her palm was still throbbing, and now the redness and pain was beginning to climb toward her wrist. To her horror, little bubbles of skin were starting to appear on her palm now too.

"I'm not going to get rid of my purse," said Wendy, clutching it even tighter. "I *won* it. It belongs to *me*."

Shades of *Lord of the Rings*.

"Wendy, if you don't get rid of that purse, your curse is never going to go away. At least— All right, try this. Put down the purse and walk away from it." Jacqueline didn't know whether applying reason to the situation would help, but what else was she going to do?

Now her arm was turning fiery red and the pain was continuing to build. More boils erupted on her hand, and they were shiny and hard. Crap. This was not a normal burn. She needed to see the crones.

"Mrs. Hudson, is Dodger up there?" she called. She could send him over to get Andromeda.

"Ain't seen the likes of him since yesterday," Mrs. Hudson replied as she came down the stairs. She was holding a small plastic bag filled with ice. "Lazy, good for noth— Good heavens! What happened to you, dearie?"

"I touched her purse," Jacqueline said acerbically. "And it's hexed."

Wendy, who'd been watching all of this with suspicious eyes, edged away from Jacqueline and Mrs. Hudson, still holding that damned (possibly quite literally) purse.

"Just put it down for a second, will you, Wendy?" Jacqueline pleaded. "Obviously I can't take it, and Mrs. Hudson won't touch it, will you?"

"Certainly *not*," replied the landlady.

"I think if you put it down and step away from it, you might feel a little...better," Jacqueline continued. "Can't you see—there's something wrong with it? A normal purse wouldn't cause this." She held up her swollen, burning, bubbling hand.

"It's because it's *you*," Wendy retorted. But she sounded a little less certain. "Egala said you'd try to get it from me, so she protected it."

"Why do you think she doesn't want me to get it from you?" Jacqueline replied impatiently. "*Because it's cursing you.*"

"No, it's protecting me from you," Wendy said. "Things would be even worse if I didn't have this. It's like a shield."

Jacqueline was so upset from both pain and frustration that she nearly screamed. But she managed to hold it in, though her eyes bulged from the effort.

Perhaps it was her wild, frantic expression that cut through Wendy's hesitation. She looked at Jacqueline, then at Mrs. Hudson, and put down the purse on a table of books.

And, thankfully, the books did not erupt into flames. Or boils.

"Thank you," Jacqueline said through teeth gritted with pain. "Now, can you just put some distance between you and the purse?"

Wendy, who already looked a little less tense, nodded jerkily and took two steps away from the table.

Just then, the sound of boots pounded down the stairs. Dodger came into view, but before Jacqueline could speak, he took in the situation.

He leaped the rest of the way down, missing the last seven or so steps, and lunged for the purse. He swept it off the table in one glorious move, did a perfect-ten tumble, and landed on his feet holding up the bag in triumph.

Wendy shrieked and lunged, but Dodger held it high above her grabby hands. "I got it, mu'um! I got it!"

"You *bitch*!" cried Wendy, spinning onto Jacqueline. "I *trusted* you!"

"Dodger. Put it down," Jacqueline said, her jaws tight from the pain. "It's all right. Put down the purse. I need you to go get Andromeda—down the street at Camellia House. *Now*," she said, trying to keep from crying...the aching was *so bad*. "Please."

Dodger gave her a very confused look, but he did as she requested and set the purse on the counter.

"Wendy, please...don't pick it up again," Jacqueline said through tears. The bubbly skin was beginning to erupt on her wrist and up her arm. "See, I made him put it back. No one is going to take it."

The fact wasn't lost on Jacqueline that Dodger had snatched the purse but it hadn't burned him. Surely Egala had put her own extra-special little present for

Jacqueline on the purse, knowing she'd try to get it away from Wendy.

Clever bitch.

And a coward, too—not having had the decency to do any of this destructiveness in person, but to use Wendy as her unwitting tool.

Dodger didn't hesitate, thankfully. He ran out the door and dashed down the street.

"Move a little further away," Jacqueline suggested to Wendy. Her voice came out in embarrassingly whiny from the pain. "How are you feeling?"

Her ex-friend eyed her suspiciously. "Fine."

The ice did help, Jacqueline discovered belatedly. But it didn't keep the boils from erupting on her arm, and now she was feeling the burning along her upper arm and into her shoulder. If Andromeda didn't get here soon and fix things—please let her be able to fix things!—Jacqueline didn't know what she was going to do.

"You need to lay down somewhere, dearie," said Mrs. Hudson. She cast an accusing look at Wendy.

"But the shop..." Jacqueline began, then caught herself. She was in no condition to wait on customers.

"Where is that Danvers creature?" Mrs. Hudson said furiously. "She's never—" She bit off her fuming as none other than Mrs. Danvers made her appearance.

"I was attending to the litterbox," said the housekeeper from between stiff lips. Her eyes flashed with fury, then, when they lit on Jacqueline, her anger faded a little. "What has happened?"

"A hexed purse is what has happened, you stringy old bat," Mrs. Hudson exploded. "And where were you when this was all going on?"

The next thing Jacqueline knew, the two women

were bundling her off into one of the back rooms as they shouted accusations and insults at each other.

"Can't have the customers seeing you like this, now, can we?" said Danvers in an almost motherly tone. Yet there was that ever-present hint of condescension in her words as well. "I'll see to the front while *you*," she said loftily to Mrs. Hudson, "attend to this. I'm certain a cup of tea will do the trick," she added sarcastically.

Mrs. Hudson huffed and snapped back, but Jacqueline hardly knew what was going on at this point. She was in so much agony that the waves of pain drowned out whatever was going on between the two women. She didn't know where Wendy was—or her damned purse, for that matter—and all she wanted was relief. She closed her eyes, willing away the pain...

The next thing she knew, there were low, murmuring voices and cool hands touching her. The fiery pain began to ebb, and she found she could move her fingers again.

Prying open her eyes, Jacqueline discovered herself surrounded by the three crones. Zwyla and Pietra were muttering something that could be a spell of their own, or simply instructions or commentary—but who knew? Andromeda was applying a thick salve to Jacqueline's injured arm, and had pulled away the collar of her shirt in order to rub some on her shoulder, neck, and chest, where the angry rash had begun to spread. Already the fiery pain was cooling. The scents of lavender and rose filled her nose.

Tears of relief stung Jacqueline's eyes, and she whispered, "Thank you."

And then she closed her eyes again.

~

SHE DIDN'T KNOW how long she'd rested, but when Jacqueline opened her eyes, she felt no pain. Her fingers moved, her hand looked normal again, and she was alone on the sofa in her flat.

She sat up and heaved a great sigh. A glance at the clock on the microwave told her it was just past noon. Good—so she hadn't been out of commission for very long.

Jacqueline rose from the sofa, sorely tempted to do what she should have done first thing this morning: dive under the covers of her bed to read *The Nonesuch* or *The Grand Sophy*. But she thought better of it, because she really needed to find Wendy and give that woman a *serious* piece of her mind.

At this point, Jacqueline didn't even care whether her ex-friend sent her drafted emails to everyone in the entire bookselling world, or took out an ad in the *New York Times* or *Chicago Tribune* about how sucky Three Tomes Bookshop was—she was going to ban Wendy from ever entering the store again, even if she had to apply her *own* curse.

Furious all over again, Jacqueline nevertheless remembered that she had a sort-of date in a couple of hours. She checked in the mirror to make sure she didn't look like a hag—she didn't, actually, which pleased her—but she did put in a sparkly little barrette to hold back some of her curling red hair and reapplied eyeliner and mascara (since most of it had been smudged or cried away during her ordeal). She couldn't do anything about her soft, beginning-to-sag jaw line or her moon-sized pores, however.

Jacqueline changed her clothes too, opting for a long, lightweight blue sweater over stretchy denim leggings and a pair of soft brown boots she'd once splurged on at Nordstrom. A long pendant necklace that hit at about her diaphragm completed the look.

"Not bad for an old bitch who just about died from a cursed purse," she told herself, looking at her reflection. The crescent-shaped array of seven freckles on her cheek were still slightly raised, as they'd become during her first few days here in Button Cove. She had accepted them as the mark of her changed life and an honoring of her croneness.

Feeling somehow strengthened by all of this, Jacqueline took the tiny elevator down to the second floor. She stepped out into the tea room and found Mrs. Hudson deftly managing the small cadre of customers in the space. To Jacqueline's surprise, Dodger and Cinderella were there as well. They weren't working, however; they were sitting on two chairs near the pantry where Dodger had kept his stash, heads together and *holding hands*.

Oh dear.

In fact, Jacqueline had half expected not to see Cinderella again, hoping that the girl had remained in her book. Which reminded her that she'd seen the book on the floor and put it behind the counter. Maybe Cinderella didn't know where it was so she could go back in.

"Oh, there you are, dearie," said Mrs. Hudson before Jacqueline could mention it to Cinderella. "You look much better now, don't you, ducks? But you'll be needing a nice, strong cuppa, now, won't you, then?" She shoved a teacup across the counter at Jacqueline and filled it with whatever was in the teapot she held. "It's Lady Grey—a trifle less bold than her lord the earl, and good for a bit of bracing after fighting off a curse, if I do say so."

Jacqueline took the tea—she had no choice—and said, "What happened to Wendy and the purse?"

Mrs. Hudson pursed her lips and lifted her nose like she smelled something awful. "That woman took off when the ladies got here. But she left her bag, she did."

"She left it?" Jacqueline sloshed her tea and just missed spilling it on her "date" sweater. She couldn't believe Wendy had abandoned the purse. "Where is it?"

"Why, the ladies took it with them, of course," said Mrs. Hudson, as if Jacqueline should have known. "Asked *me* to put in a bag for them, of all things...but I did, and then they went off with it."

Jacqueline nodded. Obviously the crones didn't want to take the chance of touching the handbag themselves. She wondered whether Dodger and Mrs. Hudson didn't feel any pain when they touched the bag because they were from books, or because the curse Egala had put on it was only directed at Jacqueline and the ZAP Ladies. Or maybe Jacqueline was the only lucky recipient of the boiling hand curse.

"All right, thank you. And thank you for this," Jacqueline said, gesturing with the tea. Its contents did smell quite nice: a little flowery, with a hint of bergamot. She might even drink it after she added twelve packets of sugar.

Down on the main floor, she found Mrs. Danvers capably ringing up customers. Jacqueline reflected yet again how lucky she was that Danvers and Hudson could almost run the place without her. Having them around had its negatives, but right now, the positives had them far outweighed.

"Can I help you find something?" Jacqueline said

to a woman who seemed to be waiting for Danvers to be available to assist.

"Oh, yes, thank you! I'm looking for a really girly sort of picture book for my niece's four-year-old daughter. I only had boys, so she's the only reason I have to buy something frothy and pink and princessy." The woman smiled. "She's really into princesses and ballerinas and things like that."

"Oh, I have just the thing," said Jacqueline, gesturing for her to follow her up the stairs. "The children's picture book section is up here by the tea room."

She led the way to the large, sunny room adjacent to the café. There were lots of poufs and pillows on the floor, and short, toddler-sized chairs and tables. An adult-sized rocking chair was arranged in the corner for "story time," which Jacqueline hadn't yet started up again but was determined to do very soon. The low, child-height shelves were painted primary colors and the walls were decorated with a Dr. Seuss mural that ran all the way around the room, onto the floor, and splashed onto the ceiling.

She knew exactly where the book was she wanted —she'd just shelved two copies of it yesterday. It was a gorgeous rendition of "Cinderella," illustrated by an up-and-coming artist who lived near Chicago and who had done a book event at one of the libraries. It was only coincidence that Jacqueline walked past the real Cinderella when she went through the tea room, a fact that she declined to mention to her customer.

But when she got to the section, the book wasn't there. Neither of the copies.

"Oh dear," said Jacqueline. "It appears we've sold out of the book I had in mind. But I do have this one, which is also very popular for the frothy, pink, feminine types." She pulled a copy of *Angelina Ballerina* from a nearby shelf and offered it to the woman.

"Oh my gosh, this is *adorable!*" said the customer, flipping through it. "And look at the colors!" The woman closed it and clutched it to her chest. "I almost want a copy for myself," she said with a grin. "Thank you. This is perfect."

"Very happy to assist. The other book I had in mind is an exquisitely illustrated edition of 'Cinderella,'" said Jacqueline as they walked back down the stairs. "I'm happy to order a copy in for you if you like —I can get a copy signed by the illustrator."

"'Cinderella'?" replied the customer. "I'm not familiar with that one. Is it about a cat or something?"

Jacqueline nearly stumbled. "'Cinderella,'" she said clearly. "I'm talking about the glass slipper and the stroke-of-midnight fairy tale."

The woman shook her head, still looking blank. "No, I'm sorry. I'm not familiar with that one. Glass slipper? Who would want to wear shoes made from glass? That would be *so* uncomfortable. Anyway, this will be just perfect. Thank you so much," she said, moving toward the counter and Mrs. Danvers as Jacqueline gaped at her.

It was pretty impossible for someone not to have heard of "Cinderella," wasn't it?

Unlikely, but not impossible. Still...Jacqueline had a very funny, weird feeling, and as soon as the customer left with her purchase—which also included the last-minute addition of the Mexican cookbook on display—Jacqueline edged Mrs. Danvers away from the computer and logged in to check on the status of the Cinderella book she'd been looking for.

She stared at the computer.

Nothing. Absolutely *nothing* came up when she typed in "Cinderella."

Not one thing.

Her chest felt tight, and Jacqueline fairly dove under the counter where she'd put *Grimms' Fairy Tales.*

It was still there, thank goodness...but her fingers fumbled a few times before she actually grasped the book and pulled it out.

"What the hell is going on with me?" she said, looking at her fingers—they still worked—and the book, which was there, but it seemed blurry and sort of faint, even though it was in her hand.

That was a weird thing, but she knew her eyes were getting worse every day.

"Is something the matter, ma'am?" asked Mrs. Danvers.

"I was looking for that 'Cinderella' book with the illustrations by Darby Wright," Jacqueline told her, setting the old Grimms' book on the counter. "I shelved two copies yesterday, but they're not showing in the system and they aren't on the shelf."

"'Cinderella'? Well, of course you can't find them," Danvers replied.

"I guess you sold them," Jacqueline said, heaving a sigh of relief. She'd half expected the housekeeper to say, "What's 'Cinderella'?"

"No, ma'am. I certainly did not. They're gone."

"What do you mean, they're gone? Did someone *steal* them?" Jacqueline couldn't imagine someone stealing two children's picture books. There were many other books in the shop that were worth more than a twenty-five-dollar picture book.

Danvers gave her a cold look. "They're gone, ma'am. What did you expect after your behavior last night?"

Jacqueline stared at her, knowing her gaping mouth and goggling eyes made her look like a fish. "What are you talking about...gone?"

Before Danvers could answer—and from the expression on her face, it would have been *quite* the lecture—the front-door bell jangled and Nadine burst in.

"How are you, Jacqueline? I'm sorry I haven't been over since the grand opening! I've had classes all day, and my daughter's car broke down, so I had to drive down to Grand Rapids and bring her some things yesterday evening. *OMG*, those boots are *amazing!*"

"Thank you. I splurged on them a few years ago. So is it going to be expensive to fix? Danny's car?" Jacqueline asked. Nadine's youngest daughter was a freshman in college.

"Probably. I told her to call her dad. He's the one who makes the big bucks," Nadine said with a shrug. "It won't kill him to spring for a new set of brakes. Anyway, your party was absolutely fabulous. Such a success! Congratulations."

"Thank you," Jacqueline said.

"So whatever happened with the lady whose husband is trying to kill her? And the love potion?" Nadine's eyes sparkled with fascination. "Suzette told me all about it."

"Oh, well...you won't believe this, but I made Amanda—that's the one who's trying to keep from being murdered—a protection amulet. I have no idea if it's going to work, but I followed a recipe in an old spell book, so we'll see." Jacqueline spoke lightly, as if she were talking about making a sponge cake, because Nadine was just that kind of person: she took everything at face value and with a wide, open mind.

"OMG, that sounds so cool. You need to tell me *everything*, but not now. I've got a slow flow class in ten minutes—I love doing them after lunch—but I *had* to come over and tell you I finally met the hearse driver. He's kinda hot in a nerdy sort of way, and kinda interesting, too."

"You mean Gerry Dawdle? I met him too, just this morning. He seems nice." Jacqueline made a swift decision. "So, did I tell you about those new beautiful editions of 'Cinderella' we got in the other day?"

"Editions of what?" Nadine asked.

Jacqueline's heart sank. "'Cinderella.'"

"Cinder-who?"

Crap.

"I don't know what you're talking about, Jacqueline," Nadine went on in her bubbly way. "But you know I'm not as well versed in books as you are. Just don't have the time." She grinned. "But you're being a great influence on me—I finally did watch *Rebecca* the other night after pizza—the Hitchcock version. You're right," she said, leaning closer and dropping her voice, "that Mrs. Danvers is a real creepy-ass piece of work. Do you think she's the one who set Manderley on fire?"

Jacqueline glanced over her shoulder at the crow-like woman who was straightening books on the shelves beneath the stairway. "Probably."

"Me too. Anyway, *I'm* not going to ask her," Nadine said. "Well, I just wanted to run over and let you know I missed you and, oh, to see if you want to come over for a glass of wine tonight. I know it's not Sunday, but we have lots to catch up on—we can order in from Lupe's. I want to hear all about the protection amulet and the love potion and everything else."

Like "Cinderella" disappearing from the world?

Jacqueline stifled a groan. It wasn't her fault. It couldn't be. How horrible would it be if a librarian was responsible for destroying one of the most enduring, familiar, *beloved* fairy tales of all time?

No, that was surely an exaggeration. Things were weird, but it didn't mean "Cinderella" was completely gone. How could it be?

"Wine and Mexican? That sounds great," Jacqueline replied, feeling relieved about the idea. She would tell Nadine everything because Nadine would believe it all. She had to tell *someone* who was normal. "I'll tell you all about my coffee date with Miles Massermey, too."

"Yass!" Nadine did a fist pump, then gave Jacqueline a high five. "If I can't have him, you should!"

Jacqueline faltered. "What? I didn't think he was your type..."

Nadine laughed, waving her hand at Jacqueline. "No, no, I'm totally kidding. He's not my type at all. There's no, you know, *zing* when I talk to him. I just dig the Viking vibe, you know?"

"Yes, I do know," replied Jacqueline, feeling better. "See you later tonight, then."

"Looking forward to it."

Jacqueline waved off her friend, then hurried over to the counter and began to flip through the old *Grimms' Fairy Tales*. Her heart beat faster when she couldn't find "Cinderella" in the table of contents, and she began to feel very sick when she couldn't find anything in the book with that title.

Holy shit.

Maybe things *were* that bad.

Grabbing the book—it took a couple tries, and now she began to understand why: the book was getting *squishy*, as if it were dissolving—she stormed upstairs to confront Dodger and Cinderella.

Something had to be done.

17

Jacqueline thrust the old book at Cinderella. "Your story is gone."

The girl looked at her with crystalline blue eyes and nodded. "I know."

"You *know*?" Jacqueline just barely remembered to keep her voice down so as not to upset the customers. "Well, you have to go back in!" She thrust the book at Cinderella.

"But I don't want to marry Prince Anton," said Cinderella. "I'm not going back in there because I have no choice in the matter. I want to be free."

"But...but..." Jacqueline spluttered. "You *can't* destroy one of the world's best fairy tales!"

Cinderella rolled her eyes, reminding Jacqueline that she was still a teenager. "It's not that great of a story, really, Miss Jacqueline. It's all a lie—the dress, the magic, the love potion perfume. That's what made Anton fall for me. It wasn't real. And I certainly didn't like him. He probably doesn't really even like me."

"But... *No*—it's not about that. It's about how Cinderella gets away from her terrible stepmother and stepsisters and starts a new life," Jacqueline went on. "And how the pigeons and the mice and the birds help her...and how she marries the prince and lives happily..."

Her voice trailed off.

Dammit, the girl *was* right. Happily-ever-afters just didn't happen. And there was no such thing as Disney princes—or any perfect prince. Princes Philip, Andrew, and Charles of England, among others, had handily proved *that* over the decades.

But that didn't mean the story shouldn't be told. That the famous tale should be forgotten.

"I thought maybe Kara would like to stay and take my place—"

"*No!*" This time, Jacqueline didn't keep her voice down low enough, and some of the customers glanced over.

She looked around, then opened the pantry door and dragged Cinderella inside. Dodger, of course, followed. He was uncharacteristically silent, but she read the worry in his eyes.

"Absolutely *not*," she seethed from between gritted teeth. "You cannot, you absolutely *cannot* take a real person and put them into a book."

Cinderella sighed and folded her arms over her middle. "Then the story is gone forever. Because I'm not going back in and sitting at the castle all day and letting Anton—yes, he does have *horrid* breath—kiss me and whatever." She shuddered.

"Wot if it were a girl from a different story was put in?"

Jacqueline swiveled to look at Dodger, ready to lay into him too. And then she stopped. A little prickling along her arms made her consider this radical and yet very interesting idea. Her breathing went shallow as she contemplated it. "Did you have someone in mind?" she said in a mild voice.

"Nancy," said Dodger, his eyes wide with hope. "Then she won't be shot by that Bill Sikes."

Jacqueline snatched in a sharp breath. *Nancy*. Her favorite character not only from *Oliver Twist* but also from the musical *Oliver!* To save Nancy from being killed would be *amazing* because her death never failed to make Jacqueline cry.

But...

"It would change the story too much," Jacqueline said reluctantly, thinking of what Zwyla had warned her about going into stories being like time travel. You couldn't mess with the plots.

But would that be a bad thing? Saving the character in *Oliver Twist* who stepped out of her comfort zone and took a personal risk for her own safety to do the right thing in order to save Oliver?

Jacqueline shook her head. No. It was Dickens' choice to make that happen, and it wasn't right for anyone to change it. He was the author.

"I would love to save Nancy," she said, seeing the desperation blazing in Dodger's eyes. Her own stung a little because...*Nancy*. She *deserved* to be saved. "I really would. But it would ruin the whole book—and it might even affect you, Jack Dawkins. No, it can't be Nancy. But..." Another thought struck her. "What about Bet?"

Bet was Nancy's slightly younger friend. In the book, both girls were prostitutes and hung around with Fagin and his gang of pickpockets. In the musical, it wasn't obvious they were streetwalkers, but one could certainly infer their occupation. Either way, they both lived rough lives on the street.

If Nancy couldn't be saved, maybe Bet could be.

Jacqueline was trying to remember what happened to Bet in the book, but Dodger was already leaping onto the idea with alacrity.

"Oi, mu'um, 'at's a fine idear! Poor Bet, she's the one wot idennifies Nancy's body after Bill shot 'er, and she goes a little mad. They take 'er off to the asylum. Don't never see 'er again."

Jacqueline hesitated. It might not be a good idea to take a madwoman from Charles Dickens and put her in as Cinderella.

"She weren't really mad, mu'um," Dodger said earnestly. "She were jus' sad over losin' Nancy. Nancy was like a big sister to 'er. We all was sad over losin' Nancy." His mouth drooped.

"All right, then," Jacqueline said cautiously. "How about you see if you can bring her here—it has to be *after* she gets taken off, *after* her last mention in the book. Do you understand? You'll have to break into the asylum and get her out. Can you do that?" Asking a thief to break in somewhere was really quite logical, wasn't it? Though an asylum was quite different from a man's pocket or a fancy house in Mayfair.

Dodger stood up so quickly that he knocked over the box that had contained his stash. "Yes, mu'um," he said, giving her a snappy salute. "Cinderella 'ere can go wi' me."

"No...I think Cinderella needs to go back into her book—*just temporarily*," Jacqueline said firmly as she picked up the box. "Just to, sort of prop up the story while we wait to get Bet, all right?" She was not happy to see there were still items in the box from Dodger's pickpocketing spree the other day. "What are these still doing in here? I thought we'd put everything in lost and found and they'd been claimed."

"Oh, those're just things no one wanted, mu'um," said Dodger.

"Can you even do that, Cinderella?" she said, giving the girl a steady look. "Go back into your story —even though it's gone? Is it possible?"

"Yes, of course it is. I'm the main character, aren't I? As long as I'm in the book, my story will be there."

Jacqueline felt a wave of relief. "So you'll go back in?" She hoped that would work to keep the story from completely and irrevocably disappearing. "Just temporarily."

"I will do that, Miss Jacqueline, but I won't stay long," said Cinderella reluctantly.

"Thank you. Now, what's this?" Jacqueline pulled the small wing nut that had been tangled among some cheap gold necklaces in the bottom of Dodger's box. She could see why no one wanted the jewelry; the chains were tarnished and tangled. There was also a child's pacifier and a broken lanyard. "Where did it come from?"

"I dunno, mu'um," said Dodger. "Pulled it out o' a man's pocket, I did. Was curious, I was, 'cuz I saw—"

"All right, well, I'll take these downstairs and keep them under the counter in case anyone comes in looking for it," Jacqueline said, aware that she had cut him off, but she'd already wasted too much time talking about fixing Cinderella's problems when she had plenty of her own.

"Yes, mu'um," he said.

"Are you going to go into *your* book and take care of this now? Bring Bet back? I want to meet her and talk to her before you put her in Cinderella's story, do you understand? We can't have a madwoman taking over the—the character role, no matter how desperately you want her to." She gave both of them a forbidding look.

"Yes, mu'um," said Dodger, giving her another salute.

"And you'll go back into yours for just a short while," she said to Cinderella.

"Yes, Miss Jacqueline," said Cinderella.

Jacqueline glared at them for another second or two for good measure, then, feeling slightly relieved over this possible solution, she left the pantry.

A check of the clock told her she had plenty of time to visit the ZAP Ladies before she went off to meet Detective Massermey.

"Are you all right if I go down the street for a moment?" she asked Danvers as she slid Dodger's stash box under the counter.

The woman gave her a haughty look. "Of course, ma'am."

Was Jacqueline imagining it, or was there a little less condescension in the woman's tone and expression since she'd seen Jacqueline's arm covered in burning boils?

No, it was still there.

With a sigh, she ducked out the front door and began to hurry down to the end of Camellia Court, where the ZAP Ladies lived at the very top of the circle in a Victorian house as ornate and layered as a wedding cake.

It was a gorgeous spring day, and Jacqueline was almost too warm in her lightweight sweater, thanks to her aging hormones. The sun shone in a brilliant blue sky dappled with the occasional fat, cottony cloud. The air was scented with lake from the bay a few blocks away, and trees were beginning to leaf out. Spring was definitely here!

There were many pedestrians making their way along the block: young people walking along in pairs or clusters, mothers pushing strollers, older couples taking a lunchtime walk, dog walkers and office professionals, and several bicyclists and runners as well. Jacqueline had been delightfully surprised at how consistently busy the shops were here on Camellia. There was definitely something special about this street.

She noticed some activity around a small shop in the opposite direction from which she was going, just two doors down from Sweet Devotion—Suzette's bakery—and wondered what was going in there. Whatever it was, she hoped it fit with the atmosphere and vibe from the other establishments on the block...and that it would be run by another "cool" female.

Camellia House was easily identified by the sign hanging just beyond the wrought-iron gate. Studded with gables, a long veranda that curved around to the back, and even a tower room, the house was a robin's-egg blue with ornate trim in lemon yellow and shutters painted lavender.

Even though it was still early May and too early for planting, the ZAP Ladies' yard was a pleasing tangle of greenery, including some improbably blooming flowers and sprawling herbs. Only a very small patch of grass flanked the walkway; the rest of the grounds consisted of garden made up of trellises, arbors, pots, and plots. A pea-gravel pathway led to the front steps, then angled off and trailed through an arbor that would soon explode with roses. The walkway led to the backyard, which Jacqueline knew was also bursting with herb, vegetable, flower, and even some spice plants. In early May.

There was no question that Andromeda had something special going on there with her gardening.

Jacqueline walked up the path, and before she could even knock on the front door, it opened.

Pietra smiled out at her, her cheeks flushed with pleasure. "Come in, come in, Jacqueline. I'm so relieved you're doing better. We thought you needed a little rest after all of that."

"I wanted to come over and thank you all for helping me today," Jacqueline said, stepping inside. "For coming when I needed you."

"Of *course* we did," said Pietra, grasping Jacqueline's hand and giving her a steady, affectionate look. "Of course. You're one of us now."

The front foyer fed into a large living room, which looked just like a combination of 1960s hippie/flower child meets IKEA meets...something else. Disco pop culture?

Color exploded, creating a feast for the eyes that was somehow relaxing rather than discordant. Scarlet, purple, golden yellow, cobalt, vibrant orange, and more all melded into improbable harmony.

There were wall hangings of embroidered or painted canvas, macramé, and batik, along with long, low pine and oak furnishings. Plants grew everywhere, including a viny pothos that seemed prepared to take over the entire room, crawling along the edge of two windows and draping from some artwork on the wall. A tall green lava lamp sat in the corner, and there was a faceted disco ball about the size of a beach ball hanging next to it. Shimmering love beads hung from floor to ceiling in the arched doorway that led to a narrow hall. A shelf held a curious display of platform shoes and over-the-knee vinyl boots in a variety of colors, and a vintage record player sat on a table between two of the windows. Candles anchored nearly every surface, and the floor was covered by a collection of mismatched woven rugs and one big, furry pink swath in front of the long, low sofa. The air held the faintest scent of sandalwood and clove.

"Is that Jacqueline?" Andromeda poked her head out from behind one of the tapestries. "Oh, you look so much better now!" she said, smiling. "Come on back—or as the Brits say, come through."

Jacqueline followed her through the doorway that was semi-hidden behind the tapestry depicting the Witches Three from *Macbeth* on a fanciful background including unicorns and mermaids. As she knew from previous visits, the archway led to a Brother Cadfael-type herbary-slash-kitchen area where she was fairly certain food didn't actually get cooked but other things were stewed, strained, steeped, and stirred.

There was a long, scarred wooden table in the middle, and along two sides of the room were built-in work counters with shelves above them. A variety of mortars and pestles in wood and marble and of many different shapes and sizes lined the shelves, along with two electric coffee bean grinders, a food processor, a dehydrator, stacks of plates, beakers, tubes, vials, bowls, cups, pitchers, and more. Knives, athames, scissors, forceps, scalpels, tweezers, and other tools rested in flatware organizers. Dried herbs hung in bunches from the ceiling, and pots of living herbs adorned a long windowsill. There were jars upon jars of other ingredients as well: some things one might find in a normal kitchen—cinnamon, sage, dried seaweed—and others, like snakeskin and mourning dove feathers, not so common.

And along the shortest exterior wall was the built-in fireplace with a large cauldron hanging inside from a sturdy metal rack. There was currently no fire burning.

When Jacqueline stepped inside the room, she hardly noticed any of these things, for her attention was immediately drawn to the woman at the long table sitting next to Zwyla.

"Wendy!"

Jacqueline knew her exclamation must sound both accusatory and shocked, but seeing her old friend sitting there like she'd been invited to dinner was the last thing she expected.

And in front of Wendy, in the center of the table, was the rosy-pink leather purse that had caused all of the trouble.

"Jacqueline." Wendy sounded uncomfortable. She rose from her seat. "I..." She blinked rapidly. "I'm sorry about the burn. I'm glad you're all right."

"So am I," Jacqueline said, uncertain how to feel about Wendy and her seeming chumminess with the ZAP Ladies. Why did she feel so put out by the fact that her former friend—the one who'd tried to sabotage her, curse her, and who'd slandered the *shit* out of her—was just sitting there, easy and comfortable, with *her*, *Jacqueline's*, crones, in their special workshop?

"Jacqueline," said Zwyla with a warm smile as she looked at Jacqueline's hand. "You seem to be completely healed. I'm so glad to see you've fully recovered."

"Thank you," Jacqueline said, feeling as if she'd crashed a party and interrupted some sort of gossipy game. "Um...this looks cozy."

"We broke the curse," Pietra burst out.

"*We?*" said Andromeda, lifting one slender brow. "I hardly think your use of that pronoun is fair. It was my skill at identifying the essence of foxglove that made it obvious how to—"

"Well, you never would have thought to look

under the lining for the curse if I hadn't pointed out—"

"I would have found it soon enough, Petey," Andromeda said evenly. "And besides, you were so busy making spice cupcakes that—"

"*Someone* had to provide fortification," Pietra retorted. "It's not like you have the faintest clue in the kitchen anyway. If it were up to you, we'd all starve."

"That's *completely* not true," Andromeda responded. "You know I make a mean pesto—"

"Woman cannot live on pesto alone," Pietra proclaimed. "Especially when she's my age and has digestive issues."

This might have gone on for another few minutes if Zwyla had not intervened. "Regardless of how, and by whom—the curse has, in fact, been disabled," she said in a very loud, stern voice. "With no further casualties." She looked at Wendy. "Your handbag is now safe for you to use. And for anyone to touch."

Despite this good news, Jacqueline was still unsettled. She looked around the room. Somehow she felt cheated. They'd fixed the problem—abolished the curse—without her even being there, without her presence or assistance or information or anything.

It was just...over.

She sighed. Real life definitely wasn't like books, where no threat was resolved without a fight or a big ordeal.

"Well, I'm glad to hear that," she said weakly.

"Jacqueline," said Wendy, who was still standing. "Can I walk with you back to your bookshop?"

Jacqueline didn't really want to be around her former friend, and she wasn't certain she was ready to leave quite yet, but Jacqueline didn't see that she had a choice without looking like an ass, so she agreed.

"We'll talk later about the other things, Jacqueline," said Zwyla as she escorted them to the front door.

"All right," Jacqueline replied. By the time that happened, hopefully she'd be able to tell them that the Cinderella issue was resolved and that the love potion was dealt with and that Amanda Gauthier was safe and sound with her protection amulet.

With this in mind, Jacqueline felt a little better. She might not have been involved in the curse's lifting, but she'd resolved several other problems.

As soon as the front door closed behind them, Wendy said, "Jacqueline, I don't know how to apologize for my behavior...for everything. I hope...I hope that someday you'll forgive me."

"It wasn't your fault," Jacqueline said in an admittedly stilted voice. "Egala can be very persuasive and very cunning. I'm glad that it wasn't really you saying those things."

They walked through the gate before Wendy spoke again. "Thank you. You're being more generous than I deserve because...well, it wasn't all Egala. Part of it *was* me, and how I was feeling about what happened with you. I never really believed it about you and Desmond Triplett. But I lashed out at you on the day you were fired because...because I was jealous."

"You were *jealous*?" Jacqueline stopped, staring at Wendy in incredulity. "Of *what*? Of me getting fired? Of false rumors going around?"

Wendy's face was red. "Because obviously Desmond was attracted to you and wanted you...and no one wanted *me* anymore. Not even Richard." Her voice choked off into a sob. "I lied earlier. Richard asked me for a divorce over a month ago—the night before you got fired. It was still very raw that morning, and I was hurt and angry, and I—I let that affect me in the worst way when I heard the rumor about you and Desmond. And...and I let my own rumor about me and Desmond get started. To try to make myself feel better. I don't know what was wrong with me. I'm really sorry, Jacqueline. *Really* sorry."

Jacqueline clamped her lips closed so that she didn't say anything she'd regret. Inside, she was boiling...but after a moment, her rage ebbed.

People did weird things. They reacted badly, irrationally, irresponsibly all the time. She'd done her share of mucking things up.

"It's all right," she said after a few more steps. They were almost to Three Tomes. "I can understand why you were sort of reeling after Richard did that."

Wendy sniffled and swiped at her nose with a tissue. "I feel like shit for the way I treated you—then, and just these last few days. Zwyla told me that was why the curse worked so well, and why the purse gave you such a bad reaction when you touched it. I was...I was fueling it. *Inadvertently* fueling it because of my own feelings."

"I see," Jacqueline said. They'd reached the door to the bookshop. "Well, again, thank you. I accept your apology. I'm grateful Zwyla and Andromeda and Pietra were able to set things right. No lasting harm done." She couldn't force much warmth into her words—she was still shocked and saddened by her friend's confession—but she did mean them. For the most part. After all, she didn't have to interact with Wendy or even ever see her again. It was no skin off her back to accept the apology.

Wendy gave her a watery smile. "Thank you, Jacqueline. And good luck with your shop."

"Good luck with Richard," Jacqueline replied. "And whatever happens there."

She gave a little wave and opened the door to the bookshop, inordinately pleased that Wendy didn't make any move to follow her inside.

She needed some time and space away from the situation—in fact, just some time and space away from everything related to curses and potions and amulets and story jumping...

She just wanted a little taste of normal life for a while.

"Goodbye, Jacqueline," Wendy said. "I'll be leaving Button Cove now, and heading back to Chicago to pick up the pieces of my life. Wish me luck."

Jacqueline smiled, and this time her words were fully genuine and filled with warmth. "I wish you all the best of luck. Let me know how everything goes. Good luck, Wendy."

JACQUELINE HAD no trouble finding Better Grounds for her meetup with Massermey. But she had to admit to damp palms and a little nervous squiggling in her belly as she walked down the block to the café.

She couldn't remember the last time she'd been on an actual date. Sure, she had had her friend with benefits, Lester, back in Chicago, and they often accompanied each other to events like weddings, business dinners, parties, and so on...but there wasn't any real spark between them. It was just a convenience.

But this was a different story. Even if it was just coffee.

She and Massermey arrived at the same time, and

Jacqueline felt her cheeks warm a little when she saw the glint of pleasure in his eyes.

"Glad you didn't get caught up in anything at the shop," he said by way of greeting.

Oh, if he only knew!

"Glad you didn't get called to a murder scene or something," she said with a smile.

"That makes two of us. Want to grab a seat while I go up to the counter? What can I get you?"

Jacqueline sighed, looking at the menu. "I really want a seriously strong, sweet cappuccino, but I can't drink coffee after three if I want to sleep at night. So make it a nonfat decaf capp with honey, if they have it."

A few moments later, Massermey returned with their drinks, along with a plate-sized muffin. "I skipped lunch," he confessed, "so I could slip out early enough to meet you."

"That was nice of you," she said, feeling a pleasant little jolt in her heartbeat. "And thank you for the coffee."

"My pleasure. The muffin is big enough to share," he said, producing a plastic knife. He cut the pastry into quarters and picked up one of the pieces. "I don't feel so bad about having a muffin for a late lunch when it's carrot."

Jacqueline chuckled. "Well, that's one way to get your veggies. So, can I ask if there's anything going on with the Amanda Gauthier case?"

He nodded, swallowing. "I can tell you a few things. There's nothing really confidential going on, to be honest. Everything that's happened seems to have been an accident that could be construed as something more."

"I agree about the inhalers going missing—sort of

—and the almost being run down on the road being questionable," Jacqueline said, cutting a sliver of muffin. "But the fireplace leaking gas?"

Massermey nodded, and his mustache bristled with the pursing of his lips. "That's the only thing that makes you go, hmmm. A small part of the fixture—a little nut—is missing, and that's what caused the leak. Could be an accident—maybe it got loose, fell off, and got vacuumed up...or maybe someone removed it."

He picked up another quarter of the muffin, and Jacqueline realized he had nice hands. Not too long and skinny, not knobby at the knuckles, not too hairy, and not too stubby. Just...nice and solid and square.

He shook his head. "I don't get any vibe from the husband, though. Nothing rings wrong with him at all. The wife—well, she comes across as a little scattered—"

"Because she's a woman?" Jacqueline asked gently. "Most women, if they thought their husbands were trying to kill them, would be a tad anxious."

"No," he said, drawing out the answer firmly. "Because she's changed some of the details of her story a few times. Nothing major, just, you know, scattered in her descriptions. And she's really insistent that we look for the missing inhalers, and the piece missing from the fireplace. She thinks he hid them somewhere at their house."

"Oh." Jacqueline popped a piece of muffin into her mouth. She'd just thought of something she wanted to say...something in the back of her mind. But then she tasted the muffin and all thoughts went away because she hadn't had much lunch either. Only a cup of yogurt and an apple. "Oh, this is good. Not as good as Suzette's cranberry spice muffins, but really good."

"Getting my vitamin C for the day," he said,

holding up the last untouched quarter of the muffin. "See, there's even pieces of grated carrots in it. So it's not just one big, fluffy carb."

She laughed. "Hey, you don't have to justify it to me. I've been known to have a scone for breakfast and then another one for lunch. If it has blueberries in it, I figure I've had my fruit for the day."

His eyes crinkled and his mustache and beard twitched. "Not gonna hear any arguments from me. So, Jacqueline...what—and who—did you leave behind in Chicago to come to Button Cove?"

Her face heated at this very obvious and very direct question, but Jacqueline ignored the flush and hoped he didn't notice.

It wasn't fair, really—Massermey had light skin and strawberry-blond hair, but he had a lot of freckles along with a natural ruddiness that helped to hide any change of color. Aside from that, he was a detective, which meant he was used to not only interrogating people for a living, but reading them too.

"I left behind a librarian job of twenty-five years that I loved, a darling little house I rented for ten that was sold out from under me with no notice— I'm still bitter about that—and a friend-with-benefits who was a CPA...which tells you about how exciting he was." She smirked a little, surprised at how free and flirtatious she was feeling, and watched him over the rim of her mug as she sipped her cappuccino.

Massermey's brows lifted as he contemplated her for a moment, as if unsure what to make of such a blunt answer. "A friend with benefits, huh?"

"They weren't exactly stellar benefits," she went on blithely. "Just enough to... Well, just convenient. Neither of us were all that torn up about me moving four hours away. I haven't talked to Les since I left Chicago."

"Good." Massermey gave her a smile that looked a little feral, and Jacqueline felt a sudden, surprising dart of desire in her belly. "I— *Crap.*" He pulled out his phone. "It's work— Oh, *fu*—"

Jacqueline laughed. "You don't have to censor the F-word for me."

His face was grim when he looked up. "I wasn't censoring, I was— It's Big Bay Winery. There's been a shooting. A fatality."

Jacqueline felt all the blood drain from her face. Massermey was already on his feet, and she was right there with him.

"Can I come with you? Please?" Her heart was pounding like a tom-tom, and she felt sick.

No. It can't be.

So much for the protection amulet.

"You really shouldn't—"

"I promise I won't get in the way, but...Miles"—it was the first time she'd used his name, and she added a lot of pleading to her voice—"I can't help but feel responsible. A little. And—"

"All right," he said gruffly. "Come on. But you stay in the car unless I tell you otherwise."

She hurried out after him, barely managing to keep up with his longer legs.

They were both silent as he navigated his Bronco Sport out of town and up into the hills to the winery as fast as possible. Jacqueline could hear all sorts of snatches from the radio in his car, with lots of codes she didn't understand. The only thing she knew was that someone was dead up at Big Bay Winery from a gunshot.

And she was terrified that she knew exactly who

it was.

There were police cars and an ambulance in the parking lot where she'd parked only yesterday. The infamous Tesla was in its place, along with several other vehicles.

A small crowd of people gathered on the small patch of lawn in front of the house-like office building. Some were probably tourists; others were likely employees at the winery.

Massermey pulled into a spot, glanced at her, and said, "All right, you can stand on the lawn with them. But that's the closest you get, understand?"

Absurdly pleased that he'd read her mind and made the offer, Jacqueline nodded. But her flash of pleasure evaporated when she remembered why they were here. She climbed out of the vehicle.

He'd stridden into the building, flashing his badge, by the time she approached the group on the lawn. It didn't feel right to start asking questions like a gawker, so she hovered and tried to listen to what people were saying.

"I can't believe it! She was just talking to me a little while ago," someone murmured. "Everything seemed *fine.*"

"Far too young," another person was saying. "Just impossible to believe."

"Whose gun was it, anyway?"

"It was his, I guess," replied someone else. "I just can't believe it..."

Jacqueline felt sick to her stomach. *Why* hadn't she done more? Why hadn't she insisted Massermey do more?

And, apparently, her taking a stab at making a protection amulet had failed miserably.

A witch I am definitely not.

The door to the office building opened, and the murmuring stopped as everyone looked up to see what was happening. Whispers started up again as two figures came out, one being a police officer with her arm around the other person.

It took Jacqueline far too long to recognize that the second figure, the one being led out, was Amanda Gauthier.

She gasped, staring in shock. Either Amanda heard her or noticed her, for she looked right up and at Jacqueline.

Amanda pulled away from the police officer who'd been helping her and rushed over to Jacqueline.

"Oh, thank you...thank you!" she cried, taking Jacqueline's hands. "It worked. It worked! The amulet saved me!"

18

"So it *wasn't* Amanda who was shot?" said Nadine.

Jacqueline was on her second glass of Pinot Gris, and was prepared to move on to a third. It had been one *hell* of a twenty-four hours. "It wasn't Amanda. It was Kenneth, her husband. She was trying to get the gun away from him—apparently, he'd lost his temper or something and pulled it on her—and accidentally shot him in the process."

"So the protection amulet really did work," said Suzette in an awed voice. "That's kind of wild."

"Wild isn't the word I'd use," said Nadine, who'd just drained the last of her wine. "*Lucky* would be my choice. But now that we know you have at least some witchy ability, Jacqueline, can you make me a love potion?"

When Jacqueline swiveled toward her with a shocked, outraged expression, Nadine burst out laughing. "Gotcha. Fill me up, will ya, Suze? Did you see the look on her face?"

"You're hilarious," said Jacqueline, snickering in spite of herself.

"I try," said Nadine.

The three of them had gathered at one of the small

tables in Sweet Devotion because Suzette had a catering order and was making extra bread bowls for the next day. She hadn't wanted to miss out on the wine and conversation, so they'd met in her place instead of Nadine's apartment next to the yoga studio upstairs.

"So Amanda is safe now," said Suzette. "But her husband is dead. How awful to know the person you're married to has been trying to kill you. I mean, it was bad enough splitting up from Dean, but if he'd been trying to kill me, how much worse would *that* have been?"

"I wonder if she'll move forward with the plans to open the inn," Jacqueline said. "If she'll stay here in Button Cove or go back to... I think it was Chicago Kenneth said she was from."

"If it were me, I'd want to get far away from this place," said Nadine with a little shiver. Then the frown dissolved from her face just as quickly as it had come. "Well, now that you have that problem figured out, tell us what's the latest with Cinderella. Have you figured out why she's here? Why she came out of the book?"

Jacqueline felt a rush of relief that Nadine remembered Cinderella now. Apparently, the girl had gone back into the book as promised and had saved her tale —at least temporarily.

"I guess we have a lot of catching up to do," Jacqueline said with a giddy smile. She took a fortifying drink of the crisp white wine and launched into a summary of Cinderella's refusal to marry Prince Anton, her kidnapping of Kara into her book and Jacqueline's own visit to the ball, the revelation that a love potion in the form of a perfume had been used to capture Anton's love in the fairy tale, and ended with an explanation of how they planned to resolve the issue.

By the time she finished, both Nadine and Suzette had forgotten their wine and were staring at her, open-mouthed.

It was a full two minutes before either of them could speak, which gave Jacqueline the opportunity to finish the rest of her enchiladas suizas, which had been in danger of going cold during her long speeches.

"Two things," said Nadine finally. "One: your life is crazy."

"Tell me something I don't know," replied Jacqueline.

"And two: *you were at Cinderella's ball?* Was it amazing? Was it just like you expected it to be? I'm kind of jealous."

"Exactly like I'd always imagined it. Her dress was —well, the only word is magical. I've never seen or even imagined anything like it," Jacqueline said. "It was amazing, I have to admit—even though I was terrified I'd never be able to leave."

"It makes sense that it was all a love potion, or a spell—not just the dressing her up, you know, in the fancy clothes, but the insta-love from the prince," said Suzette. "Now that I know it, it makes perfect sense."

Jacqueline couldn't even think it was strange that they were talking about a fairy tale as if it were actual history. She merely nodded wisely and forked up the last bite of enchilada.

"So no one noticed it wasn't Cinderella who was dancing with the prince? That it was someone else? That it was Kara?" Nadine asked. "Isn't that kind of weird? And how do you think it's going to work when they put in Bet instead? Won't people notice? Or will they put her in from the beginning of the story?"

"And by the way, can I just say I'm *devastated* that

you couldn't save Nancy?" Suzette broke in. "My sister played Nancy in *Oliver!* in high school, and I walked around singing 'Oom-Pah-Pah' and 'As Long as He Needs Me' for weeks. It was awful every performance when Bill Sikes killed her."

She seemed genuinely upset, and Jacqueline reached over to pat her on the hand. "I wish we could. But it would mess with the story line and possibly destroy it. We can't take the chance."

Nadine was frowning. "Okay, so let me get this straight. You're going to put Bet into Cinderella's place in the story...permanently? What if she doesn't look anything like her? What if people realize it's not her? Won't that mess things up?"

"I'm a little worried about that too, but I think it'll be all right. See, when I went into the story, the ballroom scene was *exactly* the way I'd always imagined it would be. The way I'd pictured it in my head—not the way I'd ever seen it in a book or movie.

"And isn't that true for every book? Every story? We all imagine the details, the visuals in our heads when we read or hear a story—and it's personal and unique for each one of us. And so it doesn't really matter what Cinderella actually looks like, or the prince—or even how Dickens imagined the Artful Dodger would look when he wrote the character—"

"Because they're going to look to each of us just how we imagine them!" Nadine exclaimed. "I get it! And it makes perfect sense."

"Right. At least, that's my theory," Jacqueline said.

"It makes sense to me— Hey, Jacqueline, are you expecting someone at the shop? It looks like someone's at your door," said Suzette.

Jacqueline looked out the window, and a little

shiver went down her spine. "That's Egala. I'd better go over there and find out what she wants."

"Too bad you don't have your own protection amulet," Nadine said. "Want us to come?"

"No. I have a feeling it'll be just fine. But if anything goes haywire, go for help, okay?"

Jacqueline slammed the last bit of her wine and, with that fortification, left the bakery. She darted across the street—it was after nine, so there wasn't any traffic.

Egala must have heard her coming, for she turned to greet her. "Jacqueline," said her very distant cousin.

"What do you want?" Jacqueline said.

"I'm not here to cause problems," said Egala, holding up her hands.

Jacqueline barely managed not to flinch—after all, the woman was a witch; who knew what could spurt out of her fingertips? "You've caused enough already, haven't you?"

"That's why I'm here," Egala said. To Jacqueline's eye, she appeared a little cowed. "I wanted to say, things got a little out of hand with your friend Wendy. It wasn't my intention that the, uh, curse would fry you up that badly."

"Then what was your intention?"

"Just to...well, make things a little uncomfortable for you. That's all."

"You're not getting the bookshop," Jacqueline said sharply. "Even if I wanted to give it to you—which I don't and won't—it belongs to me."

"Yes, yes, I realize that now. I just came to tell you that you won't have to worry about me, uh, messing with you anymore. All right? I've given up on the shop."

Jacqueline believed her. Her shoulders relaxed a little. "All right. Good."

"I'm going to be opening my own place here on Camellia Court," said Egala, glancing up the street.

Jacqueline knew exactly what she meant. The little shop two doors down from Sweet Devotion. "I see," she said without enthusiasm.

"So I just wanted to let you know, since we'll be... well, colleagues, I guess." Egala smiled, but it looked forced.

"What kind of shop?" Jacqueline asked suspiciously.

"I'm going to sell accessories. Purses and—"

"Oh, no you *aren't*. No *way*. No *freaking* way—"

"They won't be cursed. I promise," Egala said hastily. "But they are special."

"Special how?" Jacqueline demanded.

But Egala just smiled and said, "You'll have to buy one to find out." And with that, she gave a little wave and started off down the street toward her new shop.

Jacqueline blinked, and the next thing she knew, Egala was gone. But there, hanging from the building of her new shop, was now a sign that read: EGALA'S.

19

Jacqueline opened up the shop the next morning with a minor headache—she'd gone back to Sweet Devotion and had a little more wine—along with a feeling of optimism.

For some reason, she believed Egala's contention that she was done trying to wrest the bookshop from her. Jacqueline didn't necessarily believe that her relative wasn't going to cause problems in the future, but she suspected whatever they might be, they wouldn't include skin-searing curses or sabotage.

Amanda Gauthier had experienced a horrible event, but she was safe now, and that put Jacqueline's mind at ease, despite the fact that a man had been killed.

Wendy was, hopefully, on her way back to Chicago as promised.

Jacqueline expected to see Dodger and Cinderella soon, and, presumably, Bet with them.

And when and if Kara came in, asking about the love potion, Jacqueline would continue to lead her through the "natural" love potion process and hope that other inspirations would come along to help guide her in dealing with the lovelorn teen.

All in all, it had been quite the productive week, Jacqueline thought as she flipped the CLOSED sign over.

And it was only Thursday.

The morning went smoothly. Customers came in, purchased books, teas, pastries, crystals, incense, and more.

It wasn't until noon that Dodger and Cinderella made their appearance. Fortunately, Jacqueline wasn't busy at that moment, so she was able to join them up in the tea room.

A young, waif-like woman was with them. Her clothing certainly appeared as ragtag as Cinderella's did, but she had much darker brown hair. Or maybe it was just dirty. Bet looked as if she hadn't had a decent meal in her entire life, but beneath the ashes and grime was a pretty face with a pointed chin and delicate nose. There was also a determined glint in her eyes that gave Jacqueline hope that the plan she'd hatched with Dodger and Cinderella would actually work.

"You understand the situation?" Jacqueline asked Bet.

"Blimey, yes I do, milady," said the girl. "I'm gonna be Cinderella, I am! Forever!" Her eyes sparkled. "I ain't never dreamed such a thing, milady."

Jacqueline didn't have the heart to correct her form of address. Instead, she smiled and said, "I hope you enjoy every bit of it." And she meant it. Helping a woman get out of a difficult life was a balm to her soul, even if the woman was only a fictional character. She turned to Dodger. "You had no problem getting her out of the asylum?"

He gave her sly grin. "Well, now, mu'um, I

woulden say *no* pro'lem, but we got 'er 'ere, now didn't we?"

Jacqueline decided not to ask for any details. "Very well. I suppose you'd best take her on inside and see what happens. Not you, Dodger. You have to remain here. Let Cinderella do it. The less cross-pollination between stories, the safer everyone will be. All right?"

He grumbled and started to argue, but Cinderella spoke up. "Miss Jacqueline speaks the truth. Bet and I will go, and I'll be back as soon as I can."

Having resolved all of this, Jacqueline assigned Dodger to carry some heavy boxes of books out from the back room, and went down to retrieve the Grimms' book—which was even softer and mushier than it had been yesterday. She'd just handed it over to Cinderella when the bell over the front door announced a new arrival, and Jacqueline went down to find out who it was. To her delight, it was Detective Massermey.

"How did everything go yesterday?" Jacqueline asked. After she saw Amanda coming out of the house, she hadn't had the chance to talk to Massermey other than a quick text to tell him she'd seen Amanda and had gotten a ride back with one of the police officers. "Tragic about Kenneth Gauthier, wasn't it? But at least Amanda is safe and all is as well as it can be."

Massermey's smile of greeting faded. "Well, I'm not so sure everything is 'well.'"

"What do you mean?"

He sighed. "I really need to talk to Amanda Gauthier again—I still have some questions about how everything went down yesterday—but I can't seem to locate her. She was supposed to come in and make a statement today. No one knows where she is, and she's not responding to her cell phone. I stopped in, partly to mention to you if you do see her to let me know—if she happens to drop by. And partly to see if you've got any coffee stashed away anywhere," he added with a grin. "The crap at the office is undrinkable."

"I do have some coffee—but it's upstairs in my apartment. If you don't mind running up there with me, I can get you a mug."

"Sure thing," he replied. "I haven't seen the place since you moved in."

"It's a lot nicer without the dead body," she said, eliciting a laugh from him.

"I'll bet."

"Hey," she said as she started up the stairs to the second floor. "I just had a thought...Dod—uh, Jack, I mean—one of the—uh—people who works here found a little wing nut on the day of my party, when Amanda and Kenneth were here. It's a long shot, but it just occurred to me that maybe it's the missing piece from the fireplace at Amanda's office. Jack said he got it from—" Jacqueline shut her mouth when she realized she was just about to inform the detective that she had a pickpocket on staff.

"From where? What makes you think it has anything to do with Amanda Gauthier's fireplace?"

"Oh, uh, well, he said it, um, fell out of a well-dressed man's pocket here the other day—it's possible it came from Kenneth Gauthier's pocket. He was the best-dressed man here that I recall; everyone else was in casual clothing, but he was wearing a really nice suit. It might be proof that he removed the nut and was trying to kill her."

"Long shot is right, but sure, I'll take a look, see if it could fit. How about if I sit at this table here by the window? I can drink my coffee—if you can slip it past Mrs. Hudson—and take a look at the part. I also should take a look at my email. I've been avoiding it all morning. Maybe you can show me your secret coffee maker in the apartment another time...when we're not so distracted." He gave her a *very* warm smile.

Jacqueline smiled back. "I love that idea." She called down to Dodger to bring up the lost-and-found box then went up to get the coffee.

As she came back down, she glanced out the front window and saw Amanda Gauthier getting out of Gerry Dawdle's rideshare hearse.

Perfect.

She'd go down and meet Amanda, and get her to come upstairs to talk to Massermey.

She was going to tell him this when she delivered the coffee (Mrs. Hudson was, thankfully, in deep conversation about the advantages of Chinese tea over Indian tea), but he spoke first.

He was holding up the little wing nut with a funny smile on his face. "Jacqueline, I think this *is* the missing piece from the fireplace. I don't know how you knew, but I think you're right. And you say it fell out of Kenneth Gauthier's pocket?" He frowned. "That seems strange, but it's strange that it's here in the first place, so who am I to look a gift horse? Can I talk to the kid who found it?"

"Oh, sure," Jacqueline said. She'd have to coach Jack first so he didn't get himself arrested, but she couldn't decline Massermey's request without making a big deal about it. "Also, I think Amanda is about to come in here. I just saw her getting out of the hearse— you know, the rideshare car."

Massermey's attention sharpened. "Don't tell her I'm here. She might get spooked. Could you just get her to come up here and I'll try to talk to her?"

"Sure," Jacqueline said uncertainly. "Um...is something going on?"

He heaved a sigh, then spoke in a low voice. "All right, I'll tell you: I don't know if I believe her story about what happened yesterday. I just need to clear a few things up."

"Okay. Well, you said she was scattered," said Jacqueline, feeling confused.

"Right. That's why I want to talk to her again. Just...play it cool and get her to come up here if you can. If she doesn't come in—"

The bell jangled downstairs. "I bet that's her," Jacqueline said. "I'll be right back. I hope."

She hurried down the stairs to find Amanda standing in the front room of the bookshop. For a woman who'd shot her husband—albeit accidentally —when *he'd* been trying to kill *her*, she looked great. Well rested, beautifully dressed, perfectly made up.

"Jacqueline!" cried Amanda, rushing toward her for a big hug. "I just can't thank you enough for everything you did for me! It's all because of you and the little...*ahem*...you gave me," she said, patting the pocket of her mustard-colored cashmere jacket. "It protected me from everything!"

"I'm so sorry about what you had to go through," Jacqueline said, a little taken aback by Amanda's gleeful mood. "It must have been terribly frightening...not only to have your suspicions proven, but also to...well, to have had to protect yourself like you did."

"It *was* awful," Amanda said, her smile fading. "I never want to live through anything like that again. And now I won't—now that I have this." She patted her pocket again. "It's never leaving my side. I'm thinking about having it made into a pendant necklace, or maybe even a ring."

"I'm sure that would work just fine," said Jacqueline. "Um...would you like to come upstairs and have a cup of tea? Relax a little?"

"Oh, that would be wonderful. But I also came in to buy a book. I misplaced the copy I bought the other day when we were here for your little gathering. Oh, that reminds me—I still have to have that case of wine sent over. Do you want Chardonnay, a Sauvignon Blanc, or half of each? I'll definitely send the vintner's reserve of whichever you prefer."

"The Sauvignon Blanc would be great. Which book were you needing?" Jacqueline said.

"*Gone Girl*," replied Amanda. "I remember walking out of here with it, saying goodbye to Kenneth—he had to go to a meeting, so we went our separate ways because my car's still in the shop—and then I did some more shopping and ended up at home without that bag."

Jacqueline smiled. "As a matter of fact, someone brought the book here because you left it in the rideshare hearse the other day, still in its bag. I'll go get it."

"Well, how lucky is that?" said Amanda. "Maybe this works as a good-luck charm too!" She waggled her pocket, eyes dancing.

Jacqueline hurried down the hall to the back room where she'd put the book. On her way back up to the front, Dodger hissed at her from inside the romance room.

"Mu'um," he said. "*Mu'um!*"

"What is it?" she said, a little impatiently.

"T'at's the lady," he said, gesturing out toward Amanda. "T'at's 'er."

"What do you mean? The lady who...what?" Jacqueline said.

"The lady wot put t'at thing in the man's pocket."

"What thing?"

"T'at little metal thinga-bob, wot was in my box."

Jacqueline stared at him as the words sank in. Big, hairy prickles erupted all over her body. "What are you saying?"

"The lady put the thing in the man's pocket," said Dodger, enunciating clearly for once. "Real secret-like, an' I was wonderin' wot it was, so I took it out."

"You're saying...you're *certain* of this...that she—the lady out there—put the little metal thing that looks like it's got wings on it—in the man's pocket? *She* put it in *his* pocket? Without him noticing?"

"Oi, mu'um, 'ow many times I have t'say it? Aye! She put it in 'is pocket, real sneaky-like. I *saw* it."

Jacqueline felt the world fall away in front of her as her body went numb. It was impossible...wasn't it? Completely, utterly *impossible*. Why would Amanda do such a thing? Take off the wing nut in her own fireplace?

Then Jacqueline laughed—short, hard, bitter. What book was she holding in her hand? What book had Amanda Gauthier bought? *Gone Girl*.

The damned truth had been there all along.

"All right—go upstairs and tell Detective Massermey what you just told me," she said, coaching be damned. "He's the big blond guy sitting at the table by the window. I'll keep her busy for a few minutes, but get him to come down right away."

Jacqueline came back out into the front room smiling cheerily. "Here it is! I'm so glad you came in for it."

"Oh, thank you. Not that I would have minded buying another copy—after all, I really owe you,"

Amanda said, tucking the book and its bag into the large leather tote she carried.

"It's a great book. Have you, uh, read it?" Jacqueline asked.

"Oh, yes. It's a favorite of mine. I really enjoyed the movie, too. But I lost my original copy a while back, and I thought it was time to get a new one. Sort of a...I don't know, a memento, I suppose." She smiled, and that was when Jacqueline knew without a doubt that her suspicions were correct.

At that moment, heavy steps came down the stairs and Massermey came into view.

"Oh, Mrs. Gauthier," he said heartily. "There you are! I've been trying to reach you all morning. Are you feeling better today?"

"Why, yes I am," Amanda replied. Her smile faltered a little, but then she patted her pocket, and the grin brightened again and became almost catlike. "But I'm sorry—I really don't have time to talk to you right now, Detective. I'll get back to you soon." She turned to Jacqueline and said breezily, "Thank you again! Without your help, I never would have been able to get through this nightmare."

"Um, Mrs. Gauthier, I really do need to talk to you right now," Massermey said, moving between her and the door to cut off her escape.

"I'm sorry, Detective, but as I said, it's not a good time." Amanda's smile remained in place as she started walking toward the door. "My ride is waiting for me. See? The hearse pulling up down the street? Such a charming idea—a hearse for a taxicab."

She walked around Massermey as if he weren't even standing there, and to Jacqueline's shock and surprise, he didn't make any movement to stop her.

The expression on his face was one of consternation and confusion and internal struggle.

All at once, Jacqueline realized what was happening. *Holy shit.* That protection amulet was working even better than she'd imagined. Massermey couldn't make a move toward her.

"Oh, wait, Amanda," she said, thinking quickly. "I have *one other thing* for you." She gave Amanda a steady, meaningful look, then dropped her gaze to the pocket where Amanda kept her protection amulet and gave a slow nod. "I can't believe I almost forgot about it."

Amanda stopped with her hand on the door. "You do? What is it?"

"It kind of goes with that, you know, stone you're going to make into a pendant?" Jacqueline said, careful not to look at Massermey. "It, uh, makes it work better. If you know what I mean. Can you wait just another minute while I get it?"

"Oh, *sure,*" said Amanda enthusiastically. "I'll just text the driver— Oh, look, here he is right now."

Sure enough, Gerry Dawdle had just appeared at the door of the shop. "I thought that was you," he said to Amanda. "I went home to get them—you left your inhalers in my car the other day." He was holding a small brown paper bag.

"My inhalers?" she said, doing a very good impression of being confused. "Are you saying someone left a bag of inhalers in your car?" She spun to Massermey, who was still sort of frozen in place. "Do you hear that? My husband must have left them in this man's car!"

"I don't think so," said Gerry. "I'm pretty sure it was you who was riding with me right before I found them."

"I always keep an inhaler in my purse," Amanda said calmly. "But I wouldn't have left an entire bag of them in your car. You've probably got me mixed up with someone else." She looked at Jacqueline. "Will it take long?"

"Oh, no, I'll be right back."

"No worries! I'll be just fine till you get back," Amanda said gaily.

Jacqueline groaned inwardly. Yeah, she sure would.

On her way back down the hall, Jacqueline snagged Dodger from the romance room—unseen by Amanda, who was still near the door—and hustled him to the back door of the shop. She told him what she wanted him to do, then shoved him out the door.

Now she had to find something to give to Amanda...

Grateful for back stairwells, she dashed up the steps to the second floor and hurried into the New Age room. She grabbed the first thing she saw that looked special: a smooth, flat white quartz about the size of a nickel.

Then she walked serenely down the main stairs from the tea room. "Here you are, Amanda," she said with a conspiratorial smile. "This should help everything."

"Thank you *so* much," Amanda replied. "I really do owe you everything, Jacqueline. Um, I don't think I'll be needing that ride after all," she added, looking at Gerry. "It's such a nice afternoon, I'll just walk! Goodbye now! Goodbye, detective!"

"I'll look forward to that case of Sauvignon Blanc!" Jacqueline said as she waved Amanda out the door. When she saw Dodger lurking down the street, she smiled to herself and ducked back into the shop.

"What in the *hell* is going on here?" exclaimed Massermey as she closed the door. He gave her a furious look, but Jacqueline grabbed him by the arm. "Are you *crazy*?"

Jacqueline didn't take offense to his fury. In fact, it was kind of sexy, seeing him all wound up. "Just wait a sec, all right? Trust me. You only know about half of what's going on here."

"That sounds about right," he said, giving her a very piercing look.

"Please...just give it a few minutes. Trust me. In the meantime, should we take a look at the bag of inhalers? That was nice of you to bring them back," she said to Gerry Dawdle. "Sorry it cost you a fare."

"Aw, that's all right. I got a real bad vibe from that woman anyway. Mollie told me I shouldn't trust her, but I couldn't not return her inhalers. People need their medicine."

"Mollie?" Jacqueline asked as Massermey—who didn't seem to be able to go out the front door yet—went over to the counter and picked up the bag of inhalers.

"One of my ghosts," replied Gerry, as if he were talking about a cat.

"I see," Jacqueline replied.

"They ride with me," he explained.

"Gotcha." She nodded and met his eyes to show that she didn't think he was crazy.

"Well, look here," Massermey said. He'd dumped the contents of the bag on the counter. There were five inhalers and a bottle of Magenta Marvel nail polish.

"That's her nail polish!" Jacqueline said, picking up the bottle. "We were talking about it the other day, and she went to dig the bottle out of her purse to show me and couldn't find it. She must have accidentally stuck it in the bag when she grabbed all the inhalers."

"That will certainly help with the evidence," Massermey said. "If I can ever get my hands on her. What the *hell* was going on there?"

Jacqueline shook her head. "You wouldn't believe me if I told you, but— Ah! Here he is."

The front door of the shop burst open and Dodger slipped in, looking *very* pleased with himself. He opened his palm to reveal a small onyx crystal. "She didn't notice a thing."

"Good for you. Detective," Jacqueline said with a smile, "I'm pretty sure you'll have absolutely no problem talking to Amanda Gauthier now."

20

"So Amanda Gauthier has been arrested for the murder of her husband," said Nadine. "And for trying to frame him for *her* murder. Who'd have thunk it?"

"I should have known when I saw her looking at *Gone Girl* that first day in the bookshop. But why would I have been suspicious?" said Jacqueline.

"Why would you indeed?" said Nadine. "I mean, you can't assume everyone who looks at a book is about to put the plot into motion. If you did, everyone who bought an Agatha Christie would be in jail."

"True dat," said Jacqueline.

"You know the funny thing—I was going to tell you that Wes just mentioned today that he was going to be doing some work for Big Bay Winery. Working on designing a little inn for the property," said Suzette. "It seemed weird to me when Kenneth had just been killed, so I was going to ask you about it."

The three of them were sitting in Jacqueline's living room, decompressing once again after another crazy day at the bookshop. Tonight's snack of choice was a huge bowl of buttery popcorn and root beer floats. Because Jacqueline deserved them.

"I'm guessing Kenneth Gauthier was the one with the ten-million-dollar life insurance policy," Jacqueline said, using her straw to stir her float. "And Amanda couldn't even wait till he was cold in the ground before starting to spend it."

"I'll bet you're so right," Suzette said wisely.

"And I'm sure Amanda completely set up the fireplace thing to time it with our appointment. She turned on the gas and just waited until she heard me at the door, then lay down and pretended to be passed out. She probably was sitting on the patio outside her office while the gas was filling the room. Then when she heard me, she slipped inside."

"Makes sense. And the other stuff she could have just lied about—the car almost running her over, and she could even have faked the asthma attack," said Suzette. "Obviously, she was the one who removed all of her inhalers."

"And left them in Gerry's hearse," said Nadine. "Either accidentally or on purpose."

"Exactly," said Jacqueline.

"Okay, so I just need to back up here for sec. You're telling me Massermey literally couldn't move when Amanda was walking toward the door?" said Nadine.

Jacqueline shook her head. "Nope. It was so weird. I could see the expression on his face; he was very confused. At first I didn't understand what was happening, but then I realized he was struggling to move and couldn't."

"But Dodger was able to get close enough to her to pick her pocket and steal the stone," Nadine went on. "How?"

"Yes. Either it was because she wasn't aware of the threat he was to her, or, probably more likely, the magic didn't affect or work on him because he's a literary character. The cursed purse didn't affect him or Mrs. Hudson either," said Jacqueline. "I'm just guessing here, but that's the only explanation that makes sense." She sighed. "I really almost screwed things up royally by making that protection amulet. If I hadn't figured out what was going on and send Dodger after Amanda, she would have gotten away with murder. And it was my fault."

"You had no way of knowing," said Nadine.

"I know...and that's what worries me. What about...what if something happens in the future and I get asked for help? How am I going to know whether to believe or trust the person or not? Amanda lied and manipulated me."

Nadine patted her arm. "Yeah, that is a tough question. I guess you're going to just have to take it one step at a time. Trust your instincts, too. Maybe there's a no-lie amulet you can make for yourself or something to help ferret out people who want to scam you."

Jacqueline sighed again. "Maybe. I guess I'll have to figure it out."

"I've got a question," said Suzette. "How did you explain things to Massermey after? Was he really mad at you for letting her go?"

"No, he wasn't mad—how could he be when *he* couldn't move?" Jacqueline replied. "Anyway, I just told him he probably wouldn't believe it, and to just go with it. I think he was happy enough to let it go at that. I'm pretty sure he doesn't *want* to know."

"Probably not," agreed Suzette. "I mean, I don't know if I would believe it if I didn't know you and hadn't been present for some of the other freaking weird things going on around here."

"So what happened with Cinderella? Are we good? Can we still moon over glass slippers and fairy godmothers?" asked Nadine, popping three kernels into her mouth in rapid succession. "God, I really don't need this, but it's so good." She scooped up a huge handful.

"You don't even want to know how much real butter and salt I put on it," Jacqueline told her. "And yes, everything's good with Cinderella—obviously, since you asked about it, you remember her and the story. Bet settled in just perfectly. She was ecstatic, according to Cinderella, and didn't even mind Anton's breath. I guess she's smelled a lot worse on the streets of Victorian London." They all giggled. "The books are back on the shelf, the Grimms' book is fully intact, and all is right in the literary world once more."

"Whew," said Suzette. She looked around. "I can hardly wait to see what happens next."

"Well, you won't have to wait too long—Egala's opening her own shop down the street," Jacqueline said. "It'll definitely be interesting to find out what she's going to do."

"Well, all I have to say is, it was a damned good thing you had Dodger here to help," said Nadine, diving in for more popcorn. "How incredibly convenient."

"Believe me, I've been thinking the very same thing. And how perfect it was that Cinderella was here to assist with the love potion situation too," Jacqueline said. "I guess that's one lesson to take from all of this: the characters who come out of the books have a job to do. A role to play."

"There's one other lesson I can take away from this crazy week," Nadine said.

"Which is what?" asked Suzette.

"That Jacqueline makes a damn good protection amulet!"

ABOUT THE AUTHOR

 **Colleen Gleason** is an award-winning, New York Times and USA Today bestselling author. She's written more than forty novels in a variety of genres—truly, something for everyone!

She loves to hear from readers, so feel free to find her online.

~

Get SMS/Text alerts for any
New Releases or **Promotions!**

Text: **COLLEEN** to **38470**

(You will only receive a single message when Colleen has a new release or title on sale. *We promise.*)

~

If you would like SMS/Text alerts for any **Events** or
book signings Colleen is attending,
Text: **MEET** to **38470**

~

Subscribe to Colleen's non-spam newsletter for other updates, news, sneak peeks, and special offers!
http://cgbks.com/news

Connect with Colleen online:
www.colleengleason.com
books@colleengleason.com

ALSO BY COLLEEN GLEASON

The Gardella Vampire Hunters

Victoria

The Rest Falls Away

Rises the Night

The Bleeding Dusk

When Twilight Burns

As Shadows Fade

Macey/Max Denton

Roaring Midnight

Raging Dawn

Roaring Shadows

Raging Winter

Roaring Dawn

∼

The Draculia Vampires

Dark Rogue: The Vampire Voss

Dark Saint: The Vampire Dimitri

Dark Vixen: The Vampire Narcise

Vampire at Sea: Tales from the Draculia Vampires

∼

Wicks Hollow Series

Ghost Story Romance & Mystery

Abandon the Night

Night Beckons

Night Forbidden

Night Resurrected

Tempted by the Night (only available to newsletter subscribers; sign up here: http://cgbks.com/news)

The Lincoln's White House Mystery Series

(writing as C. M. Gleason)

Murder in the Lincoln White House

Murder in the Oval Library

Murder at the Capitol

The Marina Alexander Adventure Novels

(writing as C. M. Gleason)

Siberian Treasure

Amazon Roulette

Sanskrit Cipher

The Phyllida Bright Mysteries

(writing as Colleen Cambridge)

Murder at Mallowan Hall (Oct 2021)